# THE BIG BREAKUP

# THE
# BIG
# BREAKUP

## ENERGY IN CRISIS

by

John R. Coyne, Jr.

and

Patricia S. Coyne

**SHEED ANDREWS AND McMEEL, INC.**
SUBSIDIARY OF UNIVERSAL PRESS SYNDICATE
KANSAS CITY

Library of Congress Cataloging in Publication Data

Coyne, John R
  The big breakup.

    1.    Petroleum industry and trade—United States.
2.    Energy policy—United States.   I.   Coyne,
Patricia S., joint author.   II.   Title.
HD9566.C73      338.2'7'282      77-22394
ISBN 0-8362-0711-4

# Chapter One

1970905

Although they remained no match for the Israelis militarily, the Arabs made a discovery during the October War of 1973 that would soon alter the shape of international politics and directly touch the daily lives of every citizen of the world's industrialized nations. They discovered the oil weapon.

Americans quickly learned just what a potent weapon it could be. During the autumn of 1973, in rapid succession, Arab states embargoed crude oil shipments to the United States and suddenly, many of us were unable to fill our gas tanks. Some gas stations closed down, others cut back sharply on hours, and the lines at stations with supplies of gasoline often stretched for miles.

Many states set up their own allocation systems, and in Washington the Nixon Administration printed up millions of coupons in anticipation of a system of national rationing. Had not Richard Nixon grown leery of doing anything politically controversial, there might well today be federal rationing of gasoline.

It was a time of unprecedented inconvenience for many Americans. We had grown accustomed to a limitless supply of unrealistically inexpensive energy to fuel our lawnmowers and motorboats and airplanes and air conditioners and automobiles. But that all changed nearly overnight and by November of 1973 there was doubt, not only about energy for conveniences, but also about sufficient supplies of heating oil to make it through what promised to be a severe winter.

Suddenly, many of us began to see things differently, and it was symbolic of our altered national state of mind that one of the first acts of the newly appointed energy czar, William Simon, was to ask Americans not to decorate their homes with Christmas tree lights that winter. A minor matter, to be sure, but a gesture, coming as it did during one of our happiest and most hopeful holidays, that dramatized just how rapidly and radically things seemed to be changing.

As it turned out, it proved to be a relatively brief period, and for most of us it all seemed, in retrospect, to add up to little more than a few months of personal inconvenience. But there were intimations during the autumn and winter of 1973 and 1974 of what an extended period of curtailed oil supplies could mean to the quality of American life.

Because of soaring fuel prices and fertilizer shortages, for instance, combined with crop shortfalls and the Russian wheat deal, farmers were forced to raise prices. As a result, supermarket prices began to soar and for the first time in decades there were sudden scarcities of what we had come to view as staples. Again, perhaps a minor matter in an overfed nation. But the implied warning was there, a warning that flashed again during the winter of 1976. A way of life based on an abundance that we had

2

grown up taking for granted might, in fact, be built on very flimsy foundations.

Another direct and inevitable result of the crisis of 1973–74 was the politicization of the energy issue. Richard Nixon, desperate to distract national attention from the spreading scandal that would soon destroy his presidency, promised us energy self-sufficiency within a decade, a promise that Gerald Ford was to echo. (Today we are importing three times as much foreign oil as we imported when the 1973 energy crisis broke.)

Some politicians suggested sending the Sixth Fleet to Arabian shores to show the colors, and Washington was swept with rumors of contingency plans for airborne drops on oil fields. Other politicians suggested that we begin to edge away from Israel, a suggestion that many of us believe Henry Kissinger immediately took to heart.

There was, politicians believed, political mileage in energy. One such politician was Sen. Henry Jackson, already off and running for the presidency. Jackson, long known as the man from Boeing, had been searching for some issue that would lend his strong establishment image a tinge of populism. In the energy crisis he thought he'd found it.

This was the period of the Agnew resignation, of Watergate, of political and corporate corruption, of televised hearings. The antiestablishment mood, which was first successfully tapped by George Wallace and which Jimmy Carter rode to the White House, had begun to coalesce into a powerful political force and Jackson and other politicians—Birch Bayh, for instance, also out to validate his populist credentials—set out to capitalize on that mood.

Many of us who watched Jackson's performance during the televised hearings on the involvement of oil companies in the energy crisis were somewhat startled. Jackson is not widely regarded as a man of charm and wit. But he is an intelligent man who knows that the real cause of the shortages and the price hikes of 1973 and 1974 was the Arab embargo. Nevertheless, during the hearings, Jackson treated oil company representatives as if they were members of a second-string mafia family, and many Americans came away from those hearings convinced that the oil companies rather than the Arabs were primarily responsible for our energy problems.

The hearings had ostensibly been scheduled, as congressional hearings generally are, to arrive at a broad understanding of the problem and to suggest legislative remedies. But, in fact, they were to turn into an attack on the oil companies and, primarily through implication and innuendo, to accuse them of all the worst that had been suspected.

At various points during the three-day hearing, the senators managed to link the industry to each of the concerns and scandals of the Nixon-Agnew era. Senator Percy, for instance, reported that his constituents believed the whole crisis to be the result of a conspiracy between the companies and the government.

Senator Ribicoff also charged conspiracy and coverup, expanding the conspiratorial circle: "You oil companies have been in a conspiracy and I use the word 'conspiracy' with the Middle Eastern oil-producing states."

Ribicoff had no doubt about the solution: "The American consumer is being taken and taken badly and he knows it. I think the time has come for the Congress of the United States to move against the major oil companies. . . ."

In addition to conspiracy and coverup, Senator Percy also managed to play on another theme of the period. "Is the energy shortage to be a sort of domestic Vietnam, where we are asked to sacrifice for a cause we are told is just but don't really know whether it is so?"

And then, of course, there was the inevitable reference to Richard Nixon. "I think," said Senator Percy, "you [the oil companies] have the same kind of credibility problem the President of the United States has today in whether he is paying a fair proportion or amount of his income in taxes."

Through it all ran an acute consciousness among the politicians of the media. Said Senator Roth, upon taking his seat: "I am delighted to be a member of this subcommittee, particularly with all the attention the media gives this hearing."

This sentiment was echoed by each of the senators, and it became obvious that all of them—and Senator Jackson, in particular—were playing the media coverage for all it was worth.

"Most Americans," said Jackson in a typical comment, implying that he was speaking for a majority of us, "seem to believe that the shortage has been contrived by the oil industry in order to raise prices, reduce competition, and force a retreat in environmental standards."

Throughout the hearings, Jackson took pains to tell us that this wasn't necessarily *his* view. Perhaps it wasn't, and perhaps a majority of Americans did feel this way, although one suspects that perhaps they may not have realized they felt this way until Jackson told them they did.

Jackson's method was to make assertions while posing as nothing more than a simple reporter of the people's views. "There are millions of Americans," he said, "who are watching this and they want to know how come these terrible increases in profits. I am not commenting one way or the other. They want to know how come these terrible increases in profits . . ."

Now Senator Jackson may, in fact, have believed he was not commenting here. But he's an intelligent man, and it's difficult indeed to believe that he didn't realize that a word like "terrible," used twice in one statement to modify the phrase "increases in profits," is worth a volume of comments.

It was this technique—making assertions while insisting that he was nothing more than the simple reporter of the views of the people—that Jackson used with devastating effect.

The seven oil company representatives who appeared before Jackson's permanent subcommittee on investigations in the Caucus Room of the Russell Senate Office Building had been told they would function as a panel to advise the senators on energy problems. From the beginning, however, it was apparent that advice was not what Jackson had in mind.

"We meet here this morning to get the facts about the energy crisis," said Jackson. "The facts are—we do not have the facts. We are not here to get anyone."

He then proceeded to do just that.

"The American people want to know if there is an oil shortage.

"The American people want to know why the prices of home heating oil and gasoline have doubled when the companies report record high inventories of these stocks.

"The American people want to know whether oil tankers are anchored offshore waiting for price increases or available storage before they unload.

"The American people want to know whether major companies are sitting on shut-in wells and hoarding production in hidden tanks and at abandoned service stations.

"The American people want to know if this so-called energy crisis is only a pretext, a cover to eliminate the major source of price competition—the independents.

"The American people want to know if scarce petroleum products are being exported during the period of shortage.

"The American people want to know why the oil industry benefits from special tax incentives that no other business or industry enjoys."

That, in a nutshell, was the bill of particulars drawn up by Jackson against the oil companies. It was an effective one.

True, each of these charges has either been proved false—loaded ships anchored offshore, for instance, or gas hoarded in abandoned service stations; or misleading, as in the charges that profits reflect more than the federally approved pass-through of costs of production, a charge which in large part resulted from a basic confusion about inventories; or unfounded, as the charge that independents suffered at the hands of the major companies during the crisis; or irrelevant, as the assertion that oil companies enjoy unusual tax benefits.

The charge that companies exported oil during the crisis is partially true. Because of existing agreements, some petroleum was moved abroad. But, as now has been well documented—although little publicized—the oil companies, more significantly, kept shortages minimal here during the crisis by diverting huge quantities of oil earmarked for Europe and Japan to the United States, a practice which endangered their working relationship with the OPEC nations.

Nevertheless, although many of these charges were refuted two years ago, and although most of the others can be effectively refuted today, they continue to make up the basic arguments for breaking up the oil companies advanced by national politicians.

The notion that breaking up the companies could in any way solve our energy problems is an absurd one. But there is political mileage in it, for it allows politicians to escape responsibility and propose easy solutions. The problem is that we have grown accustomed to an apparently endless abundance of natural resources and an unlimited freedom to waste them. Thus, for instance, we were stunned by the natural gas shortages of last winter that energy experts had been warning of for years. And one immediate reaction, just as during the Arab embargo, was to search for a convenient, short-range answer that would enable us to avoid coming to grips with our long-range problems.

And so, as the politicians tend to encourage us to do with every shortage that inconveniences us, from coffee to canning lids, we searched for evidence

8

of collusion and conspiracy to withhold supplies and fix prices, rather than facing up to the real problem. This is in many ways understandable. Our suspicion of conspiracy and collusion, dating back to the trust-busting days of Theodore Roosevelt, enjoys the status of a great American tradition. And in recent years this suspicion has been intensified by the politicization of conspiracy theories dating from the Kennedy assassination and running down through Watergate. It was this deeply ingrained suspicion that shaped much of the reaction to the embargo of 1973-74. And it was this suspicion that shaped much of the reaction to the natural gas shortages of 1976-77.

Because such reactions are essentially emotional, they frequently subside as rapidly as they rise. Thus, early in 1976, many Washington observers believed that the drive to break up the oil companies, which had been fueled primarily by emotion, had lost its momentum. But then came the winter of 1976-77 and the natural gas shortages, and suddenly all the old charges of collusion and conspiracy within the energy industry were raised again. Except for the deadly effects of governmental regulation on both oil and natural gas, there was no direct relationship between the shortages of 1973-74 and 1976-77. But during both periods emotions ran high, and somehow big oil seemed centrally involved in it all. Many oil companies are involved in natural gas development. And as some of us shivered in our homes, Liberian tankers seemed to be breaking up on some sort of mysterious schedule. The Argo Merchant breakup, for instance, was treated as one of the great calamaties of the century, and the television networks covered it as thoroughly as the Watergate hearings. Later, we were to discover that the spill did almost no damage, the oil either congealing into hard harmless balls and sinking to the bottom or diffusing and floating out to sea. Several weeks later, in fact, no one could locate the oil. But the *New York Times* found two sea birds, their feathers clotted with oil, to photograph and feature on its front page.

Such incidents had nothing to do with the structure of the oil industry, of course, nor did the natural gas shortage. And not even the severest congressional critics accused the oil companies of bringing on the bad winter. But the word "oil" had once again been pushed into the forefront of the national consciousness, emotions ran high, and there had to be someone to blame for what few of us cared to admit had been a shameful and unthinking waste of irreplaceable natural resources over several decades.

And then, almost precisely at the moment when energy and oil were uppermost in American minds, a book entitled *The Control of Oil* appeared on the market. The publication date was propitious, and the reviewers applauded. *The New York Times Book Review* gave it a front-page spread, and it became a minor literary sensation in Washington, where, as of this writing, it continues to ride high on the bestseller lists.

The author, John M. Blair, who died shortly after finishing the book, had served for fourteen years as the chief economist of the Senate Subcommittee on Antitrust and Monopoly, from which forum he and the late Senator Philip Hart waged protracted warfare against much of corporate America.

Blair's book is in large part a massive compilation of the evidence and arguments for breaking up the big oil companies that he sifted through during his tenure on the antitrust and monopoly subcommittee. It has, therefore, the strength of being well researched, but the weakness of any purely partisan argument. Blair believed passionately that the oil companies should be broken up, and the arguments and statistics he marshalls are thus chosen to advance that cause. As a member of Senator Hart's subcommittee, his job as he viewed it was to make the case for his cause, and that is what he set out to do in this book. *The Control of Oil* reads like a prosecutor's indictment of the oil industry, like all indictments intended to make the defendant appear as guilty as possible. And in the process, like all good indictments which make an effective case, Blair's book totally ignores the opposing point of view.

In conjunction with the emotional winter through which we have just passed, Blair's book helped to refuel the divestiture debate. Yet *The Control of Oil,* which a *New York Times* reviewer called "the definitive book on oil," adds nothing new to that debate, consisting as it does primarily of a rerun of old arguments, in many cases painfully out of date. Many of these arguments have been discredited. Others are no longer relevant. But in light of the latest emotional flareups, they have gained new life.

As a result, Washington again buzzes with talk about breaking up the oil companies. The House is working on a number of divestiture bills, among them one introduced this spring by Representative Udall, and there is divestiture legislation pending in the Senate. (The Bayh bill, which was considered by the Senate during the last session, considered primarily a farewell present to retiring Senator Phil Hart, was too badly drawn to stand much chance of passage. But the very fact that it reached the floor means that subsequent divestiture legislation will be taken seriously.)

Politicians believe they are on to something here, and they are. For a variety of reasons, Americans find it extremely easy to buy the charges made by Senator Jackson and critics such as Blair wholesale. Part of the reason is the disrepute in which American business today finds itself—a disrepute, as in the matter of bribes, which it has partly earned. Part of it is the antibusiness ethos which has been steadily growing over the past half-century. Part of it is the inability of American business in general to explain its positions in nonboosterish language. Part of it is our tendency to search for conspiracies and collusion. Part of it is the growth of a new populism, along with a zero-growth, smaller-is-better, politics-of-limitations philosophy. And part of it is a basic, healthy American distrust of bigness.

Something about bigness raises American hackles, and the oil companies are big, the largest of them involved in each of the major steps of energy production. They find the oil and get it out of the ground; they transport this oil to their refineries, where it is turned into a usable product; they then transport this product to gas stations or other outlets which they own and lease and where we buy it.

By combining these operations—discovery, production, transportation, refining, and marketing—the companies believe they can synchronize and

12

streamline the whole process and, by so doing, provide consumers with oil products efficiently and at minimal cost. And they also believe that this integrated process, which is called vertical integration, makes them the logical choice to discover and develop the alternative sources of energy which must be in place and functioning on that day in the not too distant future when we've finally used up the last drop of the earth's oil.

The most common charge leveled at the oil companies is that they are monopolistic. But the figures simply don't support this charge. There are, for instance, more than nine thousand smaller companies working with the larger ones to bring the crude oil to market, and the number of such companies continues to rise significantly. And those critics of the industry who charge monopoly invariably buttress their case with figures which involve twenty of the top companies, a self-defeating exercise, since twenty competing companies, by any definition of the term, just can't be called a monopoly.

Nor is the fact that the oil companies engage in more than one phase of production in any way illegal or even unusual. The farmer, for instance, who plants his crops, harvests them, transports them to a roadside stand, and sells them there, is doing precisely the same thing, albeit on a smaller scale. This sort of combined operation is a time-honored way of doing business and has been sanctioned in the courts. For Congress to pass legislation outlawing the practice by only one of our industries, say opponents of divestiture, would be inconsistent, arbitrary, and unfair.

Also, they argue, such congressional action would

be economically irresponsible. Congress itself has done no comprehensive study of what breaking up the companies would do to our nation's energy resources and our economy. But financial experts almost unanimously agree that the results would be disastrous.

For one thing, they say, the very process of dividing the pipeline segment of the industry from the production segment would be laborious, complex, and costly. The two phases of operation are intricately intertwined and heavily interdependent, and experts agree that if they can in fact be separated—and many doubt they can be—the process would take at least ten years. And in the meantime, pipeline production would grind to a halt. No sane oil executive is going to allocate funds to expand a pipeline operation which, in a few years, he will be forced to sell at a loss. And no sane investor will be willing to gamble large sums of money on an industry caught in the throes of the sort of chaos brought on by legislatively mandated self-fragmentation.

And all this, of course, would occur at precisely the moment when the nation desperately needs to be allocating money for new energy development. Even as matters now stand, it is estimated that energy will not be able to attract the kind of money necessary for the sort of new oil development we need if we are even to begin to approach the goal of national self-sufficiency. And if the oil companies are forced into the internal upheavals that would accompany divestiture, the prospects for future development are bleak indeed.

Then there is the problem of what would happen in the not inconceivable case of another war in the

Mideast. We now import nearly 50 percent of all the oil we use. If foreign oil were denied us either through embargo or the cutting off of our shipping lanes, then the energy crisis would reach desperate proportions, not only causing massive personal inconvenience, but also threatening public health and safety. And, of course, such a situation could effectively immobilize the equipment upon which we depend for national defense.

Finally, say divestiture critics, given a fragmented oil industry, a condition of national emergency would inevitably lead to a total federal takeover of the industry. With private investments unable to finance a self-sufficient energy policy, governmental intervention would be unavoidable. And even without a national emergency, governmental intervention in a vital industry, weakened by legislatively mandated chaos, is, if not inevitable, at the very least a distinct possibility. It's something few thoughtful Americans care to see.

If we have learned any one lesson over the past decade, it is that centralized government is not the most efficient or economical instrument for meeting our needs. Yet, according to industry defenders, this is what the oil-company legislation currently pending in Congress could eventually lead to—total nationalization of the oil industry.

No matter how you view it, divestiture is a bad idea whose time is past, a nonsolution, its appeal totally emotional, unviolated by reason. Nevertheless, that emotional appeal can be politically attractive, and as matters now stand the whole future of divestiture as an issue may depend on what stand Jimmy Carter intends to take on it. Thus far, Carter's public pronouncements on vertical divestiture have been relatively reassuring, although he has been less reassuring in another area.

Until very recently, most proposed divestiture legislation had been aimed primarily at dismembering the oil companies vertically. Now, however, there is a growing interest in horizontal divestiture—that is, prohibiting the oil companies by law from engaging in the development of alternative forms of energy. Thus far, Carter has not sounded totally unsympathetic. But that may be because he has not yet digested what horizontal divestiture could mean. Consider: according to some estimates, the world may have only another twenty-five years' supply of traditional hydrocarbons left. That is no doubt a pessimistic estimate, but that supply will eventually run out and when it does we are going to have to be ready to shift to coal, oil shale, and nuclear, solar, and geothermal energy.

At present, the oil industry is heavily involved in the development of such energy sources and it believes it has the unique expertise and experience to develop them. And for the time being, that's a claim that few other industries, and certainly not the federal government, can make. At a time when programs for alternative energy development should have been running in high gear for at least a decade, it seems shortsighted indeed to prohibit the only people in sight capable of gearing up those programs from doing so.

In later chapters we will write at length on the problems involved in developing alternate sources. But perhaps this quote from a former presidential adviser on energy policy best sums it up: "We should not forbid the oil companies from engaging in research in other forms of energy or in acquiring other energy resources. They have the capital and the experience to develop them. More importantly, they know that if they do not find other sources of energy, they will die when they run out of petroleum—and most of them see that day approaching. I don't think we have any interest in killing them and if they are allowed to diversify they will have powerful incentives to develop new energy sources."

# Chapter Two

---

The idea of divestiture had been kicking around the Senate for the past ten years, primarily as the personal project of the late Senator Philip Hart, a liberal Democrat from Michigan with strong populist leanings, along with his economic adviser John Blair, who always distrusted any large profit maker. For a decade Hart and Blair had been trying to push through committees a divestiture bill designed to split up the major companies into separate producing, pipeline, and refining-marketing companies.

But until the embargo, the shortages, and the price hikes, Hart's proposal, which Blair helped to craft, was looked upon primarily as a personal hobby horse, with little more chance of being translated into serious legislation than Everett Dirksen's crusade to make the marigold our national flower.

But then came the Yom Kippur war and the Arab embargo. Suddenly a public which had come to view total automotive mobility and cheap gasoline as inherent rights began to look for the culprits behind what seemed like a direct threat to the American way of life. Senator Jackson's permanent subcommittee on investigations told them where to look, and the hobbyhorse of Hart and Blair suddenly lost its marigold status. It became instead a distinct legislative possibility, with apparent widespread popular support.

It was also an issue which many politicians believed they could parlay into national prominence or higher office. Senator James Abourezk, for instance, a newcomer to the Senate, hoped to make it his issue. (By attempting to do so, he offended many constituents, and the immediate reaction in Washington was that this is why the Democratic leadership in South Dakota insisted he not run again.) And Senators Jackson and Bayh both saw in it a powerful issue which could fuel their drives for the presidential nomination in what most political analysts were calling a populist year. And the public seemed to be responding.

Archie Bunker, in an "All in the Family" episode which appeared about that time, went down to the basement and found the oil in the heating tank had run out. Archie slapped the tank and muttered, "Goddamn A-rabs."

Archie's pronunciation may not have been quite elegant, but according to public opinion samplings, his reaction was enlightened. One survey, for instance, commissioned by the American Petroleum Institute in 1976 and designed to sample opinions on the oil crisis and to analyze how those opinions were formed, discovered that "there was almost total lack of information on the responsibility of the Arab members of OPEC for the embargo and the shortage and on the responsibility of all OPEC members for the price increases. The oil industry is at fault; little if any blame is put elsewhere."

The report also discovered that the hostility toward the industry was intense and almost universal. "It was a reaction quick to the tongue and deeply held by almost all respondents."

This hostility, said the report, grew directly out of personal experiences during the embargo. People still vividly recalled waiting in lines at gas stations. There was also "fear of change, ill-feelings about being upset and inconvenienced, and a feeling that their way of life was being threatened. The 1974 experience is still very much in their minds."

These feelings are understandable, of course, for the embargo and the price rises and the perceived threat to a way of life hit us at precisely that moment when a great wave of national outrage and despair had begun to crest.

Spiro Agnew, the personification, as James Reston put it, of "the old American verities" for millions of Americans, had just resigned and was sitting in disgrace in his transition office. The Watergate drums had begun to beat. Ehrlichman and Haldeman were gone, and others were going—and often as not, going to jail. There was a feeling throughout the nation that our government was totally rotten and about to topple over on us all.

If the government seemed rotten, so did the American business community, which many Americans had come to view as a working partner with that government. Televised hearings, newscasts, papers and magazines—all poured out a flood of stories of corporate corruption. There seemed an endless supply. There were stories of illegal campaign contributions, of bribery, of aging men running through Washington clutching brown paper bags stuffed with laundered corporate money.

20

Babbitt, born again in the fifties as a soulless man in a gray flannel suit, had reemerged in the seventies as a white-collar grafter. These grafters no longer sported boaters or made grammatical fluffs or called themselves boosters, and the suits were now Brooksy pinstripes. But underneath it all was that same old figure without soul or center, motivated wholly by greed.

It was not lost on many Americans that the bright young men of the Nixon administration who paraded in front of the television cameras, apologizing abjectly for their transgressions, would have looked completely at home in almost any corporate vice-president's office. And for those who didn't get the message, there were plenty of commentators and analysts willing to point it out to them.

It is not the purpose of this book to explore the antibusiness phenomenon in America. It has always been with us and during certain times of crisis it has traditionally been translated into political action. During the past decade, however, it seems to have taken on new dimensions.

In the sixties, our first mass-produced generation of college students joined battle for the first time with corporate-industrial America, taking on what had been dubbed, ironically enough by the most pro-business president of recent years, the military-industrial complex. Their protests, at the height of the unrest brought on by Vietnam, were given daily publicity by the mass media, another new partner in the antibusiness lobby. It was as difficult for corporate recruiters to visit campuses as it was for representatives of the CIA or the military.

There was for a time a strong counterreaction

from what in those days we called middle America, and for a time, when hard-hat marches made front-page news and when Spiro Agnew became a hero to those marchers, it seemed that a new alliance was being formed—working and middle-class Americans joining with conservative Republicans and members of the military-industrial complex, up against students, academics, media men, and old-line members of the liberal establishment. We used to call it the New American Majority.

As it turned out, however, that New American Majority, just about the time we began to use the term, was rapidly on its way toward becoming the old American minority once again, and the scandals delivered the coup de grace. But in the early 1970s, when the economy began to crumble, the handwriting had already begun to appear.

Those working and middle-income Americans who a few years before had responded to Spiro Agnew now began to feel the effects of inflation on their daily lives and to grow concerned that the comforts and gains in economic well-being that we believed would come automatically if we just worked hard enough might no longer be waiting for us.

After many years of guns and butter, the war which had long been the source of our apparent economic good health was winding down, and many working Americans found that suddenly they could no longer make it economically.

Thus, an understandable search for the culprit. Many believed it was the government. Many believed that it was corporate America's uncaring search for ever greater profits that was at the heart of the problem.

It was decidedly in the interest of politicians in Washington to push the latter view. "There was," says the American Petroleum Institute's report, "a clear feeling of distrust of oil companies, a feeling that first the people were lied to in 1974 about the existence of a shortage and then 'ripped off,' in the current parlance, by high prices that produced unjustified profits."

This feeling of hostility toward the oil companies was just too good a thing for Washington to ignore. Every Washington politician, liberal or conservative, feared that Watergate had painted them all with the same brush. Hostilities had to be transferred from government to the oil companies. Yet in the last analysis, government played a much larger role, through regulation, in bringing on the energy crisis than had the oil companies.

But the thing for a politician to do was to feed that distrust of big oil, to play the advocate of the little people against big oil, and by doing so to blur the role that government had played in bringing on the crisis and to obscure the fact that no one in government, whether in the Executive branch or in the Senate, had done anything at all about developing a national energy policy which might just steer us toward self-sufficiency.

Thus, out of a welter of emotions, political expediency, and a changing national mood, a divestiture bill, once the private marigold of a lone senator, came suddenly to be a vital issue in American politics. And because of the winter of 1976–77, it has been revitalized.

Part of the totally unexpected success the bill's proponents enjoyed in getting it out of committee was due to the legislation's very marigold quality. Phil Hart, a loved and respected member of the Senate who suffered from cancer, was giving up his seat and the senators arguing for the bill did so by asserting that it would be a fitting memorial to the career of a distinguished colleague.

"No greater tribute," said Senator Abourezk on the floor of the Senate last year, "to his perseverence, foresight and creative thinking could be paid than passing this bill and overriding the inevitable veto by the end of this session."

That tribute wasn't paid last year, however, and the Senate went home to campaign without passing the divestiture bill. This happened largely because its sponsors couldn't convince Mike Mansfield and the Senate leadership that it was worthy of serious consideration. That opinion was reinforced by editorials opposing the bill in most major American newspapers, among them the *Washington Post,* generally viewed in the capital as the official voice of establishment liberalism.

Nevertheless, the prodivestiture forces will try again, either with more carefully drafted legislation or with piecemeal bills which will break up the industry bit by bit over an extended period. Breaking up the oil companies is, many politicians believe, an idea whose time has come. In 1975, Senators Abourezk and Gary Hart offered a divestiture amendment, tied to a bill to deregulate natural gas, which was supported by forty-five senators. That total startled nearly everyone, including many of the senators themselves. During the primary campaigns of 1976, a candidate's stand on divestiture became something of a liberal litmus test. Birch Bayh was for it, as was

Mo Udall, who made support for divestiture one of the conditions for his support of Jimmy Carter.

Because of the condition of the economy, there will be reluctance to introduce any divestiture legislation in the 95th Congress as sweeping as the marigold bill. Nevertheless, there will be divestiture legislation, each bill perhaps more modest in scope, but each with the ultimate aim of eventually breaking up big oil. And underlying each of these pieces of legislation will be the same basic arguments and premises that underlie the marigold bill.

The most basic of these arguments is that the oil companies are simply too big. And they are big indeed. Five of the major companies are listed in the first ten of *Fortune's* 500 and eight of them are included in the top fifteen.

Yet, despite a certain understandable discomfort it causes, there is nothing inherently wrong or undemocratic in bigness itself, and the industry maintains that bigness is essential because of the great scope of its job. This is not to say that a single company in any field cannot become too large. But the only way to determine that is within the context of the field itself and by analyzing just how much of the market in that field a single company corners. Exxon is the largest of the oil companies; it controls less than 10 percent of the market.

In the U.S. alone, the industry has to invest about $600 for every man, woman, and child to get us the oil and natural gas we need. And that investment is skyrocketing. And if they are to continue to produce enough energy to keep the country running through the next few decades, the companies insist, they must remain large. Otherwise they simply could not attract the sort of investment capital they will have to attract for future energy needs.

Virtually all the experts agree that our energy bill will be enormous. We are at the point at which vast amounts of capital are going to be required to find more oil and develop new energy sources. Consider one recent discovery and the cost of utilizing it, for instance. To carry oil from Alaska's North Slope to a location where it could be transported to refineries, it was necessary to build a pipeline from Prudhoe Bay to Valdez. The cost of that pipeline: more than $8 billion. Only large companies could possibly raise that amount and if we are to discover new sources of oil, we will discover them in places as remote as the North Slope or under the ocean, where it will be extremely expensive to bring the oil to market.

Prodivestiture politicians tend to sidestep the whole argument, however, by asserting that we'll just have to learn to get along on less energy. The small companies they favor creating could simply not finance the operations necessary to bring us oil from the earth's remote places. Therefore, because the big companies must be broken up, and because there will consequently be no one to supply us with oil, the only answer is to do without.

Illogical? Perhaps. But it fits perfectly within the context of the little-is-better philosophy which has crept into the national consciousness and which has gradually come to inform much of our political debate. Morris Udall, in a recent roundtable discussion, put it this way:

"I grew up in an era in which part of the great American myth was that everything is going to get bigger and better. If you have two cars, your children are going to have four cars. If you have a four-room house, they are going to have an eight-room house. Everything is going to get bigger and better. . . . I think the day is going to come, and this may sound un-American, when we are going to have to ask ourselves whether we can really afford, in terms of energy, the belief that everything should get bigger and better all of the time."

This kind of world-weary cynicism concerning the American myth, or what we used to call the American Dream, is very much with us just now. Where it came from is difficult to determine, although there is much in it of the campus revolt of the sixties —the Greening of America, the New Left, communal living, participatory democracy, organic foods, Barry Commoner. But it has left the campuses now and moved out into society, and much of it has been institutionalized into one of our major political parties. It floods the editorial pages of newspapers and the television talk shows, and a generation is growing up which, in large part, unquestioningly accepts its precepts.

Ironically enough, this attitude comes at precisely that historical moment when a majority of scientists believe we are on the brink of a breakthrough into vast new energy sources. The development of these resources would allow us to continue to improve the way of life which most Americans still prefer to the life of lowered expectations that the Barry Commoners and new breed of politicians like Jerry Brown hope to impose on us.

Estimates of how long the oil left in the earth will last vary from twenty-five to one hundred years. We can continue to use that oil at present levels and we

27

can, in the meantime, develop alternate sources of energy—if the politicians allow it.

It simply is not true that we must radically curtail our way of life, as Udall advocates, because we will eventually run out of energy. There is probably sufficient oil to carry us through into the period when we will benefit from dramatic breakthroughs such as large-scale solar and wind energy and the safe and economical use of nuclear energy.

True, we can expect shortages during the next few decades until the new technology catches up with demand. But those shortages are not symptomatic of dwindling energy supplies. Instead, they are symptomatic, just as the crisis of 1974 was symptomatic, of something else—the cumulative effects of increasing government encroachment into the market. The government, for instance, until the OPEC price hike, artificially kept the price of oil down. This sort of price restraint provided consumers with fuel well below market value, and therefore naturally encouraged waste. It also insured that the oil companies could not expand in the ways they should have to in order to bring to market domestic oil lying offshore and in capped wells.

Another complicating factor is that governmentally legislated environmental controls either slowed down or curtailed domestic development of oil sources which would have softened the impact of the embargo and would a few years from now carry us through the coming shortfalls. Environmental considerations have also made further exploration more costly, and because the price of gasoline could not compensate for the extra environment cost, exploration continued to decrease.

Now few would argue that we must, therefore, in the name of all-out development and exploration, abandon all concern for the environment. But there is an interesting contradiction in the philosophy of the smaller-is-better politicians who argue for curtailment of energy in the name of environmental concerns. Although Morris Udall committed verbicide on the term during the primary season, most of these politicians consider themselves liberals. And one central concern of the contemporary liberalism has always been the condition of the poor. But the liberal position on the issues of energy and the environment tend to run directly counter to this concern.

If the price of energy rises, most of us who consider ourselves members of the middle class—and that includes politicians—can muddle along. The poor, however, are hit first and are hit hardest. In general, many of the concerns of the environmentalists are essentially elitist concerns, springing primarily from aesthetic considerations. But the environment is pretty far down on the list of priorities among those citizens who are economically deprived, while the price and availability of energy is very high indeed. A poor person is far more concerned with the price of gasoline than he is, say, with the natural landscape of Alaska. Yet a raft of environmental measures inevitably drives the price of that gas up.

The fuel he puts into that car may even have begun its trip to the market through the Alaska pipeline, the construction of which was infinitely more expensive because of stringent environmental requirements that many believe unnecessary. Or that oil could have been offloaded from a super-tanker far from the continental United States which could not unload directly because of environmental concerns. Again, a complication in the delivery process mandated by the environmentalists which adds to the cost and therefore the price. That oil might also have been treated in a refinery operating under tight new pollution controls which add dramatically to the costs. And if that poor person is also driving a newer model, he'll have to fill it up with unleaded gas, a more costly product which some believe is creating as many problems as the leaded variety.

But perhaps he won't be driving a new model if he's poor. The antipollution devices on those new models, again mandated by the environmentalists, are making car prices prohibitive. And perhaps, deep down inside, the environmentalists don't really believe the poor should be driving cars at all. Perhaps only politicians making over $40,000 per year should be driving cars.

But the discussion of how environmentalist liberals tend to act to the detriment of the poor is in itself the subject of a book. The point here is that those energy problems that were brought to a boil during the boycott were in great part brought on by federal intervention into a free market system. And now, those politicians who were responsible for those controls and who today are working for further controls tend to talk as if the reduction of energy resources is a natural disaster, like drought and earthquakes.

In fact, with careful planning, the energy crisis needn't have happened at all. And in the future, with a wealth of new energy technology on the horizon, the kind of society foreseen by the spokesmen for the smaller-is-better philosophy need not evolve. All that is necessary is that government restrain itself.

But that doesn't seem quite likely, and the gloomy predictions about future energy resources threaten to become self-fulfilling prophecies. If the articulators of the new philosophy can convince the country that expanding our energy resources can only be done at the expense of the environment, they may well extend the period of inaction in developing a coherent energy policy to that day when the oil is finally gone and no new sources have been developed to replace it. And if they can convince the nation that the industry uniquely equipped to develop those new resources should be broken up and devitalized, then we will indeed have that society of lowered expectations that the smaller-is-better spokesmen advocate.

Says Morris Udall: "We've all heard the old story about good news and bad news. Well, there will be two kinds of news in the next few years, bad news and terrible news. There just isn't going to be any good news. It is all bad news. We are in trouble."

Perhaps. But given Udall's political views and the image he has constructed among his constituents, one suspects that he has a vested interest in seeing that prediction come true and he leaves his listeners with the distinct impression that if that gloomy future were not realized, he'd be very disappointed indeed.

"Putting myself out in the future," he says, "as if I were a grandfather holding my grandson on my knee, I can imagine the boy saying—'Tell me, grand-dad, about those crazy old days when electrical utility companies used to advertise to get people to buy more appliances and burn more electric heat, and when gas stations would give away glasses and stamps to get you to use more gas. Tell me about all those strange things that used to happen.'"

Now a cynic might say that either Congressman Udall foresees a future in which children frame radically different sorts of questions in radically different speech patterns, or he foresees uniquely eccentric grandchildren. But aside from that, Udall is a sincere and perceptive man and he no doubt believes in that future he foresees. He is also an intelligent man, so there is no doubt that he realizes that that future need not be. If the oil industry were given a free rein to develop domestic supplies of oil and future energy sources, he undoubtedly under-stands, then that future would never arrive.

It must be then, given his intelligence, sincerity, and perceptiveness, that he believes it would be better for us all if it did arrive. Why? That, of course, is the question, a question to which there is yet no comprehensive answer, involving as it does a whole new way of looking at things, a whole new view of our national purpose and way of life, a whole new philosophy which, except perhaps during the age of Thoreau, has never before been central among the men who shape the course of American life.

As we said earlier, that philosophy grew up on the campus in the sixties, when communal living, back to nature, Eastern mysticism, and unquestioning acceptance of the views and the way of life of Third World nations was central. We saw its first manifes-

32

tations off the campuses in the streets of Chicago, and we saw it made respectable and institutionalized in a major political party with the McGovern candidacy.

What precisely is the shape of that new philosophy? As yet we see only the symptoms, perhaps because the center has not solidified. But some of the manifestations are apparent. It is, for one thing, an obviously romantic philosophy, harking back—as liberals used to accuse conservatives of harking back—to a simpler nation, when life was more manageable and people were more tuned in to the basics of living and were according to the romance better and closer.

We saw this manifested in the rage among the university young for communal living, their chosen political form being participatory democracy. If we just could get rid of nonessentials—cars, appliances, conveniences, air conditioners, for instance—and live closer to, and thus more in harmony, with the things that sustain us—air, water, plants, trees, animals—then we would find the selves that are presently buried beneath the superfluities of contemporary life.

It's an attractive philosophy, but the sort of country it envisions would be difficult to bring into being. For one thing, we'd have to get rid of, or at least sharply limit, industrial capitalism, since it is industrial capitalism that creates the superfluities which separate us from our better selves. Thus, the antibusiness thrust in general and the strong distaste for successful giant industries such as big oil.

Oversimplified, to be sure. But we are dealing here with something amorphous, something still struggling for shape, and its exponents for the most part give no indication that they have attempted to follow through to its logical consequences the philosophy they have embraced. Perhaps that is inevitable in dealing with a neoromantic philosophy. But think for a moment, if we can speculate without sounding excessively frivolous, what life for those who most ardently embrace the new philosophy would be like after their world was born.

Most of the new romantics are decent, attractive, and interesting people. And most of them are also middle-class or upper middle-class people, educated at universities. Life has always been relatively good to them and they are accustomed to having their toilets flush and their automobiles start without concerning themselves greatly over whoever or whatever it is that brings these phenomena about. Because such things have always been, the tendency is to believe they always will be, perfectly flushing toilets being just as much a part of the natural order of things as, say, redwoods. The complete conservationist, said one United States senator to us recently, tends to be the man who has just bought his first vacation home.

But in the new world of sharply limited expectations, it would be highly likely that those toilets wouldn't flush at all and those cars would no longer automatically start. Now perhaps, because the automobile is a nasty beast, that wouldn't be all bad. But it would make it more difficult to get to that vacation home.

And if you decided to pursue that philosophy to its extreme ends, you'd find yourself in a number of soul-searching predicaments. Say, for instance, that you've thrown out your appliances and eschewed electrical heat, as Mr. Udall's eccentric grandson apparently has been forced to do. And say you want a piece of toast. Well, one thing to do, as a prominent thinker who threw out his toaster recently suggested, is to toast your bread in the oven. But what fuels the oven? We've gotten rid of electricity, gas is outré, and coal, of course, pollutes the atmosphere. And so what do you do? 1970905

Solar development never got off the ground, microwave cookers cause cancer, and nuclear energy has been outlawed. So, until something else comes along, you're stuck with wood, which means that you've got to go out and murder a tree. So what's the solution? Perhaps the toast isn't necessary after all. The FTC was never too high on bread, anyhow. But you still have to find a way to heat that house.

And suppose a more substantial hunger arises. You could always go hunting or raise livestock. But again, that would mean murdering a fellow creature. You could, of course, become a vegetarian. But without fuel for transportation that would mean raising your own crops, something one suspects the most ardent of our political environmentalists have never set their hands to. And if they did, one suspects that after a few sets of blood blisters and chronic backache, they'd be secretly praying for the good old-fashioned interstate transport system, supplied with fuel from the now defunct oil companies, to set food on the table.

Exaggerated, no doubt. But plausible, given the thrust of the new philosophy. And it is understandable that millions of Americans are puzzled about it all. As Eric Hoffer points out, we are the first society on earth to develop machines which will finally relieve all men of the necessity to do back-breaking work. And just when we have freed men from that physical and mental serfdom that only such work can dictate, the temper of the times seems to be demanding that we make it more difficult, and perhaps eventually impossible, to obtain and use the fuel that makes those machines run.

# Chapter
# Three

"What is most disheartening about the advocates of divestiture," says *Fortune* magazine, "is their appalling economic illiteracy."

Perhaps nothing is more symptomatic of that illiteracy than the endless recurrence of the phrase "obscene profits" in the discourse of the divestiture lobby. The phrase was used first by Senator Jackson in connection with the oil industry, but since then it trips quite easily off the tongue of each of the political enemies of big oil.

It's one of those niggling phrases that gets under the skin of industry defenders, in much the same way, say, that Robert Dole's continual use of "the Democrat party" irritated Democratic loyalists during the presidential campaign of 1976. But there is more than semantic needling involved here, and when Senator Abourezk used the phrase on the floor of the Senate some time ago, one of the oil-state senators challenged him to define obscenity as that term applies to profits, and to come up with some figures to substantiate what appeared to be his charges.

Abourezk replied that "obscene" means "well above average."

Now that in itself is peculiar enough. If you say, for instance, that *Hustler* is an obscene magazine, does that mean *Hustler* is a magazine well above average?

But we quibble. Senator Abourezk obviously means that when "obscene" modifies "profits," it means profits well above the average level of profits—a definition, incidentally, that could also be applied to the salary he himself earns. If this definition is applied consistently, then the proposition, "Senator Abourezk makes an obscene salary," is a true one since Abourezk's salary is not only "well above" but actually more than twice the nation's average salary. The same, however, cannot be said of oil company profits in relation to the average profit in the U.S.

Amplifying his definition, Abourezk said that "in the last two or three years, [the oil industry's] profits have been exorbitant." He then admitted that he didn't have the figures at hand, but promised to submit them for the record "as soon as I can get a call over to the office to get them."

"Telephone service must have been unreliable in Washington that day," speculated *Fortune*, "because the Senator didn't supply those pornographic numbers—and seven months later he still hasn't."

In fact, the year in which the senator from South Dakota was referring to oil company profits in terms usually reserved for X-rated movies and pornographic magazines was 1975. And in that year oil company profits had fallen by an average of 25 percent, accounting for more than half the decline in the earnings of the entire *Fortune* 500.

Senator Abourezk's problem here is the problem faced by most intense critics of the oil industry.

Nineteen seventy-three and four were, in fact, years of extraordinary profits for the oil industry. But those were unique years, and the problem the critics face is to demonstrate that those years were typical rather than atypical.

During those two years the oil companies made extraordinary profits, in much the same way, say, that a man who earns $15,000 a year, and who bought a house for $30,000 a decade ago and sells it today for $60,000 can be said to have made an extraordinary profit.

Now that same man, in most cases, is likely to take that $30,000 "profit" and invest it in another home, the price of which has probably risen at the same rate at which the price of his first home rose. And this is much the same thing that happened to the oil industry. It had the unusual reserves of crude oil on hand that had been purchased for the usual $3 to $4 a barrel. Then, suddenly, came the OPEC mandated price rise, and those same reserves were suddenly worth $12 to $13 a barrel on the market.

So what do you do under such circumstances? The man who finds that his $30,000 home is suddenly worth $60,000, for instance, could sell that home for an amount that would guarantee him a profit based on the original dollar figure. He could, in other words, sell that house for $35,000, thus enabling him to realize a $5,000 profit according to the going price of a decade ago.

But if he did so, he would be unable to buy another house with that $35,000, equivalent in any way to the home he just sold. The prices of all the houses in his area would have been inflated in precisely the same way the value of his original home had been inflated.

Obviously, then, he will be most likely to take the $60,000 and plow it back into a home the price of which will be comparable to the going price for his old home. He won't have realized any real profit. But he will be keeping pace. And if he were to take that first choice mentioned above—to sell for $35,000 because it guaranteed him a paper profit at the prices of a decade ago—he certainly could not be said to be interested in "obscene profits." He just might, however, be a prime candidate for psychiatric consultation.

In a way, the same thing that happened to our hypothetical homeowner happened to the oil companies. The dramatic events of 1973 and 1974 telescoped a decade into less than one calendar year, and oil prices overnight reached the level that they might have reached naturally and without traumatizing the nation had they risen at the same level as other prices.

But they had not done so and overnight the price of crude oil rose dramatically. After this price hike, the oil companies, like the homeowner, could have sold the oil they had in storage for the going pre-embargo prices, thereby making a normal paper profit, in preprice-hike terms. This would have allowed them to dodge the charge of making "obscene" profits.

But once that oil had run out, they would have had to restock their reserves at the new $12 per barrel rate and the profits realized from selling at the $3 to $4 barrel rate would simply not have allowed them to have replenished those reserves at the new going prices without taking heavy losses. (Perhaps losses of this sort could be called "obscene."

But it seems more likely that, given the current fashionable antibusiness mind set, the only acceptable modifier with losses for Senator Abourezk and his followers would be "divine.")

The comparison here between the homeowner and the oil industry is of course simplistic, for although the basic principles are similar, numerous other factors are involved when discussing big oil. These factors are incredibly complex and it is extremely difficult for oil spokesmen themselves to explain them to the general public—to say nothing of senators—when attempting to discuss the sorts of complications involved in their profit figures. There are, for instance, the various sorts of taxes oil companies pay, domestic and foreign, and the various trade-offs among them. There is the relationship between money taken in, exploration expenditures, research and development outlays, and actual profits. There is the way inflation distorts the meaning of dollar figures and the way in which billion dollar figures, seemingly so massive, are much less impressive when consideration is given to the fact that these multinational companies are spreading those figures throughout scores of countries.

Because the figures are complex and open to misinterpretation—indeed, the companies themselves, as witness the Jackson hearings, often seem to the rest of us unable to understand them—it is a simple enough matter for critics to talk about a 58 percent increase in profits, or a 75 percent increase, or a 125 percent increase, or whatever figure happens to be in current use. And because consumers see the price of their gasoline and their heating oil and their electrical rates rising in what seems to be relative to the figures being quoted at the time, it isn't too difficult for them to decide that oil companies are gouging them for profits.

And that's the way it seemed during the crisis.

Those profits during 1973 and 1974 were, on paper, unusually high. But in 1975 and 1976 profits leveled off again. And even those 1973 and 1974 profits were not funds which translated into folding money to be used by oil executives or even stockholders. The companies used those profits to replenish those reserves which had been exhausted during the embargo and its aftermath. And what was left over was plowed back into finding new sources of energy.

Between 1973 and 1974 the net income of oil companies increased by 40 percent. During the same period capital and exploration expenditures rose by 52.7 percent. The industry used what profits it had left after increasing industry costs and increased taxes and inflation to find and develop new domestic sources of energy.

And the money to find new domestic sources did not come solely from American pocketbooks. The profits that were made from American sales all went into discovering and developing these sources. But the industry also financed much of this exploration with foreign sales, a practice that has been in effect since 1970. Thus, not only did nearly every cent of profits on American sales go toward developing domestic sources; a considerable portion of foreign profits were also financing the development of new sources to meet our future domestic energy needs.

And how about those profits themselves? Were

they really on the face of it exorbitant, as the critics charge? Were they in fact "obscene"? We don't use obscene in the Fanny Hill sense here, but in the Abourezk sense—that is, not raunchy, but "well above average."

Not at all, if figures supplied by the Federal Trade Commission can be trusted. In terms of return on invested capital, the oil industry's return is a very chaste and tasteful average one indeed. Over a ten-year period, its average was 10.3 percent. In comparison, pharmaceuticals showed a 17.0 percent return, instruments and related products 14.5 percent, motor vehicles and equipment 12.9 percent, tobacco 12.0 percent, transportation equipment 11.3 percent, chemicals and allied products 11.1 percent, and printing and publishing 10.5 percent.

All of which means, apparently, that Senator Abourezk must find obscene those companies which make aspirins, cars, cigars, and books, to name just a few of the eight businesses which rank ahead of oil in terms of average return on invested capital.

In terms of return on equity, energy ranks eighteenth, with 13.0 percent. Health care consumer goods show a 17.2 percent profit, personal consumer goods a 14.5 percent profit. Financial institutions, the construction industry, food and drink, utilities, electronics, insurance, automotives—all show a higher return on equity than big oil.

In terms of return on total capital, the oil industry ranks fifteenth, with an average 8.2 percent return, outranked once again by, among others, health care products, consumer goods, building materials, metals, leisure and educational products.

If "obscene" profits mean well above average,

then the modifier hardly applies in the case of the oil industry over the period 1964 through 1973. And what of the big leap of 1973–74? There was a leap, to be sure, and the leap was a big one—53 percent. But was it obscene? Certainly not if you consider that 1972 was an unusually depressed year for the industry and the first half of 1973 was a period of unusually low profits. Had those profits been included in a ten-year average, they would not have seemed huge at all.

The industry's "windfall" gains of 53 percent seem not quite so dramatic when contrasted with the profits of other industries during the same period —industries, incidentally, those vital concerns were in no way shaped by a group of oil shieks. During that same period, for instance, according to the FTC, the metal working machinery industry realized a 396 percent increase in profits. The primary nonferrous metals industry realized a 101 percent increase in profits. In the aircraft and parts industry, the increase was 109 percent. A Treasury Department study of profits during the period places the oil industry tenth out of twenty-nine industries. Above average during that brief period, yes. But, in comparison to the rest of the business community, quite modestly so.

And, as we have mentioned earlier, most of this increase resulted from factors over which the oil industry simply had no control. The increase in profits was the result of an increase in the value of the oil it was holding in storage. And the increase in the value of that oil was caused by the OPEC price hikes, combined with inflation and the devaluation of the dollar. The bulk of the huge profits realized by the industry, then, were primarily paper profits. The oil in reserve had to be replaced by oil at the new OPEC prices, thus wiping out a substantial portion of those profits. As every property owner knows, property prices adjusted upward because of inflation do not translate into money to spend.

Adding to the paper problem was the fact that Washington chose in 1973 to float the dollar. When the dollar was subsequently devalued, foreign oil holdings which had been denominated in foreign currency were immediately worth more in dollars. But as the dollar gained force, these paper profits for the most part evaporated.

Nineteen seventy-three and seventy-four, then, for oil as for other major industries, were years of unusual profits—but profits, for the most part, that were not real ones. These were one-time profits, brought on by a unique coming together of external events, over which the industry exercised no control. As the economists put it, these profits were non-recurring.

Obscene profits? Not by any sensible measure. Nevertheless, according to some, we should be worried about oil industry profits in another way. According to many financial experts they just are not large enough. Many serious economists believe that oil no longer generates sufficient profits to engage in the kinds of investment necessary to meet future energy needs.

A George Washington University Energy Policy Research Study, entitled "Competition in the Oil Industry," puts it this way: "By most recent estimates, the future capital needs of the petroleum industry would be formidable. Because it is tied to

**45**

an increasingly scarce resource, the oil industry faces increased production costs over time. In 1973, the Chase Manhattan Bank estimated that, in order to meet its projected capital requirements, the petroleum industry will need an annual increase in after-tax profits of 18 percent for the next fifteen years. Over the past fifteen, the industry's after-tax profits increased by only 7.6 percent annually. Put differently, the petroleum industry will require a 16.5 percent return on equity for the next fifteen years compared to the average 10.6 percent return on equity realized during the previous fifteen years. If the oil companies are to meet anticipated demand for their products, their operations must become more, not less, profitable." Blair in *The Control of Oil* cited as evidence of oil industry greed and corruption the fact that its executives are aiming at a 16 percent profit level. They are, however, simply trying to do what financial experts agree is necessary to raise capital for necessary energy investment.

There is still undiscovered oil, but it is oil which will be increasingly difficult to reach. It lies in forbidding and inaccessible places such as the Alaskan Arctic, deep beneath the sea, or in shale, from which our technology has developed no practical means of extraction.

There is a great time lag between when a company begins to search for this sort of oil and when that oil, if ever, is finally recovered. Capital must come first, and investors must be absolutely sure that the companies in which they put their money are solid enough to sustain losses and setbacks—that their money can be recovered in the event of unanticipated difficulties—and that the companies can afford to pay interest on that investment over that long period of years which must ensue before they can begin to realize profits.

For this reason, there is much concern in the business community and among many economists that governmental policies will, as they have done historically, increasingly deflate oil profits to such an extent that the industry will be unable to keep pace with demand and the nation will be unable ever to become even reasonably self-sufficient in oil.

The Chase Manhattan Bank has estimated that the energy industry will need to generate about $1,350 billion during the decade ahead for world-wide exploration and development, refineries, tankers, pipelines, and other facilities and services. And since the industry has doubled its ratio of long-term debt to total capital over the last ten years, the Chase Manhattan estimates that the annual rate of earnings will have to more than double in the decade ahead if funds are to be raised and if the industry is not to go disastrously in debt.

We have critical energy needs and we will feel them acutely in the decade ahead. The oil companies are the only means in the foreseeable future of satisfying those needs, and the only way they can do so is to realize sufficient profits today to raise tomorrow's capital. But we still tend to criticize the oil industry for making profits, even though it is one of our most vital industries, and even though its profits are considerably less than those of a number of other highly visible industries.

Part of the reason, of course, is that dramatic price rise and those gasoline lines most of us still remember quite vividly. And last winter's gas crisis raised strong anti-industry feelings. But in fact, what felt like a con job was really the onset of cold reality. Up until the boycott, we had been getting what many experts tell us was a dangerously unhealthy bargain for natural gas and at the pumps as well. For more than two decades, from 1950 to 1972, gasoline price increases were held well below the increases in other prices for products on the Consumer Price Index. In terms of octane ratings, the quality of the product rose steadily. But its price remained relatively stable and once taxes were stripped from the total, we were essentially still paying 1950s prices for the basic product in 1972.

All of this naturally encouraged overutilization and waste, just as would, say, buckets of beer selling for a nickel in 1977. The cars grew bigger, we used them as much as possible for recreational purposes, and the result, as the ecologists like to tell us, was a dwindling supply of accessible oil. And they are right, of course. We did use too much fuel, largely because we were encouraged to and because it cost so little.

But it does get somewhat annoying when the same people who are most vocal in their criticisms of the American energy-consuming lifestyle also tend to be most vocal in telling the consumer that he is being ripped off at the gas pump. There is something just a bit less than honest in holding to both positions at the same time. If we are to be encouraged to use less energy, then the price of gasoline should rise. That isn't a rip-off. It's simply a free market economy at work. If a product is scarce, it costs, and that simple formula lays out the single best system of conservation yet to be devised.

What are the alternatives? One suspects that those critics who simultaneously call for conservation and charge the oil companies with ripping off consumers have in mind some sort of government allocation program. This, essentially, is the statist view of the marketplace. The price of products should remain stable, with the government setting and controlling those prices and determining who can buy how much of what.

Now the people who champion government allocation theories never talk very loudly about them, for the simple reason that if they were completely explained, most Americans would find them totally unacceptable.

One of the authors of this book, during a tour of duty as a speechwriter in the Nixon Administration, frequently found it necessary to work closely with bureaucrats at the departments and agencies, attempting to find out just what they were up to and whether what they were up to, if anything, might not just make a subject for a presidential speech. The final Watergate showdown was fast approaching, and we were desperate to find anything at all, other than tapes, for the president to talk about.

One of the favorite topics was energy, and we all came to know the new energy bureaucrats well. The Federal Energy Administration—then the Federal Energy Office—had just recently been born, staffed for the most part by rejects from other departments and agencies. Some also came from the defunct Cost of Living Council and the Office of Management and Budget. But for the most part, they were not exactly the cream of the bureaucratic crop. What they may have lacked in natural genius, however, they made up for in enthusiasm and a certain frightening sincerity.

One of them is especially memorable. He visited my office in the Old Executive Office Building in early 1971, apparently sent to us to explain why it would be a brilliant stroke for the president to come out for a governmental allocation program. He was the quintessential Washington bureaucrat—well-informed, diligent, earnest, humorless. His mission in life was to do for people what they weren't sufficiently intelligent to do for themselves and he believed absolutely that once they saw the perfection of the schemes the federal government was developing to order their lives, resistance to those schemes would naturally crumble.

He talked about the benefits of such an allocation scheme as he saw them. And, of course, had he been told that not everyone agreed on the definition of benefits he simply wouldn't have believed it. He was big on mass transit, as they all are, and he thought automobiles should be outlawed from Washington altogether.

He had a scheme which he and his friends at FEO had cooked up that he knew the president would love to talk about. He could even take credit for it. There would be two different rationing systems, business and recreational. For recreational use, you'd be required to fill out a form when buying gas which would state your recreational destination.

If you were intending, say, to come to Washington to go sightseeing, the attendant would consult a mileage chart, which would automatically make allowances for the age and model of your car—of course, he said, eventually the Department of Transportation would develop one standard model for all Americans to drive (and they are actually working on one)—and you would be sold whatever amount of gas you would need to make it to a point somewhere on the outskirts of the District of Columbia. Some sort of mass transit would be waiting at this point to carry you into the city and, in the meantime, your car would be refueled at a waiting point outside the city.

He assured me that although the details were still very rough, he'd be glad to whip them up into a comprehensive proposal which could perhaps also serve as a blueprint for a pilot project.

Several weeks later, when it became apparent that I wasn't going to answer his calls, he stopped trying. But I think of him often, and when I do, I think of those considerations that simply could never cross his mind. If they did, he'd probably be unable to continue to function as a federal energy bureaucrat.

He simply could never understand, for instance, that people neither want nor need his help. Nor could he understand just how chilling it would seem to many Americans to have the government in total control of fuel and therefore in effective control of their freedom of movement. Nor would he understand the objection to allowing government to ration out energy to private industry. When government has control over a private industry's energy supply, then it has control over that industry.

But that, perhaps, was to be desired from my bureaucratic friend's point of view.

We do not, of course, hold this bureaucrat up as typical of anything much more than the bureaucratic cast of mind. But certain attitudes here, certain approaches to problems, tend to find common ground with other attitudes which are currently very fashionable and which help to account, among other things, for the singling out of oil company profits for special condemnation.

The phrase "obscene profits," as most of those who use it understand, does not, if we accept Senator Abourezk's rather hasty definition of the term obscene, really apply to the actual profits of the oil companies, as those profits compare to profits in other industries. There is something more at work here, and one suspects that in the view of those who use the phrase, "obscene profits" is one concept as, for instance, "damn Yankee" is one concept in the South. There is no such thing as a Yankee who isn't by definition "damn." And in the same way, there is no such profit which is not by definition obscene.

Exaggerated? Perhaps. But there is a distinct trend here, intensified during this decade as two strands of contemporary American thought, one emotional and one intellectual, have finally intertwined. One strand, discussed in the previous chapter, is essentially emotional, a new romanticism which grew up on the campuses and spread out through society during the sixties and the early seventies.

The romantic thrust of this new sensibility would make the movement eminently lampoonable—and it is—were it not for a serious intellectual movement that complements it and provides it with a respectable structure of ideas. This movement is called various names, but is usually known as the zero-growth philosophy of economics.

This zero-growth philosophy is not new; the problem of apparently limitless growth in a finite system has concerned thinkers since Malthus. Nevertheless, it is not a philosophy which in the past has played any significant role in the shaping of American thought. Boiled down to its simplest terms, the prevailing American belief—the belief which built us into a great industrial power—is that if there is sufficient economic growth, all the problems of living, the social problems that plague us, will naturally be cured. It is, in its essentials, an optimistic view of the world.

The other view, the zero-growth view, is, unlike the basic American faith in growth, a pessimistic view. Essentially, it says that the problems that plague us will continue to increase for as long as we continue to grow. It is only when growth ends that we stand a chance of solving those problems.

This new philosophy has much in it of the new romanticism and shares many of its unconscious biases. In fact, claims one U.S. senator who has long been deeply involved in conservation, many of our most articulate ecologists today are zero-growthers in disguise.

The zero-growth philosophy achieved respectability here first in the early seventies with the publication of *The Limits to Growth,* a computerized study carried out by a group of MIT researchers and financed by the Club of Rome's Project of the Predicament of Man. Now that's a big project, the predicament of man beginning in Eden and perplexing us through the ages. But the predicament that the no-growthers are concerned with is a bit more apocalyptic. We have a choice, they tell us. Either growth must end or civilization will.

If population continues to grow and if industrial growth continues unchecked, then our natural resources will soon be exhausted. According to the authors of *The Limits of Growth,* this will occur, unless present trends are checked, within one hundred years. Man can still live indefinitely on earth, say the authors. But he can only do so if he imposes stringent limits on himself and his industrial production.

Now millenialists have always been with us and every now and then—around tax time, say—the apocalypse may not be altogether unwelcome. But most of us don't really believe it's coming and many of us see basic flaws in these pessimistic assumptions. There is, for instance, the whale-oil syndrome, especially apropos when we consider the finite supplies left to us of hydrocarbons. It was common during the last century for people to lament the passing of the great herds of whales, whose oil kept our lamps burning. Without whales, some very intelligent people argued convincingly, lights would soon go out all over the world.

It is this sort of thing that represents the intellectual Achilles heel of the zero-growthers. They tend to hold a view of the world and man which we have come to view as liberal. Yet their liberalism seems informed by a strong Calvinistic streak. Liberals generally believe that all is change and all change is progress. But the zero-growthers have suddenly drawn a line in time and said, this far and no farther. Certain things are bad and these things will remain bad. But the question that critics of the zero-growthers ask is, why not just solve those problems such as pollution within the problem-solving structure of contemporary technological society? Why instead restructure society entirely to solve the problem? We found substitutes for whale oil and we did so because of our developing technology. We could have outlawed home lighting, of course, and that would also have solved the problem of disappearing whale oil supplies. But we didn't and at least a few of us are glad we didn't.

The problem here is a basic one, the two points of view diametrically opposed. One view holds that in the end all the world's evils—overpopulation, pollution, diminishing resources—are the fault of technological, industrial society and the only way to put a halt to these evils is to put a halt to this sort of society. Two decades ago we would have thought of persons who held such views as cranks. Today, however, the zero-growth view is fashionable not only on university campuses, but also in national politics.

This sort of world view accounts in large part for the appeal of California's Governor Jerry Brown, whose message is directed toward those who agree that "we are entering an era of limits" and that it is time "to slow down spaceship earth." There may be a good deal of political game playing here, what Brown's critics in California call "hippie jingleism." It is nevertheless apparent that Brown has struck a deep and familiar chord among many Americans, primarily those younger, educated Americans who are products of the campuses of the sixties. They were weaned on the neoromanticism of that period, and the no-growth philosophy seems the perfect complement to that neoromanticism.

Opposed to that view generally is the view held by those of us who believe that the problems of technological society contain the seeds of their own solution and that it is not necessary to dismantle the technology in order to solve the problem. Provide the incentive, we believe, and the problem will be solved. We call those incentives profits and many of us believe that profits have become too low and as a result some of the more pressing problems that exercise the zero-growthers—air pollution, for instance—are not being solved simply because industry can't afford to go to work to solve them.

There are indications all along the line that profits are dipping dangerously—shortages, for instance, for the first time in modern peacetime history. Low profits bring on shortages by making it harder for business to borrow money and sell additional equity shares. They pull back on the money directly available for expansion. And they discourage management from investing in new ventures, in new plants, and in new equipment because estimated returns won't justify costs.

It all comes down to a simple proposition. If companies are to meet our demands, they must maintain their own health. And to stay healthy, they have to make sufficient profits for reinvestment and to attract outside capital.

Yet, when the oil industry or other basic industries try to raise their profit returns, they are invariably assailed by officials in Washington as if they were conspiring to fix horse races. It wasn't too many years ago that the brother of a president of the U.S., in his role of attorney general, routed steel executives out of their beds as if they were mafia dons attending a meeting in the Catskills. Why? Primarily, because the whole issue has become politicized. It is a measure of the articulateness of the antiprofits proponents that although relatively small in number, they pack a disproportionate political wallop. Yet what are the alternatives to profits?

The government could allocate reinvestment capital, of course. Or it could simply declare a national policy of no-growth, a condition difficult to visualize, for no-growth would inevitably mean a steady blacking out of our plants and factories, a slow, certain crumbling as those things which now work eventually ceased working because no one was making replacement parts and fewer and fewer people could make repairs. No-growth must by definition lead to regression, and were it to become official national policy, our children might be on hand on that day when the last automobile stops running, the last electric light flickers out, the last central heating unit in the country finally breaks down.

The implications here are somewhat stupefying in those areas where we have become accustomed to technological benefits—medical technology, for instance, with its sophisticated devices and equipment. But, of course, that isn't something that a true no-growther, deep down inside, really believes in. In an overcrowded world there is nothing moral about preserving a human life which is not quite capable of self-preservation. The Karen Quinlans of the world should die, just as unwanted babies should die. And perhaps the old Eskimo practice of leaving the aged members of the tribe out on the ice to die isn't really all that bad an idea after all.

Thus, against such an intellectual backdrop, the

standard argument for profits is simply irrelevant. A few years ago, a Democratic secretary of commerce could put the whole case into two paragraphs and everyone knew precisely what he was talking about. In 1972, former Commerce Secretary John T. Connor had this to say to the Democratic party Platform Committee:

"Those who criticize corporate profits conveniently overlook the fact that a substantial part of corporate profits goes to pay taxes, which help support the countless programs of federal and state governments. The rest of the profit dollar is what keeps our economy regenerating itself. Part of it is paid out as dividends to the millions of Americans who have invested their savings in our private enterprise system in the expectation of getting a return on that investment. And a large part of the balance is spent directly to build new plants and buy the new equipment needed to provide more jobs, and better jobs, for American working men and women. It is this function of profits—providing the funds for continual modernization and expansion of the means of production—that is so vital to the future of our country and is so little appreciated."

But the point now seems to be that it is indeed appreciated—but among the no-growthers no longer wanted.

There is also something peripherally interesting here that seems seldom commented upon among those who analyze the no-growth philosophy. In contrast to Mr. Connor's stated concern, for instance, the interest of the no-growth intellectuals in the condition of Mr. Connor's "working men and women" is minimal, if not nonexistent.

One of the most offensive things about America to intellectuals is the way in which working people and the middle class have put together a system of production, an industrial and technological capability that has surpassed anything the world has seen without any intellectual codification of the system, of the classes within it, or theories of the state. Thus, American politicians inevitably have trouble giving those speeches in which they describe what made our system great, since it all boils down to a simple matter of people working with a maximum of freedom to make their lives better—working, in other words, for profit.

Eric Hoffer put it this way: "Nothing so offends the doctrinaire intellectual as our ability to achieve the momentous in a matter-of-fact way, unblessed by words. Think of it: our unprecedented productive capacity, our affluence, our freedom and equality are not the end product of a sublime ideology, an absolute truth, or a promethean struggle. The skyscrapers, the huge factories, dams, powerhouses, docks, railroads, highways, airports, parks, farms stem mostly from the utterly trivial motivation of profit."

Trivial, to be sure, but profound in its simplicity and distasteful in the extreme to those intellectual codifiers who cannot tolerate systems which are not, in fact, systems.

It is not a unique observation that the zero-growth movement is an elitist movement, just as the extreme ecological movement is elitist. The zero-growthers tend to be people with university roots, people who as upper-middle-class types have long been accustomed to having things done for them.

And it never occurs to them that they, just as much as any robber baron, live on the sweat and sufferance of American working people, the people who make the cars run and make the plumbing work. Without the active cooperation of these people, things would very soon cease entirely to work. The extreme ecologists conceive of plans which, in the end, harm society's poor people. The zero-growthers conceive a vision of society in which the working man and woman literally have no place, except behind the scenes, where they would be expected to be quiet and keep things running. Why? That no intellectual can say for sure. But one suspects that he may believe it to be the natural order of things.

The zero-growthers speak constantly of "rediscovering nature's laws," an idea which would appall Eric Hoffer, a man who actually knows what real work means and who believes that "dehumanization means the reclamation of man by nature." Thomas Hardy put it this way: "Man begins where nature ends; nature and man can never be friends."

Underneath it all, as they rediscover nature, one suspects that the new romantics and the zero-growthers are also rediscovering something very much like the great chain of being, in which everything and everyone has a fixed place in the natural order. And this, in the end, may be the only way that such a philosophy can prevail. You no longer offer man that "trivial motivation of profit." You tell him that he simply has to do what he is supposed to do. That's the natural order. It gave us the feudal period, which was one of the most romantic and orderly in history and in which the concepts of zero-growth largely prevailed. It was, in fact, the last great period of its sort. But there's just a chance now, if the current fashions continue, that our children may live to see a similarly orderly, no-growth period.

There is a popular no-growth story that runs something like this. An American no-growther and a Haitian are sitting on a hill looking out over the lush, pristine forests and jungles of Haiti. The no-growther sighs and says, "In the right kind of world, this will never change."

The Haitian looks toward a clearing in the jungle where a few families live in incredible squalor and filth. "I can't wait until this is all black with factory smoke," he says.

In the end, it seems to boil down to profits. The new romantics hate profits because they make the military-industrial complex go. And the zero-growthers hate profits because they are the means by which that military-industrial complex perpetuates itself and its technology. Of course, oil companies are worst of all, since it is their product which literally fuels that industrial and technological machine.

Thus, a relentless propaganda campaign has begun to take its toll. "The public attitude toward the multinational oil companies," says Morris Adelman, professor of economics at MIT, "brings me back to the bad old days of Joe McCarthy. Then, many of our people, frustrated, angry, and a bit fearful of the unreachable leaders of the 'monolithic Communist bloc,' went out determined to find and bash an enemy at home. Today, unable to do anything about high oil prices, many of our citizens are

61

inclined to take it out on the multinational oil companies."

The comparison may not be quite precise, but there are striking similarities between the anti-Communist rhetoric of the fifties and the anti-oil-company rhetoric of today. In both cases, politicians whipped up fears and frustrations and then offered a convenient scapegoat for their audiences. And in both cases, there was splendid political mileage to be gained. In politics, nothing succeeds like whipping up hate and fear.

It matters little that each of the charges made is proved later to be a canard. We know now that the oil companies' "windfall profits" were one-time profits which in the end proved to be paper profits and were, in fact, considerably less than many of the inventory one-shot profits realized during the period when controls were lifted.

We know now that oil company profits are not in fact considerably above the average of other American industries—they are in fact lower than many and they are slipping. Yet that really doesn't matter. As one English critic said of a writer who tried, and failed, to make sense out of the Jackson hearings: "He fails to take into account the kite-flying tactics which are peculiar to the American political scene, it being an accepted part of the game that even if charges are not substantiated and quietly die down, they will have achieved their purpose of personal publicity for the propagandists."

The charges have not been substantiated, but neither have they died down, the whole issue of oil company profits just too good a kite-flying—or some would say demogogic—issue to let die.

And what would replace the profits? We can continue to have them and, if we do, we will continue in much the same way we have been going. Or we can have statism, as my bureaucrat friend and those like him would much prefer. Or we can have no growth.

There are powerful ideas stirring here, ideas which if translated into political action and programs could profoundly alter the face of this society. Politicians like Senator Abourezk have caught a glimpse of those ideas, and phrases like "obscene profits" speak directly to a constituency out there which has begun to stir.

T.S. Eliot once referred to poets as the antennae of the race. Perhaps. But the role seems better suited to successful politicians, who know what the people are ripe for before the people know themselves.

# Chapter Four

Just before the elections of 1976, it seemed that the drive toward divestiture had run out of fuel.

Things had come to a head during that summer. A comprehensive bill to break up the eighteen major oil companies—Exxon, Texaco, Mobil, Standard of California, Gulf, Standard of Indiana, Shell, Atlantic Richfield, Continental, Occidental, Phillips, Union, Sun, Ashland, Cities Service, Amerada Hess, Getty, Marathon—had been introduced into the Senate and was scheduled to come up for debate in late summer or early autumn, just before the voting.

Just calling the roll of all the companies involved, each with its own products selling at different, competing prices, makes the basic grounds for the legislation—that the oil industry is a monopoly—somewhat laughable. An editorial in the *Chicago Sun-Times* put it this way:

"For one thing, the [divestiture] bill is based on a defective assumption, which is that there is a U.S. oil monopoly that sets gasoline prices. The facts can be detected by anybody willing to take the trouble to drive around the Chicago area for half an afternoon. The observant motorist will see at least a half-dozen oil companies competing for his business; he will see gasoline prices that vary by as much as a nickel a gallon."

Nevertheless, the bill, which was predicated upon the assumption that the oil companies were guilty of monopolistic practices was introduced into the Senate. This in itself didn't worry the oil industry. There had been some form of marigold legislation aimed at breaking up the oil companies kicking around the Senate even before Senator Hart first took up his lance.

But the industry hadn't yet quite come to grips with the new mood. In 1975, for instance, they completely misjudged the depth of feelings in the Senate when, in pushing for a bill that would deregulate the pricing of natural gas, they apparently failed to notice an amendment tacked onto that bill by Senators Abourezk and Gary Hart which would have resulted in full-fledged divestiture. The vote on the amendment was 45 to 54, but the significant thing was that a swing of only five votes would have put the Senate on record as favoring full-fledged divestiture.

No one believed at the time that the Senate really wanted it, and it was understood in Washington that many of the senators voting "yes" were doing so only as a gesture toward consumerist constituents, knowing that their colleagues in the House would undo any damage they had done.

The antidivestiture forces didn't find this reassuring, however. They had the votes to beat back any divestiture bill or amendment, and many of those senators who had voted for the Abourezk-Hart amendment would vote against any legislation with a serious chance of passage should the crunch come.

But what was alarming was that those senators who could normally be counted on to vote against divestiture apparently believed that there was a great deal of political mileage to be gained by going on record as favoring divestiture. There was obviously a good deal more antioil sentiment out there than had been suspected. Successful politicians are, as mentioned, the antennae of the race, and if you want to know what the country is feeling, there's no better gauge than the voting record of a successful, pragmatic politician.

The depth of the political appeal of divestiture was demonstrated again when the Senate Judiciary Committee stunned everyone, friend and foe alike, by sending the marigold divestiture bill to the floor. The *Pittsburgh Post-Gazette*, in an editorial, summed up the general reaction this way: "Why the Senate Judiciary Committee voted eight-to-seven to send to the floor a hare-brained scheme to force the break-up of eighteen of America's largest oil companies is not beyond us. It is called playing to the bleachers of American politics."

But what was troublesome, of course, was that there was that much response from the bleachers. Clearly, the American public still harbored deep misgivings about the role of the oil companies in the energy crisis of 1973–74.

The nation's newspapers, for the most part, attempted, somewhat belatedly, to point out to the public that their fears and suspicions were being exploited by self-serving politicians. "The people pushing divestiture are not doing anything to ease the energy shortage or bring down prices," editorialized the *Kansas City Star*. "They are just playing to the political galleries by trying to sock it to Big, Bad Oil." The *New York Daily News* spoke of "the vindictive prejudices of a small band of lawmakers."

The *Hartford Times* believed that "the petroleum companies . . . are being used as scapegoats as a result of Congress' inability to come to realistic grips with the nation's monumental energy crisis," and the *Providence Journal* pointed out that "the ultimate irony is that in the end they [the divestiture bills] would make worse the very conditions which their authors promise to correct."

It was generally agreed that the marigold divestiture bill was bad legislation—a bill, as Hawaii's Senator Hiram Fong put it, "based on emotion and prejudice, not facts."

"The proposal now before Congress to break up the big oil companies is not the way to handle the country's energy problems," wrote the *Los Angeles Times*. "After many months of debate, the advocates of vertical divestiture have failed to make a case, and the risks of the action they propose have become clear."

As the summer passed, the editorial reactions in nearly all the more than 300 newspapers which dealt with the divestiture bill were negative. And the prodivestiture forces saw the handwriting on the wall when the *Washington Post* and the *New York Times,* the reigning spokesmen for establishment liberalism, both came out strongly against the divestiture bill.

True, the *Post* in its divestiture editorial typically hedged its bets. "A long angry quarrel this summer over the oil companies would be an expensive luxury for this country—more expensive than we can afford.

Breaking up the companies is irrelevant. The real business confronting the country was nicely illustrated this month when, in three successive weeks, the refining industry set new records for gasoline production. The latest was a fat 12 percent above the same week a year ago. As long as the United States does nothing about its excessive and rising consumption of oil, merely fiddling with the structure of the oil companies will accomplish very little."

Now this is vintage *Post*. Breaking up the companies, we are told, is "irrelevant." What is important is that we do something to encourage some sort of conservation ethic. And here, one suspects, the *Post* would not be at all unhappy with a statist solution. But in the meantime, until we work that out, it is a waste of time to be "fiddling" with the structure of the industry. Later, perhaps . . . But the message here is clear to all the *Post's* liberal congressional constituents. Divestiture in itself is not a bad idea. In fact, it may be a very good one later on. But this isn't the time for it, and the bill currently before the Senate is the wrong bill at the wrong time.

For all practical purposes, the *Post's* disapproval signaled that the bill was dead, and the proindustry forces heaved a great sigh of relief. Yet there was in reality little to feel relieved about. True, three hundred newspapers had waded in editorially on the side of the industry, and legislative analysts were predicting that the bill would lose by ten to fifteen votes.

But the problem for the antidivestiture forces was that it never came to a vote. Mike Mansfield, heeding colleagues up for reelection who didn't want the issue muddying their campaigns, and threatened by

68

pro-oil senators with a session that would run straight through the customary preelection campaign recess, removed the bill from the calendar. And there was no serious pressure from the divestiture proponents to bring it to a vote, for they knew that they would be beaten. Were they to be beaten badly, the issue might well be dead for several sessions. And so, fearing that a resounding defeat might bury divestiture as an issue, they quietly let it die, thus turning what could have been a major victory for antidivestiture forces, supported as they were by such unlikely allies as the *Washington Post* and *New York Times,* into a stand-off.

And so, when the new Congress took its seat, the divestiture issue was still very much alive. This time round, however, the approach of the prodivestiture forces is expected to be different. There will be less concentration on any one comprehensive marigold bill; instead, the emphasis will be on less-ambitious, piecemeal legislation which, if successful, would over the long run just as effectively break up the industry as any one comprehensive marigold bill.

Thus, the oil industry is experiencing the jitters over such recommendations as those contained in a report of the House Small Business Committee. The recommendations, which call for legislation to prevent major oil companies from owning service stations, are the first-ever divestiture recommendations to come from a committee of the House. "It isn't that one recommendation by itself that troubles us," says one oil industry spokesman. "But the recommendation is part of something bigger that worries us very much."

In the end, just by getting their bill onto the floor,

the prodivestiture forces in the Senate won a victory and set a precedent which made it thinkable for the House to recommend something it had previously always shied away from recommending. That "something bigger" that the industry fears seems to be looming ever larger on the legislative horizon. And there is always, in addition, the threat of horizontal divestiture—the outlawing of oil from other forms of energy—which would, considering the fact that oil is a finite product, amount to slow homicide for the industry.

"There's bound to be a major change in the structure of the oil industry within the next five years," says FEA official John Hill. "Forces have been unleashed here that can't be stopped."

One of those forces takes the form of the junior senator from Massachusetts. Edward Kennedy is a formidable force in the Senate indeed. Kennedy has led the fight, for instance, for national health insurance, a program which nobody gave much chance of enactment just a few years back. It was too sweeping, too radical; it amounted to nothing less than socialized medicine; it would destroy quality medical care here as it had done in Great Britain; it was too expensive and would set us on the road to national bankruptcy, just as it had done to England. All the arguments were there, along with the statistics to back them up. But Kennedy, whose staff work may be the most impressive in the Senate, kept hammering away, and now that Carter is president, national health legislation is inevitable. Kennedy has done all that could be done to pave the way for it and he will be remembered as the man who made it possible.

But Kennedy now is said to feel that the propaganda battle for national health insurance has been won, and he is looking for new legislative areas to pioneer and propagandize. That is why the speculation that he would be taking over Senator Hart's Antitrust and Monopoly Subcommittee has made the oil industry very nervous indeed. Kennedy has been looking for a new target, having, to his own satisfaction, sufficiently subdued the health-care industry. And the oil industry, which will be the subject of intensive new investigations by Kennedy's new subcommittee, remains an attractive target.

Why Kennedy would want to conquer this new legislative world is another question. But in Washington, the word was that he was looking very hard at 1980. In 1980, Muskie and Humphrey will no longer be vital figures. Kennedy will be the youngest grand old liberal-populist man of presidential caliber representing his party in the Senate. And Chappaquidick by that time will be a faded memory. Even if he has to wait until 1984, by then he'll still be a sufficiently young grand old man to make the run. With national health insurance on the books, and with the scalp of big oil on his belt, Kennedy would make a formidable presidential candidate.

At any rate, Kennedy or no, Sen. Hart's old subcommittee will no doubt continue to press the charge that big oil is monopolistic.

Now this charge presents great difficulties. Most intelligent observers agree that it simply isn't true and can never be made to stick. Yet given the structure of the industry, the way it does business, and its sheer size, the charge is difficult to disprove, especially when many Americans see something inherently sinister in anything as complex and as huge as the oil industry. Indeed, one suspects that if Americans were polled as to what constituted a monopoly, size would be a common answer.

During the height of the controversy over the divestiture bill last summer, many of the nation's newspapers attempted to clear up the monopoly question for their readers. The fact that the companies were big, they explained, and that they were vertically integrated, had nothing whatsoever to do with monopolistic practices.

"Divestiture," explained the *Miami Herald* patiently, "is the name for break 'em up, or force the companies to give up either production, or refining, or marketing, or transportation of oil and its products. The theory is that the companies monopolize the trade and thus maintain high prices to the public.

"The fact is that no one company controls as much as 10 percent of the nation's refineries. No one company has more than 11 percent of production. So there is really not much to break up."

The *Pittsburgh Post-Gazette* put it this way: "Higher [oil] prices derive not from any oily oligopoly in the U.S. but rather from cartel-pricing abroad and from inadequate supplies here in the U.S. That there is no monopoly or oligopoly should be evident from the fact that in the U.S. there are operating about five giants, about seventeen other majors and hundreds of other smaller oil companies. They do engage in price competition; and, except for their good year of inventory profits—which in fact benefited the U.S. economy and American consumers —their profits in a typical year are only about average for American industry in general."

72

And the *New York Times,* in general a strong editorial friend of those most active in the prodivestiture movement, similarly chided those friends for the misconceptions about monopolistic practices which they were attempting to foist on the public.

"The proposed solution of divestiture," said the *Times,* "is based on a fallacious theory of the energy crisis—the notion that it was caused by the American oil 'monopoly' rather than the cartel of oil-producing countries. This risks diverting attention from the real problems to a dramatic and emotional non-solution."

It is, of course, a matter of historical fact that the energy crisis was brought on solely by the unilateral actions of the OPEC cartel, operating totally independently of the oil industry. As the *Miami Herald* put it, "It should be remembered that recent price increases in petroleum products reflect rising worldwide demand combined with manipulation by the Organization of Petroleum Exporting Countries—not by domestic oil interests. It should also be remembered that OPEC has boosted crude oil prices more than 400 percent in the last few years, but the price of gasoline in the United States has gone up at less than half that rate. . . ."

Nevertheless, as the *Times* points out, the tendency is to opt for the "dramatic and emotional non-solution," and perhaps by so doing to avoid a discussion of the hard issues involved in the energy crisis—foreign policy, a national program of conservation, government regulation, a national energy policy, to name just a few.

The monopoly charge is the easiest charge to make. It is not an easy charge to prove, as witness the inability of the Justice Department to develop a coherent antitrust case against big oil, or of Senator Hart's Antitrust and Monopoly Subcommittee ever to put together a convincing case.

But the attack against alleged monopolistic practices obviously remains convincing for a great number of Americans. The way the companies are structured, the phrase "vertical integration" itself no doubt raises suspicions.

Professor Wesley Liebeler, who teaches law at UCLA, puts it this way: "It is somewhat a mystery why so many observers seem to regard the vertical integration of business firms as slightly sinister when those same observers are surrounded by vertical integration in their daily lives. If we read 'slightly sinister' for 'monopoly,' an explanation may be found in Ronald Coase's remark that 'if an economist finds something—a business practice of one sort or another—that he does not understand, he looks for a monopoly explanation.'"

The phrase "vertical integration" is perhaps a bit arcane and jargonistic and doesn't trip easily off the tongue. Probably no one who sets out to drive himself to work each morning says to his wife, "Goodbye, dear. Now I'm going to practice vertical integration." But by buying his own car to transport himself to work rather than depending on public transportation, which he may find inconvenient and unreliable, he is practicing precisely that—vertical integration. And whenever a business purchases its own truck to haul its goods or when it buys its own retail outlet, then that business is practicing vertical integration.

Dr. Edward Mitchell, professor of business economics at the University of Michigan, estimates that vertical integration saves the oil industry about 20 percent in costs. Without vertical integration, says Professor Mitchell, consumer prices of oil products would probably rise by at least a billion dollars per year from what he calls the "risk effect" alone. Companies simply can't rely on guarantees such as long-term contracts to assure supply, transportation, and outlets for their products.

Perhaps the best historical example of this is provided by Standard Oil of Ohio (SOHIO). The 1911 Sherman Act had broken the Rockefeller Standard Oil trust into geographic regions. As a result, SOHIO became a small refiner and marketer operating within the state of Ohio, without crude production. It was a model of what the proponents of divestiture would like to see the major companies become.

SOHIO, near bankruptcy, attempted to solve its crude supply problems by signing a long-term contract with Carter Oil, a crude production company located in Oklahoma. Then, to transport the crude, SOHIO entered into an agreement with two other companies to build a trunk line to the source of crude supply in Oklahoma.

Unfortunately for SOHIO, it had agreed to buy the crude at a fixed price before the Depression caused the price of oil to plummet. And even more unfortunately, new, prolific crude fields were discovered in Illinois, and the price of Illinois crude delivered to Ohio dropped well below the price of Oklahoma crude. It all added up to disaster and the only thing that saved SOHIO from collapse was the willingness of Carter Oil to allow SOHIO to break the contract—but not before SOHIO took a serious financial beating.

It was not lost on SOHIO that had it owned the crude in Oklahoma, it could either have held back production until the Illinois wells ran dry or sold the Oklahoma crude locally without the added transportation expenses. As a result of the experience, SOHIO began to integrate into crude and today has become a crude-rich integrated company with enormous Alaskan production.

Transportation is an extremely important consideration here. Oil, for the most part, is transported through pipelines, and the relationship between pipelines and refining is an intricate one. Arthur Johnson, in an exhaustive study of oil pipelines, summarizes what happened in the wake of Sherman to those companies that did not own their own pipelines.

"Although the 1911 [Sherman Act] decision eventually added to the number of independent, integrated companies, it could not—and did not—end the interdependence of pipelines and refiners. None of the refining companies divorced from the combination remained without pipelines of their own two decades later, and most found it necessary to integrate backward sooner than that. The pipeline companies separated from the combination found themselves just as dependent on Standard companies' patronage as before the dissolution. Because initially the dependence was reciprocal, they made few changes in operating practices and rates. This policy, plus the changing location of oil production and consumption centers, contributed to the decline or demise of most of the independent disaffiliated pipeline companies by the early 1930's."

And just as the oil companies found control of a supply of crude and of transportation and refining essential, so did they find it helpful, if they were to benefit financially, to stabilize marketing through emphasis on brand recognition. Other industries solve the marketing problem by entering into long-term sales contracts, and such contracts serve the purpose for certain oil products. But gasoline makes up a large portion of oil sales and it would be impossible to enter into a long-term contract with each individual customer. Instead, the companies have advertised, hoping to instill brand loyalty. They offer convenient locations, credit, and repair services, in an attempt to win steady customers and, by doing so, to minimize demand fluctuations. This sort of reduction in demand fluctuation, the companies believe, leads, among other things, to stable profits for individual companies.

It is an interesting datum that those companies which are not integrated overwhelmingly specialize in oil products other than gasoline. According to one recent survey, the typical integrated company gave over 43.4 percent of its refinery production to pump gasoline; the typical nonintegrated company gave over only 27 percent to pump gasoline.

The point here is an obvious one—only integrated companies can afford to take the risks inherent in the production and sale of gasoline, a product which lends itself to often unpredictable demand fluctuations. And only the integrated companies can realistically expect to maintain low prices through competition. The oil industry, like other businesses, did not decide to integrate because it was power hungry for monopolistic control. Indeed, there is nothing in the definition of vertical integration that suggests monopoly; the terms are simply not synonymous, or even related.

Vertical integration is simply good business practice, a way of structuring the operation of your company—and only *your* company—so that you can operate efficiently and in the black. And not too many years ago, it was the only way to survive.

Professor Edward Mitchell sums it up this way: "In recent years there has been a vast literature in financial theory suggesting that riskier firms incur higher costs of capital. If vertical integration can reduce a firm's risk then it would follow, according to this theory, that its capital costs and hence its overall costs of production would tend to be translated into price reductions. Lower risks would therefore mean lower consumer prices. Consumers would be better off. On the other side, however, lower risks would mean lower rates of return to investors. But these investors would be no worse off with these lower rates of return since there would be no offsetting fall in risk. Investors in petroleum companies would be indifferent between high rates of return and low risk, on the one hand, and low rates of return and low risk, on the other. Thus, if risk is reduced by vertical integration and lower risks mean lower capital costs and rates of return, vertical integration is a boon to consumers while it leaves investors no worse off. Vertical integration would offer a benefit to society without a cost."

In other, perhaps less technical, words, without the built-in safety of an integrated oil company, the people who buy stocks in such companies would expect a higher return, since it would be risky to buy those stocks. And since the industry would be forced to pay a higher rate of return to their investors, the price of petroleum products would inevitably go up.

Vertical integration, then, is a way of organizing and coordinating a business operation so that it works at peak efficiency, providing a fair rate of return to investors, reasonable and stable prices to consumers, and, in Professor Mitchell's words, "a benefit to society without the cost." And as such, it has nothing whatsoever to do with the concept of monopoly. On the contrary, the fact that individual companies are vertically integrated in itself is an indication that the strong competition exists. And where there is strong competition there cannot by definition also be monopoly.

A company with sole control over the source and marketing of its product—a company which, in other words enjoys a monopoly—does not need to integrate. It is assured of supply and transportation of its product because there is no one else to compete for that supply and transportation. The marketing of the product is assured, for the same reason. Vertical integration, however, represents an attempt to stabilize supply and sales in the face of competition —because of competition.

And the oil industry, by anyone's standard, is highly competitive. There are 10,000 crude oil and natural gas producers, 131 refiners, 100 pipeline companies, and over 15,000 wholesalers of petroleum products. And no one company controls more than 11 percent of the industry—production, refining, transportation, or marketing—at any level of operation. The oil industry is less concentrated than other major industries such as aluminum, aircraft, automobiles, copper, or industrial chemicals. There is less concentration in the oil industry, in fact, than in twenty-five other major industries.

According to traditional economic theory, there are three basic questions, the answers to which determine whether a monopoly exists:

Do a large number of strong firms exist within the industry, and can new firms enter easily?

Do the firms within the industry explicitly agree with each other to fix prices, divide markets geographically, or harass potential competition?

Do the firms within the industry earn, over a period of time, inexplicably high profits?

Using the criteria posited by these questions, it isn't difficult to identify a true monopoly. The Organization of Petroleum Exporting Countries (OPEC), for instance, is a perfect example. OPEC members control over 96 percent of the free world's supply of oil and they meet regularly to fix prices. Because most of the known supply of oil outside the Iron Curtain lies within their national borders, they have no significant competition to worry about. And they make exorbitant profits. In 1976, the price for a barrel of OPEC oil is from ten to one hundred times greater than the costs of producing that barrel.

OPEC is a monopoly in the classical mold. But measured against the same criteria, the major American oil companies display none of the standard symptoms. They do not, for instance, have a corner on the market. According to the Federal Trade Commission, the eight largest crude oil producers control just slightly over 50 percent of the market. And the

Chase Manhattan insists that the FTC's figures are too high. The production of the eight, says the Chase Manhattan, peaked during 1970 at about 43 percent and has fallen since then. By anyone's definition, eight companies controlling half or less than half of a given market is simply not a monopoly. Nor has any legal ruling ever established a precedent under which such a ruling would be possible.

Legal cases of monopoly have always been clear cut. Alcoa, in 1945, was ruled a monopoly because it had no domestic competition and had controlled the market for twenty-five years.

United Shoe, with no significant competition, had control of the market for forty years. It was ruled a monopoly in 1953.

American Tobacco, which shared 75 percent of the market with three competitors, was ruled a monopoly in 1946 for conspiring to fix prices and exclude competition. There had been no new entrant into the market for eight years.

Grinell was ruled a monopoly in 1966 because it had no competition, controlled 90 percent of the market, and had engaged in mergers designed to prevent competition.

In each of these cases, the issue was clear cut. In the case of the oil industry, however, none of the criteria applies.

There are neither barriers to entry nor a lack of competition. In addition to thirty large firms, there are tens of thousands of smaller companies within the industry. In 1974, these smaller companies drilled 86 percent of all exploratory new wells and today they are active, along with the majors, in exploring and developing U.S. frontier regions.

Although there are no barriers to entry and although there is intense competition in the area of crude oil exploration and production, the transportation aspects are somewhat different, primarily because large pipelines are prohibitively expensive to construct. Nevertheless, pipelines are regulated by the Interstate Commerce Commission, which assures that all competing companies have equal access, and which prevents them from engaging in preferential pricing practices.

In addition to pipelines, tankers, barges, and trucks transport 25 percent of our domestic crude and 73 percent of domestic refined products. And among these forms of transportation, competition is intense. Economists who have studied the tanker market, for instance, call it one of the most competitive in the world.

The refining segment of the industry, which turns crude oil into the petroleum products we buy, is also demonstrably competitive, although not as competitive as the exploration and production segments. In 1970, the twenty largest refineries controlled about 88 percent of the market, although not one of them accounted for more than 10 percent. And although critics charge barriers-to-entry into the field because of the capital needed to build a new refinery—between $50 million and $500 million—there were forty-seven new refineries built between 1950 and 1972 and thirteen built between 1972 and 1975. And only one of those latter thirteen was built by a major oil company. Moreover, of the eleven new refineries which will open during this decade, only four will be owned by major companies.

Testifying as an expert witness before the antitrust division of the Justice Department, Professor Leonard Weiss had this to say about the barrier-to-entry theory: "I mentioned . . . the number of firms, including some independents I have never heard of, who set out to build refineries between May and July of 1973, and it is just astounding—and these were one hundred million dollars and many one hundred million dollar investments—that shook my belief in capital as a high barrier to entry quite a bit."

Even if it *were* true that new companies, because of capital requirements, could not enter the refinery market—then the integrated oil companies could hardly be blamed. They are not, after all, responsible for the condition of the capital market. This is a problem that government has caused. Nor would forcing the oil companies to divest themselves of their refineries in any way alleviate the situation.

Finally, marketing, the fourth segment of integrated oil companies, is the most competitive segment of all. Texaco, for instance, which does the most marketing business, competes with twenty-five other leading marketers, and in 1973 controlled less than 8 percent of the national market. The share of the market for refined products among the eight largest firms fell, between 1947 and 1964, from 62 to 52 percent. And between 1970 and 1974 alone, the market share of the independent companies rose from 19 to 29 percent.

After examining such evidence, the Federal Trade Commission concluded that "gasoline marketing is the most competitive area of the petroleum industry and has the largest number of independent companies."

None of the basic criteria used to measure monopolistic practices appears to apply to the oil industry. There is a thriving competition. There are no barriers to entry. And earnings are in no way exorbitant. And in the end, according to economists, earnings have always been viewed as the best evidence of the existence of monopolistic practices.

Professor Richard Mancke, associate professor of international economics at Tufts University, says that "the persistence of abnormally high industry profits over a long period of time" generally is ample proof of monopoly. Mancke continues: "Judged by the most common measure—the after-tax rate of return on equity investments—profits of most American oil companies were below the average for all U.S. industrial firms for the ten years up to 1973. Largely as a result of embargo-caused higher crude-oil prices, oil company profits rose substantially in 1973 and 1974. Nevertheless, even then they were only slightly higher than the average earned by all U.S. manufacturing companies. Moreover, they began to fall off in the last quarter of 1974 and this falling-off accelerated in 1975. The fact that unusually big profits were earned for a period of less than two years that coincided with a period of unanticipated supply shortages is not evidence of monopoly."

Because accounting data can be engineered and because there are no real criteria for accounting profit data (the oil companies have recently been accused of rigging figures), Professor Edward Mitchell set out to interpret industry's profits without reference to company bookkeeping figures. Mitchell instead calculated the profits realized by owners of oil company common stocks and concluded:

"1. American petroleum companies were significantly less profitable than the S & P [Standard and Poor's] 500 over the 1953 to 1972 period. Indeed, not one of the twenty-one American petroleum companies equalled the S & P 500's rate of return!

"2. The eight companies charged by the Federal Trade Commission with monopolizing the industry earned an average rate of return of 12.1 percent, more than 20 percent below the S & P norm for the 1953 to 1972 period.

"3. From 1960 to 1972 domestic producers realized less than half the rate of return of the S & P 500."

There is no way over a period of time, concludes Professor Mitchell, that monopoly profits could be concealed in stock figures. The oil industry, according to Professor Mitchell's research, is not earning monopoly profits. And if it were indeed a monopoly, it would be a dismally unsuccessful one indeed.

The areas of competition, barriers to entry, and profits have proved fruitless to those who attempt to make the case for monopoly—and although the lack of facts does little to discourage the political kite-flyers from repeating their charges, the more serious among them increasingly tend to zero in on the charge that companies within the industry talk things over with one another in order to set prices and to avoid competition. There exists within the industry, these critics believe, what Senator Gary Hart calls "an intricate web of intercorporate ties, cooperative arrangements, and joint ventures."

Proponents of Senator Hart's "intricate web" theory in effect charge conspiracy, a charge that is notoriously difficult to prove in all areas. But the beauty of conspiracy theories is that they appeal to the emotions, and often it is enough for those who charge conspiracy to show that a few people have at some time or another spoken together in the same room. This, essentially, is all the "intricate web" theorists have to go on. Oil industry leaders, they say, sit on common boards throughout the business world, and therefore collusion is inevitable.

Perhaps. But if we are willing to believe that industry oil executives collude in board rooms, as Senator Hart and his followers charge, then we must also believe they are among the world's stupidest men. Collusion, after all, is illegal, and you'd have to be fairly thick to commit an illegal act in a board room. There are, after all, places that are a bit more private.

The implication, of course, is that industry leaders sit on various financial boards for venal purposes, an implication that is not difficult for many to accept in an antibusiness period. But in reality, oil company executives sit on those boards for the same reasons that other leaders of various industries sit on them—those financial institutions need to know what industries are doing and planning before they can make financial decisions relating to those industries. The industry, like all industries, is there to advise, and it has no say whatsoever in the final decisions.

Illegal deals? If they were to take place at all, they'd be much more likely to take place on the golf course. Perhaps the proponents of the "intricate web" theory would do better to work for laws to outlaw golf matches among leaders of industry and finance.

And if they were conspiring in those rooms, what might they be conspiring to do? They certainly don't seem to be conspiring to fix the price of gasoline. Gasoline is currently selling several cents beneath the governmentally mandated ceiling. If industry were making price deals, then it stands to reason that companies would agree to let prices float up to that government ceiling. Because industry makes only a couple of pennies of profit on each gallon of gasoline, such a rise would be of vast significance. But such a rise has not occurred and prices continue to vary, solely because of stiff intraindustry competition.

But might not the industry be making secret deals that are hidden from the public? The "intricate web" school says that they are, but again without being specific. What sorts of deals would these be? Perhaps the most obvious, if they were in fact taking place, would be in the business of bidding. Various companies bid against one another for the rights to produce oil in various fields. Rights to individual five to 6,000-acre tracts are auctioned off by sealed bid, a practice which has benefited the U.S. Treasury to the tune of $12 billion since 1970—the sum which the companies have handed over to the government for the rights to produce on the outer continental shelf.

Surely, if they were going to conspire, this would be a prime area—"We'll bid just over you for that tract, and you can bid just over us for this one." It is an area in which vast amounts of money could be saved and substantial profits realized. It was proved that the electrical equipment industry, for instance, back in the fifties, colluded prior to "secret" bidding.

It has been done. But apart from a few successful probes of asphalt marketing, no investigation has been able to unearth compelling evidence that it has been done in the petroleum industry.

Prices that the majors have bid through the years have varied—sometimes wildly. And each oil company takes elaborate and often somewhat exotic precautions to see that competitors do not learn of their bidding intentions. In 1969, for instance, during the week before Alaska accepted sealed bids for production rights on state-owned land, one company confined all its employees involved in the bidding to a private rail car that shuttled nonstop for the week back and forth across Western Canada.

The "intricate web" theorists, in the end, can argue only from implication, the single most potent weapon in their arsenal being suspicion. It is the automatic, ingrained American resistance to bigness that buttresses the charges of monopoly—an emotional reaction and nothing more. Critics of the industry fan this emotionalism by feeding the man on the street conspiracy theories and by raising his hackles with terms like "oligopoly," which sounds sinister indeed, even more sinister than monopoly.

But whether they complain of monopoly or oligopoly, critics of the oil industry often seem confused, and perhaps their confusion can in part be traced to the problem of how they can justify the only real remedies they have to propose to correct a situation which doesn't quite exist.

Many, for instance, admit that the real monopoly at work here is the OPEC cartel, which, during the past few years, since it has taken total control of the marketing of that oil, has managed to quadruple prices.

Our own oil companies may not be formally monopolistic, say many of the critics, but they function, as British journalist Anthony Sampson puts it, as "the machinery for maintaining the OPEC cartel." That is, the large oil companies, by helping the Arabs to produce, refine, transport, and market their oil, also make the day-to-day operations of the cartel smoother and more efficient. Thus, apparently, monopoly by association, and the consequent argument that in order to break up OPEC, it will be necessary to break up our oil companies.

Now there is no doubt that the producing nations want the major companies to continue to provide technical expertise and to help in the marketing of their oil. But if the integrated companies were broken up in such a way as to make this no longer possible, there is no reason whatsoever to believe that any sort of beneficial dent would be made in the OPEC cartel. In fact, from an American point of view, quite the opposite could well be the result. The most likely result, in fact, would be that the large competitors in England, France, Holland, Italy and Germany—all of them bankrolled in part by their national governments—would rush in to fill the vacuum left by the fragmentation and subsequent departure of the major companies from the scene. And the producers, of course, would welcome them with open arms.

This seems too common-sensical and too self-evident to require discussion. Yet there are advocates of divestiture—some of them the most intelligent and articulate—who insist that a host of independents would rush in to do business with the OPEC nations once the majors were broken up, and that the resulting competition would force the producing nations to drop prices sharply.

But given the reality of the existence of governmentally subsidized companies ready to replace the majors, this is so much applesauce. The independents would be so many guppies, swimming in a sea of sharks. There is also no reason to assume that competitive independents would in any way work to hold down prices. What evidence there is, in fact, suggests quite the opposite. In 1973, for instance, when the OPEC governments decided to try some direct marketing of crude oil, at an auction in Iran, independents pushed the bidding up to a peak of $17 per barrel, more than triple the posted price. And in Nigeria, independents bid as high as $22 a barrel for low sulfur Nigerian crude. The OPEC nations then used these bids as a justification for the price rises of that winter. The independents, in other words, given the chance, accomplished precisely the opposite of what their advocates claim they would accomplish.

Yet another group of oil company critics believe that the government should establish federal oil companies to bring what they call domestic monopolies under control and to break up the OPEC cartel abroad. One such idea which has been kicking around Washington for some time is the proposal, advanced by Adlai Stevenson III and others, to establish a Federal Oil and Gas Corporation which would be used as a "yardstick" competitor, against which costs and profits of the private companies would be measured. If the private profits or costs were out of line, then presumably regulatory agencies would be empowered to force them back into the pattern established by what its advocates like to call "a competitive public enterprise." But the problem, of course, is that there can be no such animal. Such a federally funded organization could arbitrarily lower or raise prices, limit or reduce production. Since it would not be in business to make money, and since whether it makes a profit or takes a loss is irrelevant, its only real function would be the quintessentially anticompetitive one of fixing prices and discouraging those fluctuations in the market that tend to be brought on by competition.

There is also the suggestion that the U.S. establish a federal oil company to operate abroad. The proponents of this approach, however, are never able to tell us why a governmental company would be in any more effective position vis a vis the OPEC cartel than the private companies, or why the operations of such a company would result in lower prices. This has not been the case with the Italian or the British companies who do business with OPEC and whose countries help finance them. And if we have learned anything during the last few decades, it should be that government operations are simply not as efficient and economical—or as honest—as private.

And finally, there's the whole question of foreign policy, which would inevitably mean that in the case of another crisis a federal company simply wouldn't have the same room to maneuver enjoyed by private companies.

James Akins, former ambassador to Saudi Arabia, puts it this way: "Every move [of the federal corporation] would be interpreted in a political context and every agreement would be called into question if there were any political disagreements between the United States and the producer." And that, essentially, is the problem inherent in a federal overseas corporation. Just consider, for instance, what would have happened had we been dependent on such a corporation during the crisis of 1973-74.

We were able to avert a true and disastrous crisis only because the oil companies were able to maneuver. But had the government been in charge, there would have been two likely primary outcomes, neither of them desirable: we could have acceded to what probably would have been Arab demands and ceased our support of Israel, thereby insuring an adequate supply of oil by stabbing an ally in the back; or we could have stood by Israel and guaranteed a cutoff that would have been more comprehensive and of much greater duration.

But perhaps the single most incomprehensible tenet embraced by the proponents of the federalization of the oil industry—or any industry, for that matter—is that while a big, centralized private corporation is somehow reprehensible, there is nothing at all wrong with—and, indeed, even something admirable about—a big, centralized governmental monopoly. Yet there is overwhelming evidence that massive governmental intervention in any industry usually works against the consumer. In this country, for instance, a deliberate federal policy aimed at keeping natural gas prices down to an artificially low level has led to enormous demand and then to shortages, when it was no longer economically feasible to develop new reserves. Or consider the quintessential governmental monopoly, the Soviet Oil Trust, which has traditionally kept prices for Iron Curtain bloc customers at what we would consider exhorbitant rates.

Nevertheless, the idea of governmental monopoly does not seem totally distasteful to the critics of the oil industry, and one has to wonder why. Perhaps it's just a basic confusion, a contradiction inherent in a certain view of how society can best be managed —a view that no longer quite seems tenable. Just a few years ago, it seemed perfectly understandable that Senator Philip Hart would be pushing for legislation that would break up, among other industries, autos, steel, aluminum, chemicals, drugs, electrical equipment, computers, communications equipment, and, of course, oil. Senator Hart, after all, was an old-line, neo-New Deal liberal, and it was the creed of that school of thought that monopoly capitalism had brought the nation to the brink of ruin and that the only salvation lay with a large and benign centralized federal government.

There was nothing at all odd about this view. It had, in one form or another, become the dominant view of the twentieth century and many thoughtful people believed sincerely that if you could exercise total control over man's environmental and economic situation, then you could help to produce a more perfect man.

It was inevitable that with the transcendence of this view, the view of a central government as the agent for exercising that control should also become transcendent. Contemporary liberalism, as we came to know it a few years ago, was a direct descendant of that school of romanticism which began by telling us that man would be perfected by nature and ended by glorifying that state as the source of that perfection.

Gradually, however, perhaps as Lyndon Johnson seemed to be stepping up the bombing of everything that moved in Southeast Asia, one of those sea-changes began to occur that come about only a few times in each century, when a commonly agreed upon view of life and government suddenly alters radically and perhaps permanently.

Any of the best and brightest of those liberals intent on perfecting us looked up suddenly and came to realize a basic truth—a government is no better than the people who run it, and if bad people happen to take over the controls, then that government will do bad things. This was a lesson that grew, and even the diehards among the old-line liberals had to admit after their arch-foe Richard Nixon took office and gave us Watergate that it was extremely dangerous to give the government too much power.

And so, suddenly, we heard all those liberal spokesmen and pamphleteers such as Arthur Schlesinger, Jr., who just a couple of years ago were aggrandizing the Executive branch and demanding that it be ceded more power, now ranting against "the Imperial Presidency." It had become that, of course. But the irony is that it had become that precisely because the old-line liberals had fought so hard to bring it about.

In the aftermath of the disillusionment which blanketed the country like radioactive fallout after Vietnam and Watergate, there are few politicians willing to get up on their soapboxes and preach the beauties of letting the federal government do it. In fact, as the 1976 elections amply demonstrated, it's politically expedient these days to soft-pedal any views which seem pro-Washington. And this, of course, doesn't apply just to that imperial presidency. It also applies to a Congress which is perceived as ineffectual, venal, and morally bankrupt. And it applies to a bureaucracy which increasingly seems to encroach into every aspect of our daily lives. We are rapidly becoming an overregulated society in which government takes more and more from us and gives less and less in return.

The average American now officially works four full months just to pay his tax bill, and within the decade that figure is expected to reach a full half year. For many, the question of the economic structure of the private sector is rapidly becoming irrelevant. MIT economists can tell us that oligopolies cause inflation until they're blue in the face. But as the tax bite increases, and as the value of the dollar shrinks, a growing number of Americans seems to believe that the primary source of their malaise is overgrown, insensitive, monopolistic government.

# Chapter
# Five

"The FTC's complaint against the eight largest oil companies must be one of the most novel monopoly suits of recent years," said the *Wall Street Journal* in 1973 of the Federal Trade Commission's ongoing attempt to break up the oil companies. "Our own reading of the whole matter is that the FTC is playing games with us, that it has taken two years to discover there is really no conspiracy among the major oil companies, but that it hates to admit it. Pressed by Congress and others to find a scapegoat for the present shortages, it has come up with a report and complaint in which loaded rhetoric is used to describe inexorable economic forces at work."

The FTC's response to the 1973–74 energy crisis, in an apparently political move which prompted the *Wall Street Journal* editorial, had been to zero in on the refineries. The majors had fared better during the energy crisis than had the independents and the inevitable charge was that the majors were squeezing out the minors. The major companies insisted, however, that they had increasingly found the refining of gasoline to be one of the least profitable of their activities. Therefore, their plans for expanding refineries and production increasingly included only what they themselves would require for their own markets. But there also existed independent jobbers who made their living by buying cut-rate gasoline from refineries which had produced more than their companies could handle. Thus, especially during the energy crisis, some independents were unable to obtain gasoline. There were no longer any excess products for them to buy. And the majors insisted that the independents were suffering, not from unfair business practices, but from risks inherent in the business of spot-market purchase.

The FTC, however, taking the popular political line of the day, argued that the situation had resulted from a consciously monopolistic act, the purpose of which was to drive potentially competitive independents out of business. But many others, among them the *Wall Street Journal,* saw it differently. "The allegation," said the *Journal,* "simply means that the major oil companies have not found it profitable to build refineries, at $250 million each, fast enough to insure the independent jobbers and refineries all the cut-rate gasoline they could use."

The FTC further contended, although somewhat unconvincingly, that the companies juggled their books to keep profits low in refining and high in production. But what it failed to acknowledge was that none of the majors, with the one exception of Getty, was in itself sufficient in crude. And this was a central point. Each of the companies barters with the others for crude. If they kept profits, and therefore the price of crude, unnaturally high, then they'd all lose money. Only Getty owned sufficient crude for the shifting charged by the FTC to be profitable.

But Getty, the sixteenth largest company, was not mentioned in the suit.

FTC's book-juggling allegation, in short, made no sense. The after-tax losses to the average major company, had another company unnaturally raised the price of crude oil, would have ranged, according to reputable economists, from a low of three cents on each dollar of profits to a high of forty-eight cents. None of the companies charged could have borne losses of this magnitude, nor is there any reason outside of mass corporate lunacy that they should want to.

Nevertheless, the FTC was suspicious, its suspicions apparently heightened by the way in which the companies barter among themselves for crude. The system is complicated, but the industry maintains that it is necessary because of the expenses involved in transporting oil and the saving that can be realized through bartering. Suppose, for instance, that Texaco has more oil than it needs in Connecticut, but is short in Oregon, while Mobil finds itself in precisely the opposite situation. The two companies then get together and arrange an exchange. The result: Texaco does not need to send a fleet of tankers sailing from Oregon to Connecticut which might well pass a Mobil fleet sailing in the opposite direction.

This bartering process is a common and open practice among the majors, and the independents participate in it as well. But if you don't have the oil you can't barter, and this is what happened to certain independents during the crisis. To the FTC it smacked of monopoly. But to a less suspicious observer, it would simply seem a more efficient way of doing business, and one that pays off for us all. It is, after all, the man at the pump who in the end has to foot the bill for those Texaco tankers and those Mobil tankers making their separate trips and meeting half way.

Yet it seems that this sort of argument simply has no meaning to regulatory agencies such as the FTC, to politicians, or even in many cases to the courts. Part of the problem appears to be that we have lost sight of just what it is that monopoly laws are supposed to accomplish. Monopoly laws exist to protect the consumer by keeping the price of the product he buys at the most reasonable competitive price. Increasingly, however, the monopoly laws are being used to protect less efficient competitors—competitors who are too small or insufficiently ingenious to play the game. And when such competitors are protected, they are inevitably protected at the expense of the consumer, whom the laws were originally passed to protect.

Almost everyone who discusses economic matters tends to agree that increased efficiency is desirable. But the FTC increasingly appears to bring charges *because* an industry is efficient, and often, it would seem, for that reason only. Professor Wesley Liebeler discusses a recent case of this kind:

"A cement company had acquired a ready-mix concrete firm in Kansas City. The Commission sought divestiture on the grounds that the effect of the vertical acquisition would be anticompetitive. The administrative law judge found that 'the vertically integrated [firm], therefore, has decisive cost advantages over its unintegrated competitors, which if passed on in the form of lower concrete prices, could result in prices lower than competitors' costs, and force those competitors out of business.'

"This fascinating excerpt," comments Professor Liebeler, "is just one small part of an opinion that makes it clear beyond a doubt that the real 'problem' is that vertical integration can operate to *lower* prices which, of course, tends to make life more difficult for other firms in the industry."

It may be that the FTC sees its mission as one of penalizing efficiency, although there is nothing in the law to validate that view of regulatory mission. Vertical integration does tend to increase efficiency, and by so doing it also tends to hold down, rather than increase, prices. This is not monopolistic. It may also have the effect, however, of forcing less efficient competitors from the market, and it is this potential effect which most troubles the FTC and which may prompt it to bring legal action against firms which are violating no laws but are functioning too efficiently.

No doubt much of this springs from genuine concern for the plight of small businessmen. And that is a concern that most Americans can appreciate. We can personally identify ourselves with the small businessman in a way that we cannot do with a huge corporation, and we can feel it when big business seems to squeeze him out of the market.

This concern is a real one. Yet despite it, the average American makes choices every day of the week that hasten the demise of many of those small businessmen we express concern for. Everytime we buy groceries at Safeway rather than at the small corner grocery store, for instance, we help to squeeze out the owner of that small store. When we buy our appliances at Sears, our drugs at Sav-A-Lot, our clothes at one of the large department store chains, we are doing the same thing.

In many ways, then, the average American consumer is opting for what is provided by big business, not because he loves it or is loyal to the concept of capitalism, but because big business provides a wider range of cheaper and better products. This, of course, is not always the case. But in such areas as the marketing of food or appliances or petroleum products, big business can do the job better, and that, in the last analysis, is all the consumer really cares about.

Yet it is doubtful that most consumers would quite believe the choices they make in their daily lives lead to these conclusions. And here we come to one of those peculiar psychological dichotomies that invariably make the analysis of people, trends, and social issues so difficult. Most Americans, if polled, would probably say they believe absolutely that we enjoy the world's highest standard of living. As proof, a great number would point to the things they are able to buy in the marketplace—goods, food, clothes, services—that are the envy of the world. They know that nowhere in those gray workers' utopias of Eastern Europe can people ever hope to buy or own a fraction of what we take as necessities. No one believes that the average worker's wife in Poland will ever own a dishwasher, for instance, or that her husband will own a set of golf clubs, as their American counterparts do.

And most Americans also understand that these things are possible only because we have managed, despite the assaults of the last several decades,

101

to retain our system of free enterprise reasonably intact. True, it is not a perfect system, and, as the critics point out, there is an often disturbing coziness between business and those who regulate business in Washington. There is also an increasingly disturbing tendency for business not to fight the regulators too strenuously just as long as it is the competition that is being penalized.

Nevertheless, it is a system that works better than any other yet devised, and it will no doubt continue to work that way for as long as government can be prevented from taking it over completely. Without it, under any of the alternative systems today which turn its functions over to the state, most of us would be living either like that Polish worker and his wife or like our bankrupt cousins in England.

But here the dichotomy arises. Most Americans would fiercely defend the way of life that big business has made possible. But big business itself? That's another question. Part of the problem, of course, is the impersonality inherent in such a massive and far-reaching system.

One industry can explain, as it tries to do, that it's "just people, working for people." A massive food chain can refer to itself and its employees and customers as a "family" and sing warm commercial jingles about itself. Another corporation can announce over and over that it "cares." And the oil industry can explain, correctly, that the shares of the six largest oil companies in this country are owned, either directly or indirectly through pension funds, retirement plans, or mutual funds, by fourteen million Americans. And they can point out that about seven million of these people are retirees, who depend on dividends from these companies to supplement their shrinking social security incomes.

All this is true. But most Americans simply aren't impressed. Big business is an impersonal force which provides them with what they want. As long as it works in the way it should, which means to most of us as long as it keeps those things coming at reasonable prices, we don't really think about it.

But once it stops carrying out that function smoothly, once kinks develop in that system and suddenly the organizations within it and the people who run them become highly visible, then we are likely to begin to throw things.

And that, in a sense, is what happened to the oil industry during the 1973–74 crisis and the subsequent embargo. Unlike many industries—tool and die manufacturing, for instance, or textiles—oil has always been relatively visible, playing as it does such a central role in our daily lives. Thus, when the crisis hit, this industry, already more visible than most, was caught pinned up there against the ridgeline, paralyzed in the same spotlight of national attention that was being focused on Washington politicians.

The oil industry had for years been telling us in commercials what it was doing for us. Now it was having trouble doing what we expected it to do for us as a matter of course, and we wanted it to tell us why. And when the companies seemed to sputter and began to talk about complex concepts such as shortfalls and old oil and OPEC, then it was easy to bend a sympathetic ear to those national politicians who talked about monopolies and conspiracies.

Anti-big-business sentiments have fueled some of the most potent popular political movements in American history. Throughout the Carter campaign, the populist themes played just below the surface. (Carter himself is steeped in populist tradition, and one of the funniest moments of the campaign came when he had to explain to Walter Cronkite who Tom Watson was. Watson, of course, was the great Southern Populist. Antibusiness sentiments cut across ideological lines, and today the John Birch Society member is as adamantly opposed to the large corporation as is the member of the Socialist Workers Party.

Thus, given our traditional opposition to bigness —as opposed, of course, to our approval of what bigness provides—given a populist streak which is never far beneath the American surface, given the energy crisis, and given a highly visible culprit to blame, it is small wonder that a climate was created in the country which made it not only expedient but politically necessary for the Federal Trade Commission to act. The FTC is, after all, supposed to protect us against such things.

The FTC had been eyeing the oil industry for years, and the crisis provided the catalyst for action. But to prove that the oil industry was a monopoly and that therefore it should be segmented, the FTC had to demonstrate that the major companies were squeezing the smaller companies out of the market. They were doing so, argued the FTC, and were succeeding, because they enjoyed special advantages conferred by government. One of these advantages, said the FTC, was oil import quotas.

The oil import quota and the whole question of

artificially limiting the amount of oil to reach the market is an involved one, reaching back to Depression days. Critics of the industry point to it as an example—and they have a case, although not altogether a fair one—of industry and government sweethearting it in order to keep prices artificially high.

In the thirties, as the Depression dramatically eroded the market for oil and as vast amounts of oil were being discovered in the Southwest, the industry believed it had two choices. Companies could compete among themselves to sell at cut-rate prices, or they could agree among themselves to reduce the amount of the product they produced.

It was a time when the industry was just beginning to restore order to the internal chaos that had followed in the wake of the antitrust actions under the Sherman Act, and many of the most important segments of the industry were still operating on a slippery footing.

If the industry allowed all the oil it was capable of producing to flood the market, the companies reasoned, there would be such a surplus that prices would fall below production cost. One certain result of that would be the quick collapse of most of the weaker companies.

This would not, of course, have caused similar concern in normal times. Such weeding out is necessary and desirable whenever companies reach the point where they produce more than they can sell. But these were not normal times. And because the Depression was not a normal situation, and would therefore eventually end, the industry, were it to be weakened by bankruptcy, would be unable for years to supply the newly created markets. (In this case, the industry reasoned correctly. Had the companies at their weakest moment in our history allowed themselves to have at one another in a cut-throat attempt to corner what markets there were, they would never have been able to handle the energy demands of World War II.)

As a result, industry worked for a system of rationing production, approved by both the states and the federal government. Each well was allowed to bring up only a certain amount of oil, a disastrous decline in prices was reversed, and the industry survived. Governmentally legislated rationing, however, continued for decades after the Depression, thereby leading to what critics claim were unnessarily and artificially high prices.

But, to give credit to the industry in retrospect, it could be argued that oil, as a limited product, ought to be rationed, and that its price should be kept artificially high to discourage use. And it could also be argued that during this period of rationing, although the price of oil did not reflect free market conditions, it was still a relatively cheap product—so cheap, in fact, that despite rationing, America evolved into a society in which the automobile and the unlimited use of gasoline for recreational purposes dictated a new way of life.

Few Americans sufficiently well off to own a car ever considered curtailing vacation plans or recreational driving because of the price of a tank of gas. Gasoline was perhaps America's number one bargain, and because we believed that it would remain so, we built that magnificent web of interstate highways which may just one day stand as unused monuments to a way of life that has passed into the murk of history.

Despite the purpose of rationing, then—to keep prices up—it could nevertheless be argued now that the price of petroleum products during the period was in fact not high enough. The relatively low price did nothing to encourage Americans to conserve a product which, over a period of time, would be depleted and could not be replaced. (This argument, incidentally, the finite-product argument, is used effectively and with some justification by the OPEC nations as the basic rationale for maintaining artificially high prices.) The general public during this period, if they thought about it at all, assumed that the oil would never run out. The oil companies, however, involved in the business of abandoning dry wells, knew otherwise, and in one sense the industry's system of rationing can also be viewed in retrospect as a system, albeit not a particularly effective one, of conservation. It is somewhat peculiar therefore that those conservationists and consumerists who have criticized the industry for maintaining high prices don't acknowledge that such a pricing system, if applied sensibly, could bring on at least a modicum of conservation. But the critics seem unable to conceive of that occurring through market principles rather than through federally mandated rationing programs.

The industry's system of rationing threatened to unravel in the fifties. Vast amounts of oil were discovered in the Persian Gulf and by 1950 Persian oil was supplying much of Western Europe. American domestic producers, realizing that cheap Persian oil, flooding the American market, would seriously threaten their domestic production, asked the government to impose an import quota, restricting the amount of foreign oil that could be imported to the States. And in 1959, President Eisenhower complied, signing an executive order which established a mandatory national oil import quota system.

Although the oil industry put its argument to the Eisenhower Administration largely in terms of national defense, it seems doubtful that foreign military foes were the main concern of the oil industry when it persuaded the government to close the faucets on imported oil. The foreign foe about whom the industry worried probably was a mercantile rather than a military enemy. Like most American producers of everything from shoes to computers, the central concern was domestic production and the specter of a flood of goods from foreign markets where labor costs are a fraction of ours.

Nevertheless, the national defense argument, although perhaps not uppermost in industry minds, appealed to General Eisenhower. And from a military point of view it was a sound one. If our domestic oil production trickled to a halt because of cheaper foreign imports, then our national defense would indeed be imperiled. A modern fighting machine depends totally on oil for its mobility. And if that oil is owned by a potential adversary, or a potential ally of an adversary, then that machine would soon cease to move.

Nevertheless, big oil has come in for a good deal of criticism for insisting on import quotas. "What a crazy system we have had all these years," says Morris Udall, articulating the most effective argu-

108

ment against import quotas. "A kind of 'drain America first' approach."

Udall makes a telling point here, for a system which guaranteed the large-scale extraction of oil from our accessible fields, rather than first using up foreign supplies, does not now seem to have been in our best national interest. But those were the Cold War years, the Communist nations were on the move around the globe, building their imperial system, and it seemed highly possible that at any given moment we could be cut off from foreign sources, with disastrous results had we become heavily dependent upon them.

No one, at the time the decision to impose quotas was made, could have known that this might not soon be the case. In fact, all the evidence of the era, given the relentless expansion of the Communist nations, indicated that the probability was high. Perhaps then we should have exploited foreign sources during those years, but there were plausible reasons then, just as there are now, against a too heavy reliance on foreign oil.

It also seems possible to argue that the State of Israel owes its existence today in large part to our decision not to allow the Arab nations to supply us. And it is not unlikely that without American support Israel never would have survived. We have in fact become her only major remaining ally. England, with its sometimes Arabist foreign policy and its desperate pre-North Sea need for Arabian oil, did what it could to prevent Israel from coming into being. France, although initially sympathetic, has also backed off because of its petroleum requirements.

From the day of its founding, Israel could look primarily for potential support to two major powers. Only the United States and the Soviet Union were sufficiently independent in oil to thwart the Arab nations. But Russia, for reasons peculiar to the workings of that nation's murky national mentality, chose to extend its friendship to a group of dictatorships which embodied everything most appalling to the socialist dream, and by so doing to set itself up as the implacable enemy of the only progressive socialistic nation in the Mideast. No doubt it had something to do with vodka and the winter, but whatever the reasons, Russia bowed out, and we became Israel's major ally, the only nation of consequence that could not be blackmailed by the Arabs.

And it is no coincidence that our support for Israel began to show signs of eroding at the highest levels just when the Arabs found that they were finally able to use oil as a weapon against us. Almost simultaneously with the embargo, the nation's policy makers, led by Henry Kissinger, began to wonder whether there wasn't, after all, a good case to be made for the Arabs' position on Israel. We suddenly realized that we had been slipping into increased dependence on OPEC and nearly overnight there was an unprecedented burst of pro-Arabism in the country.

National news magazines blossomed out in cover stories singing the praises of the Arab nations. Many respected commentators suddenly seemed to develop a pronounced pro-Arab tilt, and Richard Nixon, off on one of his last missions as Prince of Peace, traveled to Egypt and promised Sadat everything he'd ever dreamed of.

Those of us who wrote for Nixon were told to play up our traditional love for all things Arabic and it seemed possible that an Arab task force might show up any day to carry the Washington Monument off to Egypt, where it would be installed beside the pyramids.

It is not our purpose to discuss here just how drastically the moral views of statesmen can shift when self-interest suddenly becomes an issue. But suffice it to say that had our dependence on Arab oil during the late forties reached anything approaching its level in 1973-74, the chances would have been excellent that we would not have become Israel's only ally. In fact, Israel probably never would have been founded.

To the extent, then, that Israel's existence is the result of the "Drain America First" policy that Representative Udall lampoons, it was, most Americans would agree, a good policy, perhaps simply for that reason alone.

Most Americans would probably also maintain, however, that it was a bad policy insofar as the rationing and the subsequent import quotas cost them, as consumers, considerable amounts of money. The U.S. Task Force on Oil Import Controls, for instance, estimated in 1970 that American consumers were spending about $5 billion per year because of them.

Still, when one looks at the dramatic rise in energy consumption that took place during the period of import controls, again it seems obvious that the business of gasoline rationing did not seriously inhibit the growth of what we like to call the American way of life. Nor was the development of American technology in any way hindered by the price of energy. In fact, had the government allowed vast quantities of cheap oil to glut the market during those years when cheap oil was still available, much of that oil would not have been reinvested in anything meaningful for the country's future, but would have simply been wasted in an even more conspicuous way. And that, of course, would have made it even more difficult to develop a national conservation ethic.

The consequences of rationing and import quotas could be discussed endlessly, as could the question of whether the government acted properly in establishing those quotas and allowing the industry to ration.

In its bill of particulars against the industry, however, the FTC expressed no doubt about what it viewed as the consequences of import quotas. "The import quota," it said in a staff report, "clearly contributed to profits earned in producing crude oil by elevating prices, but the quota increased profits to the majors in another way. The right to import went only to existing refineries. Thus the major companies . . . were able to purchase oil at the world price as an input for their refineries, which produced final products at elevated domestic prices."

Now there is no doubt that under the import quota system the amount of foreign crude allowed each refinery was valuable indeed, because until the OPEC price rise foreign crude was considerably cheaper than domestic oil. Foreign oil, then, would have significant effects on a refinery's profits. And since refineries were generally allowed amounts of foreign crude in proportion to their total output capacity, it would seem, as the FTC argues, that the largest refineries stood to profit most. But in fact, small refineries were allowed imported crude on the basis of a sliding scale under which they actually received amounts proportionately greater than the amounts allowed to the majors.

Professor Richard B. Mancke, a Tufts University economist, estimates than in 1969, a typical year, while Standard Oil of New Jersey was allowed 35,810 barrels of imported oil per day, and a small competing refiner was allowed only 2,060 barrels, the Standard figure represented only 3 percent of its total capacity while the figure for the smaller refinery, under the sliding scale, represented approximately 20 percent of its capacity. According to Dr. Mancke, each barrel of foreign oil, when divided into total production, gave Standard a 5.41 cent advantage while the small competitor gained a 28.09 cent advantage. The small refiner, in other words, received a per-barrel subsidy five times greater than that received by the major refiner.

Obviously, therefore, the FTC's charge that the import quota system allowed refineries owned by major companies to squeeze out smaller competitors was simply wrong. The import system had been set up in such a way as to preclude the possibility. And although it could be argued that barriers to entry did exist in the refinery industry, those barriers had nothing to do with the policies of the major companies. In fact, investors increasingly began to discover that refinery investment was risky because of federal and local environmental policies, rather than because of the alleged monopolistic practices of the majors.

In addition to the import quota system, the FTC insisted that the infamous oil depletion allowance was a prime contributor to what it viewed as the monopolistic structure of the industry.

Said the FTC staff report: "Oil depletion allowances [allowed] a crude-oil-producing firm . . . to subtract from its gross income before taxes an amount equal to 22 percent of its total revenues from crude production. . . . Under this system the major integrated firms have an incentive to seek high crude prices. The high crude prices are, however, a cost to the major firms' refineries. Thus, an increase in crude profits but a decrease in refinery profits. The integrated oil companies gain because the depletion allowance reduces the tax on crude profits, while refinery profits are not subject to the same advantageous depletion allowance."

On the face of it, this seems a plausible argument. Refineries owned by major integrated companies do not have to show as much profit as do independent refineries, says the FTC, because the major companies make their profit at the production end. And they have been able to make that profit, the FTC argues, because the oil depletion allowance allows them to do so.

Now any discussion at all of the depletion allowance here is in a sense academic, since Congress has voted to outlaw its use by the major oil companies. But it forms a central part of the antitrust case which the FTC is attempting to build against the companies, and therefore deserves attention.

Perhaps the first thing to say about the depletion allowance is that it has not been, as critics seem to imply, in any way unique to the oil industry. The

114

government allows it on all of the thousands of products that come from the earth, because such products are depletable, and profits realized on them are not total profits since they must be reinvested to find similar products elsewhere. And this, at least in the case of major oil producers whose companies must reinvest to remain in existence, is precisely what happened to those savings realized by the major oil companies as a result of the depletion allowance—they were reinvested in the business of finding more oil.

Furthermore, the central FTC argument here— that special tax breaks allowed the majors to squeeze out independent minors—just doesn't hold water. As we mentioned earlier, if the major companies had jacked up the price of crude oil unnaturally, the industry would have lost revenue.

"With the oil depletion allowance at 22 percent," says one economist, "profit-shifting would only yield profits for those companies able to produce at least 93 percent of their crude-oil needs."

These and scores of other arguments that have been marshalled against the FTC's case had been hashed over for years, and the FTC, of course, was aware of them, its suit motivated more by political considerations than by any real fear that the vertically integrated oil companies were actually guilty of monopolistic practices. And the FTC's decision to proceed with its suit even after legislative actions made its arguments moot underscores the purely political motivation here. Oil import quotas, for instance, became meaningless in the face of rising foreign oil prices and declining domestic reserves, and the import quota system was formally abolished in 1973. Similarly, the oil depletion allowance for the majors was abolished in 1975.

Thus, no import quotas, no depletion allowance, and therefore no FTC case, since these are the practices which prove monopoly. A layman, looking at the FTC's case, would probably shrug and observe that even if the oil companies had been monopolies, they could no longer be so if the primary charges against them were those brought by the FTC, since those charges are now irrelevant. And not only laymen would feel this way. In 1975, the judge hearing the case urged the FTC to forget it all and withdraw charges. The whole case, the judge pointed out, was built upon a situation which no longer existed. But the FTC, for reasons that could be explained only by the prevailing political climate, refused to do so. Like all governmental agencies, it has been coming under increasing fire for allegedly favoring those businesses it is mandated to regulate. And like all governmental agencies, it has become increasingly jittery as the barrage intensifies. Thus, like most of the other regulatory agencies in Washington these days, it will turn somersaults to prove it is not a tool of any special interest.

Nineteen seventy-five was a particularly fine year for that sort of thing. In the wake of Agnew and Nixon, the city had come very close, if such a thing is possible, to suffering a collective nervous breakdown. Watergate fallout, governmental and corporate corruption, venality and immorality—it seemed to many in government that the whole thing was about to fall apart, and thousands of bureaucrats and functionaries, along with most entrenched national politicians, suddenly suspected that the people had had enough, that they were about to rise up and run the whole crew out of Washington. It was not a time in which federal agencies cared to have the champions of the public interest, led by the consumerists and Naderites of all stripes, focusing in on them. The term "Watergate" had come to mean a great deal more than a third-rate burglary.

According to some FTC staffers, many of the agency lawyers would have preferred to drop the whole thing. For one thing, the case was just too flimsy. The section of the Sherman Act upon which it was built is one of the vaguer ones, and FTC investigators had uncovered no hard evidence of monopoly. Thus the lawyers were forced to argue that because of its structure, special circumstances, and institutional peculiarities, the oil industry had the power to *become* a monopoly. Hence, the FTC's basic problem: To a public conditioned by a highly visible and articulate cadre of industry critics to view the oil companies as quintessential monopolies, such an explanation would be worse than no explanation at all. But since it is the only one that can be offered for dropping the case, the FTC is about as likely to do so as Earl Butz is to serve as chief of protocol in the Carter Administration.

From the industry's point of view, however, the FTC case isn't necessarily a terrible thing. Spokesmen for big oil have argued all along that the courts are preferable to the Congress, and for Congress to single out one industry for dismemberment by legislative fiat rather than by due process not only is unfair but potentially damaging to a carefully built national structure of safeguards and laws. Better, the industry believes, to let it work its way carefully through the courts, where the companies will win, than to rush it through Congress on a wave of temporary emotionalism growing out of transient and often faddish contemporary concerns.

There are, of course, abundant criticisms of the antitrust, FTC approach coming from both sides of the ideological spectrum. From both the left and the extreme right, for instance, comes the charge that antimonopoly laws are never vigorously enforced. Yet in one decade, from 1963 to 1973, the Justice Department initiated 224 separate investigations and brought 40 formal complaints. The modifier "vigorously," then, commonly used by these critics, is a relative one, describing a state of mind rather than an objective condition.

Those who believe that big business is by definition immoral, that capitalism is by definition an oppressive system, that corporations and the government are in league, running the country under a system of modified fascism, no doubt also believe that the FTC and Justice aren't adequately protecting us. And perhaps they aren't. But ask an average businessman, and he'll tell you precisely the opposite. The FTC, he believes, is staffed by pot-smoking, long-haired, activist young freaks who came off the campuses in the sixties and are dedicated to tearing down the free-enterprise system.

And, of course, just as these critics who suspect regulatory agencies and business of having too friendly a relationship have some justification for their charges, so too does the businessman. The regulators and those they regulate have been a bit too chummy in the past. But that is changing fast. And the fact is that the agencies are indeed increasingly attracting a bright new activist type, a product of the campuses of the sixties and seventies, intensely suspicious of big business operations.

There is no way, of course, of gauging just how many of these young activists there are out in the departments and agencies, or how rapidly their numbers are growing. But as anyone who has worked in the Executive branch can testify, they are there and they are increasingly important in influencing policy, and they are definitely increasing.

This seems especially true of the young lawyers. Many of the brightest of them no longer think of going into a prestigious firm and making a great deal of money. Today, the drill among many of the best of the new law-school graduates is to go into some form of public service, to fight for the little man and minorities against the rip-off artists, corporate and otherwise.

A job in a regulatory agency, then, where the consciousness is rising rapidly, fills the bill nicely. It is one of those changes that cannot be documented, but anyone who works in Washington can attest to it. And many of us believe that under the Carter presidency, we will finally see a full-fledged, card-carrying consumer activist taking over at least one of the agencies. As of this writing, the betting is on the Food and Drug Administration, but it could also eventually be the FTC. And should that happen, our businessman would have justification for his qualms.

At any rate, whatever the problems with the regulatory agencies, and whatever the criticisms of the Justice Department—it is underfunded and understaffed, for instance, and it takes too long to get a decision—the industry believes that there lies its best hope.

Now no doubt there are oil company executives of the kind that Senator McGovern detests, perhaps dozing off at their desks after one of those four martini, deductible-expense-account lunches. They are dreaming of a perfect world in which domestic production and profits are up, natural gas has been deregulated, the companies are developing coal and shale and nuclear energy, the administration in Washington has actually come up with an energy policy, the FTC has just announced the whole suit business was a big joke all along, and Senators Hart and Abourezk proclaim their conversion to economic conservatism and announce publicly that divestiture legislation makes no sense and might very well deal the final death blow to our faltering economy.

But such dreams are unlikely to come true, nor, after the martinis had finally worn off, would any oilman expect them to. But of all the things the oil companies have to live with, they infinitely prefer the FTC, the Justice Department, and the courts to the Congress. In the courts they will most probably win. In the Congress, as presently constituted, they're in trouble.

# Chapter
# Six

In 1975, testifying before a congressional committee, Assistant Secretary of the Treasury Gerald
Parsky had this to say about the divestiture bills
before Congress:

"These bills collectively imply that our antitrust
agencies cannot find sufficient evidence of monopoly power in the oil industry to bring a national
antitrust complaint under our existing antitrust
laws—so Congress needs to change the law. In
effect, they want to legislate a guilty verdict and a
harsh penalty without trial."

As Parksy points out, these bills are punitive in
nature, designed to short circuit our traditional
judicial processes. And there is a raft of them. As of
this writing, none of the divestiture bills in the
Senate appears to stand a chance of passage, as
they are currently written, although one did make it
to the floor in 1976. And in the House, none of the
breakup bills has yet succeeded in getting out of
committee. But that is certainly not due to a dearth
of congressional ideas on divestiture.

There were in 1976, for instance, five different
House bills pending. One, the Petroleum Marketing
Divorcement Bill, would make it illegal for anyone

to market refined petroleum products while engaged in production, refining, or transportation.

The Petroleum and Petrochemical Marketing Moratorium and Divestiture Bill would make it unlawful for large refineries to market their products.

The Energy Deconcentration Bill proceeds both vertically and horizontally, proposing that the oil industry disengage from the production of other energy sources such as coal and uranium and natural gas, and that the production, refining, transportation and marketing segments of the industry be separated as well. The Promotion of Energy Industry Competition Bill proposes similar ends, but would limit their scope to the top twenty companies.

In the Senate, six different bills were pending in 1976, generally resembling those in the House. Major among them was the Petroleum Industry Competition Bill of 1975 (S.2387), the marigold bill that stunned everyone, including its sponsors, by making it to the floor. It is a straight vertical divestiture bill, requiring that three years after its enactment none of the major oil companies be engaged in more than one phase of the industry, the only exception being that major marketers could retain or in some cases acquire refining interests.

The marigold bill sets down a number of definitions that are useful for the purpose of this discussion and that have been generally accepted by proponents of divestiture. A "major producer," for instance, is a company producing 36.5 million barrels of crude oil or 200 billion cubic feet of natural gas per year. A "major refiner" refines 75 million barrels of oil per year. And a "major marketer" sells

10 million barrels of refined petroleum products per year.

Thus, according to these size limits, only the eighteen largest oil companies would be candidates for dismemberment, although all pipeline and transportation companies, since their parent companies fall within that category, would be required to divest.

According to proponents of the bill, the kind of radical restructuring which would result from the companies either breaking themselves up or reducing their size until they are no longer majors would have a number of beneficial effects. For one thing, it would create greater competition. Each and every stage of operation would be in competition with the others, and new and competing companies would come into being.

Also, they argue, such legislation would limit potential abuse of market power through joint ventures and exchange agreements. It would prevent the majors from squeezing out independent producers, refiners, and marketers through control of their pipelines. And finally, assert the proponents, once such divestiture has taken place, the government would be able to decontrol oil pricing and distribution. As things stand, they say, the majors could easily drive the independents out of business, should controls be lifted. But after divestiture, they insist, this would no longer be possible.

Now the abuses this legislation is designed to correct are indeed serious ones, if in fact they exist. But it has been convincingly demonstrated that competition within the oil industry is alive and thriving. It's difficult, in fact, to imagine how the industry could be any more competitive and not become what the critics like to call "cut throat." And it is that intensity of competition, more than any other factor, that has led to the demise of some of the independents—they simply didn't have what it would take to compete.

Finally, to assert that various *segments* within the industry should compete with one another is to misunderstand the nature of the business. Such competition simply cannot take place without a significant loss of efficiency and a subsequent drop in profits among those who can least afford such a drop.

Pipelines are a good case in point. In the first place, they are not set up to make profits. Their only function is to transport crude to refineries, in the same way, say, that the farmer who buys a truck to haul his crops to market doesn't intend to make a profit on the truck. The function of the truck is to move the goods. If that farmer were required to hire a trucking firm everytime he needed his crops moved, his life and his business would become infinitely more complicated. And, of course, since it would add significantly to his costs, he'd have to raise the price of his product. A second firm would now be in the middle, making a separate profit, and that second firm would in no way either encourage the farmer to be more competitive or to lower his price. Quite the contrary.

Forcing the farmer to divest himself of his truck might help a smaller farmer down the road who cannot afford his own truck. But this somehow doesn't quite make sense, being neither truly competitive nor efficient, but rather encouraging inefficiency by penalizing efficiency. And this, in effect, is precisely what those bills requiring pipeline divestiture would bring about.

The analogy between the pipeline industry and the farmer isn't precise, of course. The situation in which the farmer with a truck was in a position to freeze out his neighbor without a truck couldn't occur with pipelines, since state laws and Interstate Commerce Commission regulations require that pipelines transport crude for the independents as the truck farmer and the pipeline owning oil company operate under the same principle.

There are over 250 pipeline companies in the United States moving crude oil, light hydrocarbons, and refined products, and the fact that most of these pipelines are owned by the majors, either individually or through joint ventures, has been a matter of historical concern.

In 1966, Congress passed legislation declaring pipelines engaged in interstate trade to be common carriers. It therefore required these lines to transport oil brought to them from any source including their own competition at a fair and reasonable price. The legislation also placed the pipelines under the jurisdiction of the Interstate Commerce Commission and prohibited them from providing discriminatory service to various users of the same line.

The industry naturally objected vigorously, just as the farmer with the truck would object if he were required to haul his neighbor's crops to market. But the decision to regulate the pipelines was both sensible and necessary, for it is pipelines—and pipelines alone—which if used improperly could turn the oil companies into genuine monopolies.

Pipelines would tend, without governmental regulation, to corner markets geographically. They are expensive to build, and a small-capacity line is nearly as expensive as a large-capacity line. A company which builds a line in the first place, therefore, is apt to build it big enough to transport all the crude in the region. Thus, only major companies tend to be able to afford to build pipelines and after they have built them there is rarely any competition, for there is little economic sense in constructing competing pipelines. Without government control, the danger here is obvious. The company that built the pipeline first could, if it chose, exercise a monopoly on oil transportation, especially in those inland regions inaccessible to tankers. If a company owned the only pipeline in a region, it could also totally control production in that region as well by refusing to transport a competitor's product or by charging a price for transportation which would assure that the product would not be competitive. And by seeing to it that its own refineries were supplied either with all the crude there was to be had, or by supplying them with a much cheaper crude, a pipeline could potentially control both the production and the refining of oil.

The monopolistic potential of pipelines is very real and laws imposing a common-carrier status on the pipelines are therefore just and necessary. There are other regulations, however, which, while they may have seemed just at the time they were imposed, are no longer appropriate and could do much to bring the industry to a standstill, should divestiture legislation be passed.

One of these is the 7 percent rule. The pipelines, as common carriers, are also covered by a piece of legislation which prohibits rebates and other forms of financial favoritism. In 1941, under this legislation, the Justice Department brought suit against forty-one pipeline companies on the grounds that dividends being paid to these companies were actually rebates. The companies were shipping their own oil for less than their competitors because the profits from the pipelines they owned were being returned to them.

The courts could not, of course, demand that the pipelines be nonprofit ventures. Without profits, no company would be able to attract financial backing to build new pipelines and many would have to renege on the backing that they had received for the old ones. The courts could, however, limit those profits. It agreed to allow owners of common-carrier pipelines dividends of no more than 7 percent of the value of the pipelines' property.

In 1941, this 7 percent profit rate was no doubt a realistic one. But in times like ours, when inflation rages and interest rates soar and investors expect higher rates of return on their invested dollars, a 7 percent rate is not especially attractive. Nor are pipelines generally considered a safe investment.

"Oil pipelines," says the managing director of Morgan Stanley, a prestigious banking investment firm, "are risky investments, even for oil companies. They transport only one commodity over a fixed route in one direction. The investment therefore is inflexible and cannot be easily altered to respond to changed distribution patterns. The owners of the systems are exposed to many risks that are completely beyond their control. These include production declines, proration, governmental controls, imports, changes in fuel requirements, environmental complications, and the development of alternate energy sources. Further, since oil pipelines do not have exclusive franchises or certificates of necessity, they compete for transportation business with other pipelines as well as other forms of transportation."

In fact, Professor Edward Mitchell, director of the American Enterprise Institute's National Energy Project, insists that because the government has capped profits from pipelines, the cost of oil is higher than it should be.

Says Mitchell: "High risk, high rate of return pipelines may not have been built because the Interstate Commerce Commission and the Elkin Act Consent Decree [the 7 percent limit] do not permit rates to be charged that yield high rates of return. This has great significance for public policy because it means that a whole class of pipelines whose construction would have reduced oil transportation costs and lowered product prices have not been built. . . . Regulation of pipelines has probably thwarted the construction of new pipeline capacity and has resulted in higher prices to consumers of oil products."

In general, then, pipelines are not considered by economists or financiers to be top-drawer money makers. In fact, studies show that refiners who own pipelines make less money than refiners who do not, and the more money the refiner invests in pipelines, the less he is apt to profit.

"While there is considerable variability in rates of return within each group," says Professor Mitchell, "the average rate of return moves consistently downward from 14.1 percent to 9.8 percent as we move from low to medium to high pipeline ownership."

All of this, of course, doesn't necessarily mean that for an integrated industry oil pipelines are bad investments. If there is oil to be developed and if that oil is to reach the market, then pipelines—the most efficient means for moving oil overland—must be built. And oil companies are therefore willing to build them, even though the risks involved are increasingly high and the returns are low.

All this would change, however, if Congress passes a law which says that pipelines can be owned only by separate nonintegrated companies. A few years back, such legislation might not have posed the threat to our energy supplies that it does today. Historically, American oil has been discovered in easily accessible places—Texas, Oklahoma, Louisiana. Those days have passed, however, and if we are to have a supply of oil which is not totally foreign, then transporting that oil is going to be a high-risk venture. And it's hardly likely that there'll be any independents involved.

Environmental considerations alone would cause the average businessman to back off. He knows that any pipeline plan he presents for any region of the country will be held up for years in the courts. There are other schemes yielding higher rates of return in which business can invest without the threat that their investment will be tied up for years during drawn-out court proceedings, whose results are doubtful from the beginning.

Furthermore, if private companies could be induced to invest in new pipelines, costs would surely go up. As it is now, oil companies can get money to invest in pipelines at reasonable interest rates only because of the reputation and the fiscal security of the whole integrated firm. Independent pipeline companies, however, would by definition be less financially secure, and it is highly unlikely that they'd find money at low interest rates to invest in high-risk ventures.

Moody's Investors Service, which rates the financial stability of the various companies seeking to borrow money, has up until now given a rating of "A" or better to the majors who borrow money for pipelines. And in 1975, an "Aaa" rated company could borrow money at 8.83 percent, an "Aa" company could borrow at 8.97 percent, and an "A" company at 9.65 percent. But financial experts agree that they could give an independent pipeline company no better than a "Baa."

In 1975, a "Baa" rated company was forced to pay 10.39 percent for the money it borrowed. This difference in rating, when applied to the rarified kinds of figures involved in pipeline construction, can add millions of dollars in costs.

As of early 1975, an estimated $8.6 billion worth of new pipeline was planned for the United States. If S.2387 were in effect, and if this capital therefore had to be raised by independent "Baa" companies, experts estimate that their interest rates would run at least one percentage point higher than is presently the case with the major integrated companies. Thus, the additional costs of building the nation's pipeline system would run, at 1975 figures, $80 million more a year in finance charges alone. And these costs, of course, would be passed along to the public through higher petroleum prices. In fact, many experts believe that were the industry to be segmented, not just pipelines but all segments of the industry would have to borrow at these less favorable rates.

There are, then, many good reasons today against, and few good reasons for, breaking the pipeline segment off from the rest of the integrated industry. In the past, there may have been more of a danger of major pipeline companies squeezing out independents, for the oil in the lines was plentiful, there was competition for pipeline space, and small independents, in spite of the rules, might have found it difficult to get their oil into the lines.

But today domestic production has slowed down considerably. If a pipeline doesn't run at full capacity, it loses money, and it costs little more for a company to ship at full capacity than it does at partial capacity, just as it costs little more to run a full truck than it does a half-full truck. But, of course, half a load doesn't make as much money for the trucker. And the same is true for the pipeline company. These simple financial considerations, then, dictate that pipelines will now and into the foreseeable future be very happy indeed to ship the oil of independent companies for them.

Even if there were not basic financial considerations dictating that pipelines be used fairly, there are legal ones, and the evidence indicates that they have worked well. There have been complaints against the major companies and their pipelines. But in each case these complaints have been settled by the Interstate Commerce Commission.

Before 1922, for instance, the pipelines agreed that they would ship no less than 100,000 barrels per order. But this obviously discriminated against the small companies that didn't have 100,000 barrels and the ICC therefore mandated that the minimum shipment level be lowered to 10,000 barrels. Today, if a pipeline is running at capacity, the ICC requires that the majors reduce the share of oil they are running to leave room for competition.

There have also been other sorts of complaints brought by the smaller companies, concerning such matters as irregular shipping dates or limited storage space at the line's terminal. But the ICC, which has traditionally favored the small company over the larger has rarely found genuine abuses. As an ICC chairman recently told Congress: "Today there are so few complaints and so few problems that I must say the pipelines are one of the best run transportation systems we have. . . . It would appear that except for certain impediments brought about because of environmental considerations, pipelines have been constructed on an as-needed basis and generally provide good service. It has been our experience that pipeline rates are just and reasonable—we have received no complaints in recent years involving allegations relative to the size of tender, the failure to publish through routes and joint rates, or to provide service to independents. The Commission now possesses the authority to investigate and correct abuses if they arise. However, to the extent that the need for further controls can be documented, the Commission stands ready to enforce them."

Predictably, there have been charges that the ICC has long been in the pocket of the major companies, and that statements such as those made above by the commissioner of the ICC are just so much untrustworthy verbal smog, designed to obscure flagrant industry abuses. These charges lack credibility, however, especially when you consider that every major ICC decision has been in favor of the small companies.

But perhaps the best evidence that pipelines owned by the major companies do not discriminate against independent companies comes from the independents themselves. The Independent Petroleum Association of America, representing about four thousand independent companies, has stated repeatedly that its members have not been denied access to major company-owned pipelines. In fact, the organization felt so strongly about the subject that in 1973 its president sent a letter to each U.S. senator stating: "This is to advise you that we are not aware of any producer having difficulty selling or moving his crude oil, and we do not believe any such discrimination exists."

The Senate Antitrust and Monopoly Subcommittee, after long and extensive hearings, came up with no hard evidence that the major companies had abused their pipeline power, and was forced to resort to the guilt-by-inference arguments. Its final report repeatedly pointed out that pipelines owned by the major companies have most of the country's oil, something no one tries to deny, and from this drew the conclusion that the "majors' control of product lines places obstacles in the path of non-integrated shippers in procuring transportation for their product."

The subcommittee's flat assertion was badly undercut by the denials of the nation's largest independent producers' association, as well as by the subcommittee's staff work itself. In order to back up its charges, the staff had to resort to testimony and congressional debates from 1906 and 1931, years in which the problems of pipelines were as relevant to the pipeline problems of today as blacksmithing is to jet engineering.

The subcommittee did come up with some evidence that from time to time the lines had failed to provide ample storage facilities for independent oil which was either waiting to be pumped or waiting to be refined.

There may be a potential problem with storage facilities, although the Senate failed to come up with any evidence that the problem is pressing. And whatever storage problems do exist don't require solutions in the form of congressional divestiture bills. As Fred Allvine, professor of marketing at the Georgia Institute of Technology, puts it, "these systems could be improved by requiring the pipeline company to make available terminals that could be used by shippers without their own facilities. This is often done by independent pipeline companies and would enhance competition within the . . . system. This change can, however, be accomplished without divestiture."

Professor Allvine, coauthor of a highly critical book on big oil called *Highway Robbery,* can by no stretch of the imagination be called a friend of the industry. But since the publication of his controversial book, he has grown increasingly uneasy about divestiture and has testified against it. He still sees problems and believes, for instance, that there is not sufficient control exercised over those intrastate lines which do not come under ICC purview but are overseen by the states themselves. And he believes

134

there are storage problems, as mentioned above. But even Professor Allvine, a long-time critic who views the industry with a very jaundiced eye, can find no evidence of the abuses that the Senate subcommittee staff seems to intuit.

And it is not the case that the ICC tends to cover up abuses. The fact is that it receives relatively few complaints on discriminatory practices, since often, when a major is in the wrong, just the threat of a complaint will cause him to remedy the situation at once.

APCO, for instance, a small refiner, had won a bid for crude in competition with SUNOCO, a major company that had been the producer's previous customer. According to APCO's unverified testimony, SUNOCO's pipeline told APCO that it would not ship its newly won crude because it did not meet vapor specifications. The same pipeline, however, had moved the same crude before it lost its contract to the smaller company. APCO threatened to take the case to the ICC, and the SUNOCO pipeline capitulated immediately, agreeing to transport APCO's oil.

Now there might be little mileage to be gained from recounting this undramatic anecdote, except for the fact that the Senate Antitrust and Monopoly Subcommittee staff used it to illustrate the way in which a major squeezes out a smaller company. But if the anecdote is authentic, then surely it proves something quite different. APCO wasn't squeezed out. It didn't even have to take its case to a higher authority. Just the threat was enough to cause SUNOCO to cave in almost immediately.

Now two things could have happened here.

SUNOCO executives, on learning they'd lose their bid, could have blown up and in the heat of the moment decided APCO's oil would never moisten their pipelines. But then, once the heat of the moment had passed, perhaps they relented, realizing they'd been acting unfairly. Many Senate subcommittee staffers would point out, however, that a greedy capitalistic monopoly would be most unlikely to do so on its own.

The other possibility is that the Interstate Commerce Commission poses a very real threat to those major pipeline companies who are tempted to engage in unfair practices. All things considered, this seems somewhat more plausible as an explanation, and it tends to prove something the Senate subcommittee didn't intend to prove when it dredged the whole story up. The story was intended by the staff to show that an integrated oil company which owns its own pipelines cannot be expected to use that ownership fairly. But what the story actually shows is that the ICC seems to have made a deep impression on the industry, and the law it administers which governs the use of those pipelines is working very well indeed.

The APCO-SUNOCO anecdote was typical of the material used by the Senate Antitrust and Monopoly Subcommittee staff to build its case for pipeline divestiture. One can't blame the staff, of course. Unlike many of the men they work for, Senate committee and subcommittee staffs tend to be made up of highly intelligent, ambitious, aggressive, and resourceful people who can generally be counted on to do the most thorough job possible in building their cases. They also tend to be highly opinionated people who can be expected to bring the fervor of the believer to their pursuits. Given these qualities, then, one knows immediately that something is wrong when such a group is forced to build a case out of archaic testimony and rather aimless anecdotes that prove precisely the opposite of what they were intended to prove.

The Senate subcommittee was mandated to build as good a case as possible for divestiture by proving that the major oil companies have too much power and are abusing it. But unfortunately, in the case of pipelines, there was simply no case to be made.

# Chapter
# Seven

If the oil companies were finally broken up, the exploration and production segment would probably emerge as the industry's strongest. Pipelines and refineries have not historically been considered unusually attractive business investments. But the actual business of finding the oil and getting it out of the ground has always attracted men and money. The vast majority of oil millionaires made their money by drilling exploratory wells and finding oil in them. It is a risky business, to be sure, because drilling for oil is an expensive operation and a dry well can bankrupt an investor. But drilling continues.

In 1975, according to industry figures, the average cost of drilling an onshore well was $120,290. There were 8,894 such exploratory wells dug in 1975 and 6,767 of them turned out to be dry holes. That means that in 1975 alone, $800 million disappeared down dry onshore exploratory holes.

Because drillers are not as likely to gamble on offshore drilling, offshore exploration yields a higher percentage of producing wells. The cost of offshore drilling is a great deal higher, however.

It cost $819,241, the industry estimates, to drill an

offshore well in 1975. And of the 900 drilled in 1975, exactly half of them were dry.

Nevertheless, the dream of hitting that one big strike is still perhaps the archetypal American dream. There is, of course, a certain "made in Hollywood" quality about it—Clark Gable or Spencer Tracy, dripping with black liquid gold, fighting it out under the gushers as they come blowing in. Later, the blondes, the Cadillacs, the cigars lit with one-hundred-dollar bills, and finally, the disillusionment. Somewhat vulgar, perhaps, and straight out of second-rate never-never land. Yet it happened frequently in the past and, although the more tinselly aspects of the dream may have faded, it can still happen, although more rarely now.

There is, as we have mentioned earlier, a new philosophy growing up in the nation, a philosophy which finds its romance in the vision of man and nature united as one, neither exploiting the other, the lion and the lamb and Fred from down the street lying peacefully together. This, say the new romantics, is as it always should have been and had man made his peace with nature, had he not exploited his environment, then we would not now be faced with ugly problems such as urban congestion and pollution. The solution, then, for the no-growthers, is simply to stop growing. And for their neoromantic allies, that solution must be accompanied by a return to nature.

There is another way of looking at the relationship between man and nature, however, and another way of viewing the romance in that relationship. If the lion lies down with the lamb and Fred from down the street, chances are that only the lion will arise, considerably heavier than when he first lay down. That is not to say that nature is necessarily hostile. Positing a hostile nature may be just as anthropomorphically erroneous as maintaining that lions and birds and trees have feelings identical to our own.

Nevertheless, if we are allowed just a bit of poetic license in our adjectives, we can say that nature is by no means benign, as anyone who spends January in Fairbanks can testify. Those of us who hold to this view tend to believe that the history of human progress is the history of the struggle against, and the triumph over, nature. During that struggle, man may not have improved his flawed nature one iota. But most of us no longer eat one another and, at any rate, human nature is not something to be manipulated.

What can be manipulated, however, and what can be improved, is man's physical condition, and it is by wrenching nature's secrets from her and by applying what we learn from those secrets that we have steadily improved our condition over the centuries. We no longer go barefoot, wrapped in rank animal skins. We no longer depend on migrating herds for our food or dig rocks from the field with out hands. We have been liberated by our machines, and liberation from back-breaking, killing physical work, as Eric Hoffer points out, is the greatest liberation in human history.

Here, for many of us, the true romance lies, the struggle of man to wrench a better life out of nature. And there has seemed no more colorful or dramatic symbol of that struggle than the well brought in by the wildcatter, betting his last dollar on one big roll

140

of the dice against the tremendous odds that nature throws up.

We've become very sophisticated during the last half of this century and we'd all be a bit ashamed to admit that the old tinselly dream of bringing in the big one hits a romantic chord. But there are still thousands of small independent companies engaged in the drilling business and one suspects that it's more than just a love of outdoor work that keeps them at it. Some, to be sure, may be in it only because they hope to get rich. In fact, that's probably the primary reason that all of them are there. But is there any more romantic goal? Or any more romantic achievement than making a fortune? We once thought so as a matter of course, and in those days when we thought so, we built a mighty nation overnight.

Now, of course, the whole idea is unfashionable and somewhat distasteful, rendered so in large part by verbalists in the media and in the entertainment fields who have themselves become millionaires.

There are still men who dream the old dreams, however, and it is from their ranks that the oil industry continues to attract much of its talent. James McKie, in the *Quarterly Journal of Economics,* describes the most common ways that people enter the industry:

"Many oil-producing companies originated as successful wildcat enterprises. While a few firms may begin with a large supply of capital and immediately undertake an extensive drilling program, the typical firm got its start through a series of fortunate single ventures, often involving exploratory deals with established major or independent firms. New corporations and partnerships are frequently budded from existing ones. . . . A geologist or petroleum engineer may gain enough experience on his own, making good use of the associations he has built up in the industry. . . . An employee of a drilling contractor may work up from platform hand. . . . After operating as a contract driller for some time, he may be willing to put one of his rigs into a wildcat venture on a speculative basis. . . . In this way drilling contractors frequently become independent contractors. . . .

"Another way to enter oil and gas exploration is via brokerage. Exploration enterprise swarms with middlemen anxious to arrange producing deals. . . . A speculative broker may arrange a prospecting deal among other parties . . . and usually retains for himself a small interest in the venture. Since the technical training and apprenticeship are not strictly necessary, this route is crowded with hopeful shoestring promoters along with the experienced entrepreneurs."

For these promoters and entrepreneurs, the oil depletion tax allowance has been a bonanza. But this tax allowance, as we have mentioned earlier, is not a special break devised solely for the oil industry. It is used by all the thousands of businesses that extract depletable materials from the earth.

Yet, ironically, this tax allowance which is still intact for the small businessman, may in no way alleviate depletion allowance abuses. Say, for instance, that the small entrepreneur makes his strike. That well he has brought in will eventually run dry, and if his oil income is to continue, he's going to have to sink some of his present income into future holes, any of which could come up dry, yielding him nothing.

Nothing in the law, however, requires him to go out and use his tax savings to drill more holes. It merely encourages him to do so. Thus, if he is so inclined, he can take that money instead and buy shares in Neiman-Marcus or acreage in River Oaks. He is, in other words, free to pull out of the oil business as soon as he has hit it rich. And that's as it should be.

But large companies don't have the same option. They have historically plowed their tax savings back into exploration for a very basic reason—if they didn't, they could not continue to exist. After the oil runs out in the holes they have drilled, as it always does, there have to be new holes underway. If not, the companies would fold.

So it was especially ironic that Congress in 1975 permanently repealed the tax depletion allowance for integrated companies but retained it for small independents. Increasingly, as oil becomes more difficult to find, the independents will be spending their tax savings on other, more reliable businesses, while the major companies, which would of necessity, have plowed those savings into new oil discovery, no longer have the savings to use.

But this problem with the law will become increasingly academic, for wildcatting entrepreneurs may soon become mere historical personages. The remaining big strikes are in inaccessible places; the small firms can't get to them; and no amount of divestiture legislation will change that. But the major companies find themselves hamstrung in their exploratory efforts, not only by the new

**143**

rulings, but by uninformed congressionally mandated price ceilings as well. The industry claims, for instance, that the ceilings placed by Congress on the price of gas inhibited drilling for oil as well. In 1956, according to the industry, a record 16,200 exploratory wells were drilled. By 1971, that figure had dropped to 6,992. The reason, say the companies, was that Congress had set the amount that an oil company could get for its crude below what it cost to pump new crude. Congress justified the ceiling by pointing out that the companies were making profits from the oil they were already pumping. But they ignored the fact that new oil was becoming increasingly less accessible and that if the industry was to discover and drill new holes, the oil from those holes could not be sold at a profit. Consequently, new drilling fell off and, as oil from the old holes became harder to extract, those holes were capped as well.

Because the big strikes of the future will occur in increasingly inaccessible places, the days of the small independent drillers are numbered, while the large exploratory companies will continue to grow. Offshore oil is a case in point. The industry currently estimates that there are anywhere from 10 to 49 billion recoverable barrels of outer continental shelf oil, but only the very large companies will be able to attract the investments necessary and to take the financial risks involved in getting offshore crude to onshore refineries. One group of majors, for instance, recently spent approximately $1 billion drilling and leasing off the coast of Florida and found nothing—neither gas nor oil. Similarly, in 1973, a group of companies spent more than $700

144

million on leases alone for drilling rights in Destin Anticline in the Gulf of Mexico. As of this writing, the companies have drilled eight wells and have discovered not a drop of oil.

According to the industry, the increasingly high cost of offshore drilling and the increasing difficulty in finding financing for it are compounded by existing and threatened governmental policies. For instance, the central threat of divestiture in itself tends to scare off investors. Added to that there is the constant threat of legislatively mandated delays for baseline and land use studies. There is also the threat posed by the current attempts of governors of states contiguous to the drilling sites to obtain a three-year veto power over offshore operations. And Congress constantly plays with the rules for bidding and leasing procedures.

Moreover, investors are increasingly unsettled by the threat of a governmental exploration program competing with or replacing private exploration. At present several plans have been proposed for federal exploration of the outer continental shelf. One involves contracting with private firms, while another, discussed earlier, would establish a federal corporation which would explore for, develop, and produce petroleum in competition with private firms. Public money, in other words, would be used to compete with private capital, a situation in which, unless we taxpayers finally revolted, federal financing would be unlimited and would thus inevitably destroy private companies attempting to compete.

There are numerous other governmentally inspired threats. Controls and price rollbacks come to mind, both of which threats remain very real with a still unhealthy economy and a Congress and executive branch controlled by economic activists. Many politicians in Washington today remember the Nixon controls fondly; few remember the chaos that followed when they were lifted.

Each of these threats has a dampening effect on investment. But the most damaging threat, of course, is the prospect of divestiture. If the companies were dismembered, there would be monumental problems with getting pipelines to new oil fields and with finding refineries to process the oil once it is out of the ground. These difficulties probably would not immediately affect the production segment of the industry under divestiture. Oil which is left waiting in the ground due to inefficiencies and lack of coordination at least requires no upkeep, nor does it depreciate. But pipelines with no oil to move and refineries with no oil to process could find themselves in profound financial difficulties. And while the production segment might not experience the same problems, over the long run its difficulties could be equally profound.

There would, as mentioned, be the difficulties in attracting capital at precisely the moment in which increasing amounts of capital are necessary for exploration in ever more remote areas. And those investors who do agree to back a project such as, for instance, the development of oil off the Atlantic Coast, will increasingly insist on a higher rate of return to compensate for the risks—all of which, of course, would dramatically push up the price we pay for petroleum products.

Also seriously damaged by divestiture, says the industry, would be the research arm of the production segment. Petroleum research, although it does receive limited federal funding, is financed primarily by the industry itself. In 1974, for instance, the ten biggest companies spent over half a billion dollars on basic and applied research, without which, says the industry, both innovation and efficiency would suffer severely and long-range benefits for all of us would be lost.

The central purpose of this research, of course, is to improve industry operations and to develop new products. But its scope often transcends the immediate concerns of the industry. Laboratories carrying out basic research, for instance, are searching for and improving ways of turning petroleum into protein for animal food, and eventually for human consumption. And industry scientists have developed a mulch, made from petroleum resins, which, when applied over seed beds in thin strips, warms the soil, reduces soil erosion, and fertilizes.

But such research, says the industry, would be imperiled under divestiture. For one thing, the companies would need every penny of capital they could get their hands on to establish their positions in the newly structured marketplace. And not only would research money dry up, but the research laboratories themselves would be broken up as well. Industry research is now centralized in huge laboratories which employ up to three thousand people and in which scientists and engineers working in all segments of the industry are able to coordinate their work and to interact. Under divestiture, however, there would be no central research organization through which information could flow, and therefore problems which relate to more than one segment of the industry—synthetic fuel development, for instance, or emissions control technology, or chemical techniques for enhancing emissions control technology—would in general be ignored. Those scientists whose work overlaps industry segments would find it necessary to limit the scope of that work and they would no longer benefit from close communication with fellow scientists working with the other segments of the industry. Nor would laboratories, broken up to serve separate segments, any longer be able to justify the cost of a great deal of the expensive equipment they require—electron microscopy for chemical analysis, computer-integrated mass spectrometers, gas chromatographs, to name just a few. All of these extremely sophisticated and extremely expensive machines are now used for work that benefits all segments of the industry. But their cost would be prohibitive for a single-segment company.

Oil industry research is integrated research, and the nonintegrated companies, which operate today much as the fragmented companies would operate tomorrow under divestiture, depend totally on the majors for research results. In 1973, according to the National Science Foundation, the twenty largest American companies carried out 97 percent of all the research and development in the oil industry. Some of this research, of course, would continue after divestiture, but on a considerably smaller scale and at a much greater cost. In the Chevron Research laboratories, for instance, about 7 percent of the budget, or $3 million, is devoted to synthetic fuels. The same research, Chevron estimates, if carried out by a single-segment company, would cost several times as much.

Synthetic fuel development is not simply a refining problem, involving as it does heat transfer, fossil energy chemistry, and the recovery of solids and liquids from the earth. If the companies currently involved in its development were broken up, then scientific work on recovery, for instance, would no longer be carried out in conjunction with the process of refining the synthetic fuel, but would be done secretly, and in competition with it. Eventually, say the labs, divestiture would force them to revert to the research levels of the 1950s.

Many proponents of divestiture admit that there may initially be research problems and that industry research would be impaired. But they insist that research into broad problems could simply be transferred to the government. Eventually this would no doubt become the case, but the transition process would be a lengthy one, and in the meantime, just at that moment when important energy breakthroughs are on the horizon and when we need them the most, we would lose years of energy research. Given our escalating dependence on foreign oil, our dwindling domestic supply, and the increasingly vulnerable position this puts us in, we may not be able to sustain such a loss.

Finally, in addition to exploration and research and development, there is the effect of divestiture on refineries. And that effect would not be beneficial. In order for a refinery to make money, it must have an assured supply of crude. Therefore, many refineries integrate backwards by involving themselves in production. It is greatly to a refiner's advantage

149

to operate as close to full capacity as possible, for his income is cut in half when his plant operates at half capacity while his overhead remains nearly the same. The producer can depend on a number of laws which assure him a fair share of the market. The refiner has no such laws working for him, however, and he is totally at the mercy of his source of supply. If that source dries up, he is out of business. Therefore, the refiner believes it necessary that he own as much of that source as possible.

And the recent policies of the federal government have convinced refiners that ownership, or partial ownership of wells, is more necessary than ever. Because of government controls on oil prices, for instance, the industry now charges less for a barrel of oil than it costs to replace that barrel. As a result, domestic production has dried up, and with increasing domestic shortages, and with the industry jittery about what the government intends in the way of price controls, refiners are buying increasingly into production. And it's not just refiners. Other industries who vitally need crude products are also taking matters into their own hands by buying into production, among them Dow Chemical, General Motors, and St. Regis Paper.

Nor is it just the major companies who are made uneasy and frequently harmed by federal machinations. During the period of the first OPEC price hike, small refineries were badly damaged by governmental programs designed to help them. The oil import quotas, as mentioned earlier, dealt out cheap foreign oil to refineries on the basis of size, with the smaller refineries getting a proportionately larger share than the majors. But suddenly OPEC prices skyrocketed, foreign oil became more costly than domestic, and those refineries that had relied proportionately on foreign oil suffered in greater proportion. In 1972, for instance, under the allocation scheme, a typical small refiner producing ten thousand barrels per day, could buy more than two thousand of those barrels from the foreign market at a savings of about $1.25 a barrel. On an annual basis, this savings amounted to what was in effect a subsidy of nearly $1 million a year. But with the OPEC increase, that savings disappeared.

And then, just to make matters worse—and infinitely more complicated—there was the whole business of import tickets, issued by the government to refineries which the refineries then exchanged for foreign oil. But instead of exchanging, many smaller refineries made a great portion of their profits by selling their tickets to larger companies, largely because a small refinery in the Midwest, for instance, had little practical way of transporting that foreign oil inland to its plant. Some of these small and often uneconomic and inefficient refineries actually kept operating by selling these tickets throughout the sixties, finally closing overnight when the price of foreign oil rendered the tickets worthless. Again, an example of federal encouragement of inefficiency, ending, as always, in a painful failure. The effects could have been mitigated had not that inefficient operation been kept functioning artificially well beyond its time.

Also partially to blame for the distress of the refineries during the early seventies was the President's Cost of Living Council, which had ruled that oil companies could make only an arbitrary, limited profit. Should they exceed that profit, then the Cost of Living Council would roll back the price of domestic oil. Because of OPEC, however, the price of the foreign oil held by the major companies had risen dramatically, and the companies were unwilling to sell their reserves at prices below what they would be required to pay to replace them. But had they sold that oil to independent refineries at replacement costs, they would have made more of a paper profit than the government was willing to allow. Therefore, they abandoned many of the small refineries they had previously supplied. There was also among refineries the problem of spot buying, discussed more fully later.

There is little doubt that these and other federal efforts like them ended by harming the independent refiners that they were intended to help. But the damage they did was child's play in comparison to the damage that could be done by divestiture—and done not only to the majors, but to the independents that divestiture legislation is ostensibly designed to protect and to us all as consumers of energy.

There is a basic problem of perception here, a profound misperception of the role of government and the functioning of the market, perhaps best summed up in the testimony of Richard Boushka before the Senate antitrust subcommittee. Boushka, president of Vickers Energy Corporation, an independent refining company which is part of Esmark, told the senators that if the large firms were broken up the industry—small companies such as his own as well as the majors—would find itself in a state of chaos, with supplies threatened and prices rising dramatically. The problems of the small refiners,

Boushka continued, were not caused by the majors attempting to squeeze them out of business. Rather, he said, speaking from first-hand knowledge, they sprang from other sources altogether and they would inevitably be intensified by a federal attempt to solve them.

"There may be those in the oil industry who would disagree with my testimony here this morning," said Boushka. "I ask them to examine their corporate consciences and determine whether or not they might be guilty of trying to justify past poor management decisions by blaming them on the majors. Gentlemen, in business as in politics, all important decisions involve risk. The most obvious risks in business are economic but there are others that an effective manager must consider when charting a direction for his company. When Vickers decided to expand its refinery in Ardmore, Oklahoma, and did not own or control the volume of crude oil necessary to supply that new capacity, we assumed the calculated risk that we would be able to obtain that raw material in future years. If I come to Washington three years from now, it should not be my perogative to scream antimajor slogans regarding power or monopoly and request relief in whatever form, because I know full well when I expanded that new refinery the risks and dangers involved in crude supply. Too many times, gentlemen, you as legislators are asked to find a solution to someone's predicament which was caused by his poor management judgment and decisions. When you take action in this situation, you penalize those who exercised good thinking and prudent planning.

"Inherent in a discussion concerning the breaking

up of the majors is that others in the oil industry need a subsidy to exist. We maintain that the free market in the oil industry will allow large, small, and medium-sized companies all to coexist without subsidies which breed weakness and mediocrity. We feel that the recipient of a subsidy eventually becomes an inefficient operator and a high-cost supplier of products to the consumer."

As Boushka points out, the refinery owner views his biggest problem not as a lack of market, as do most businesses, but a secure source of supply in order to manufacture that product, for his primary concern, when he expands, is to find sufficient crude to refine. That is the basic reason for integrating "upstream," or buying into production. It is simply good business practice.

Perhaps, however, the government is not interested in good business practice. Implicit in Boushka's testimony is a feeling shared by many businessmen —and perhaps especially by owners and executives of small and medium sized businesses—that if government would only leave them alone, they could solve any problems that plague them. In the business world, they believe, there is a process of natural selection at work. And in the view of men like Boushka, it is a healthy process and one with which government should not be allowed to interfere. There are now and will continue to be, in this view, natural economic forces which dictate that certain businesses—those poorly managed or perhaps poorly attuned to public demand—will be winnowed out of the field. This process, businessmen like Boushka believe, is both natural and desirable, and the end result is the strengthening of American business as

154

a whole, and therefore the strengthening of America.

But when, as seems to be happening, not just in the oil business but in other businesses as well, the government sets out deliberately to thwart this natural process, then the natural results will be, first, stagnation, and then, inevitably, increasing governmental control. The railroads, for instance, a once-thriving concern, died as a direct result of governmental regulation. Federal attempts to revive them continue to fail dismally, as all such federal attempts, because they lack natural market incentives such as the profit motive, must inevitably fail.

Oil men, along with most American businessmen, don't want their industry to go the way of the railroads. Their beliefs, not quite fashionable these days, are based on the assumption that the corporate form of business has built the most productive society the world has ever seen. That, the businessman believes, is easily demonstrable. And what is the alternative to the corporate system we have developed? There is only one, and in the countries where it has been substituted, it has failed, just as it has failed in operating our railroads or our postal service. That alternative, of course, is government, and government cannot do business because it hasn't the motivation to do it well, nor can it be held accountable in the way business can be held accountable if it fails.

Christopher Stone, professor of law at the University of Southern California and author of *Where the Law Ends: The Social Control of Corporate Behavior,* is not, as his writings demonstrate, a champion of corporate America. Nevertheless, he feels we have no choice. "There is nothing to put in its place except government," says Stone. "And government is far less responsible than the typical corporation—which, after all, has an ultimate accountability in the income statement, the balance sheet, and the annual report."

In the end, this, more than anything else, accounts for the hostility to governmental intervention into the private sector. It's not a matter of ideology or politics, as much as a basic conviction, borne out by experience, that government can't do the job. For this reason more than any other, independent refiners, for instance, oppose a scheme which might become necessary under divestiture to set up a governmental purchasing agency that would provide them with the foreign oil. The idea, toyed with separately as well as part of a divestiture bill, is to help the independents who cannot, the government believes, compete for their fair share on the international market. Once again, however, many of the independents are begging the government not to help them. One of these independent refiners, John Buckley of Northeast Petroleum Industries, puts it this way:

"What if the central purchasing authority went out on a sealed bid and received a very attractive offer for Kuwait crude? The fact is that some two-thirds of all the refinery capacity in the United States could not operate on Kuwait crude and many of the other refineries would be able to operate on Kuwait crude only by cutting their total capability. That's because Kuwait is relatively high sulfur crude and most U.S. refineries are designed to run a sweet, low sulfur crude. . . .

"Our company is today building a 200,000 barrels-a-day independent refinery in Louisiana. . . . We expect to start petroleum production within the next three to four months. I can tell you that we have run perhaps a hundred computer programs to try to determine the optimum crude slate we need in order to produce the products that will give us the best yield in the marketplace. We have designed our plant to run heavy, high sulfur, high metal content crude oil. We can handle almost any crude in the world. Thus, we are in pretty good shape to go out and buy the cheapest crude possible.

"But if we had a Government Purchasing Agency and it went out on a sealed bid basis and happened to get a bargain from some country with a high quality crude, we would end up with a crude oil our refinery is not designed to handle. . . . With more than 240 refineries in this country, the likelihood of all of them being supplied with the right quality crude oil at the right time so that each refiner is able to optimize yields is remote at best."

Buckley insists that there are ample opportunities for independent refiners to compete with the majors on the world market: "One of our strengths is our ability to make purchases of the right product or of crude oil in the marketplace quickly. . . . I have noted in my own crude oil negotiations around the world that many producing countries who have taken over all or part of the major company operations in their country, are anxious to sell to U.S. independent refiners. I have noted that we are able in some cases to get attractive payment terms for the crude we purchase or helpful flexibility in transportation schedules."

Independent refiners, in short, simply don't need

the help of the government to secure crude. Actually, the fact that they are relatively small and flexible, in a way that is not true of the major companies and certainly not true of government, works to their advantage. They can move quickly where the majors have little freedom of movement, responding to spot surpluses and shortages, adjusting to fluctuations in consumption demands, supplies, and the weathers. The majors and the independents are actually complementary, each performing a function that the other is not capable of performing.

To assert that independent refineries cannot compete with the majors is simply to ignore the facts. If they are wisely managed and run, they can and do compete. If they are not well managed and operated, then it is in no way in the national interest, or in the long-range interest of the businesses themselves, for the government to step in and subsidize them, thereby in effect rewarding them for inefficiency.

Restructuring the industry so as to create separately owned refineries would benefit neither the major companies nor the independents. Divestiture, in fact, is a response to a problem that does not exist, and it would only intensify the problems which do exist. It might, very easily, as well create new ones, among them the very problem that the proponents of divestiture hoped to solve with their legislation in the first place. For as in the other segments of the industry, divestiture might very well end by creating actual refinery monopolies. For one thing, many economists predict that economies of scale will, in a segment industry, encourage the growth of giant refineries dominating those geographic areas in which oil is produced.

In refining, just as in most businesses, there is generally a certain pull toward geographic monopoly. There can, after all, be only one business firm per lot. And when a consumer chooses between similar products at similar prices at different business establishments, then chances are he'll tend to buy those products from the establishment nearest him. But if a product in one establishment some distance away is priced significantly below a similar product in an establishment nearby, the consumer may find it worth his travel expenses to bypass the closer business and deal with the more distant one.

Similarly, travel expenses play a significant role in a refinery's control over the market for its products. As matters now stand, it is not economical for a refinery to expand and hope to compete with another firm located some distance away, simply because the expenses involved in moving into the other firm's market would be impractical. But under divestiture, and with the increasing cost of new refineries, those refineries which already exist might find that their product is now competitive over an increasingly large geographic area. Even as matters now stand, there is a real question, given higher capital costs and increasing environmental restrictions, whether it will be possible in the near future for small companies to build new refineries. And under divestiture with its loss of assured supply and market and with its almost inevitable curtailment of pipeline construction between the field and the refinery, new refineries, without the promise of pipelines to serve them and without the assurances offered by integration, would in all likelihood simply never come into existence. Over a period of time, this would mean that existing refineries would grow up to dominate an increasingly large share of the market.

No one can say with absolute certainty that divestiture would bring on refinery monopolies, although many economists believe it would. But suffice it to say that divestiture would seriously affect costs, the availability of capital, and geographic distribution, and might even bring on a major flight overseas. Divestiture, in short, might very well end in accomplishing precisely the opposite of what its most sincere proponents hope it would accomplish.

This is nothing startling or novel. We have seen it happen, in fact, in nearly every area not naturally relegated to government but into which government has seen fit to intrude. Not too many years ago the government entered the housing field, intending to provide decent homes for poor Americans. Today the government is the world's largest slumlord; its tenants, when they occupy the buildings at all, often live in incredible squalor. And government intervention into the airline business has resulted in increasing stagnation in that industry and some of the lowest profits of any business in the nation.

Governmental intervention into an area traditionally reserved to the private sector, in other words, has historically ended by intensifying the problem it set out to solve. And because government is neither flexible nor able to undo past mistakes without alienating people who have come to have a special interest in programs which don't work, the response is invariably simply to add more programs, thus building yet another wing on a ramshackle structure squatting on a rotten foundation.

If past performance is any guide, divestiture legislation would represent only the first step in government intrusion into the oil industry. When the fragmented industry, no longer able to finance exploration or pipelines or new refineries, had finally to turn to the government for financial assistance—something it never needed before divestiture—then the government would be there. And as it doled out the money, it would take a little more control. Eventually, the oil companies would be absorbed into the state, an increasing tendency in contemporary America, and finally the distinction between majors and independents would be meaningless, for they could all be called dependents.

One of the sacred books of the antibusiness, smaller-is-better movement, to which many divestiture proponents belong, is Robert Heilbroner's *Business Civilization in Decline.* Capitalism has reached the end of its tether, says Heilbroner, and because our resources are running out, we can no longer grow at our former rate. "The end of corporate growth," he writes, "will bring the progressive elimination of the profits that have been both the means and the end of the accumulation of private property." There will be, says Heilbroner, an acceleration in central planning and the consequent growth of a society in which the corporation's role will increasingly shrink, to be replaced by a steadily expanding bureaucracy, until, as Heilbroner puts it, "the traditional pillars of capitalism—private property and the market—have been amended beyond recognition."

Now it is difficult to understand how intelligent people who have watched big government bring us Vietnam, Watergate, and the congressional scandals, or who have the economic history of the Eastern European socialist nations—or of Great Britain, for that matter—to study, could possibly hope for such a society. Does no one, one wonders, read Orwell any longer?

But there is no doubt that many do want such a system, one in which centrally made decisions replace the millions of individual decisions which structure the present market system. And divestiture legislation threatens to lead inevitably to state ownership of one of our most vital industries, which represents a giant step in that direction.

# Chapter Eight

The last segment of the industry, marketing, includes the gas stations with which we are all so familiar. And it also includes the operations which directly supply those stations and deliver fuel to farmers and heating oil to homes. Of all the segments, marketing is the least streamlined and efficient, and probably the most wasteful.

It's a complicated segment. The various dealers, and the jobbers who supply them, have a variety of connections to and arrangements with the parent companies. In some cases, the parent company both owns and manages the supplying company and the service station itself, although these cases are not the rule. According to industry figures, only 15 percent of the nation's service stations are owned and run by the major companies, and these are frequently used as training schools for future marketing managers.

The great majority of service stations—four-fifths, or nearly two hundred thousand—are dealer-operated under what is essentially a franchise system; that is, the local manager dealer leases or rents the station from the major company and uses that company's products. He benefits from advertising, promotional material, credit cards, and product reputation, and the major company benefits from having an assured outlet for its products in the community.

Then there are the independents who are, according to prodivestiture forces, being forced out of the market by the major oil companies. Now on the face of it, it should be extremely easy to determine whether the majors are gaining an increasing slice of the retail market, as divestiture advocates claim. Either they are or they aren't. Unfortunately, however, no one is quite certain how precisely to define the term "independent."

While 80 percent of America's two hundred thousand retail service stations are operated by small businessmen, their situations vary. Some sell branded gasoline, for instance, and some do not, and just to complicate matters, there are both branded and nonbranded company-owned stations. Some operators who own rather than lease their stations contract with the companies and sell under brand names. And some buy on the spot market and sell nonbranded.

This last practice is a most interesting one and has in a number of ways added to the general confusion over who is doing what to whom in the market. This independent occasionally takes advantage of the name-brand benefits. But he often finds that he can buy on the spot from both the majors and the independents and, by doing so, save money and attract customers who are less interested in brand names and services than saving money at the pump. The stations that practiced spot buying eventually were to profit significantly from the embargo and the price rise. But initially they suffered, often dramatically, and it is on this period of initial suffering rather than on the subsequent period of high profits that congressional advocates of divestiture tend to focus.

Buying products on a spot market rather than under long-term contract can be highly profitable. If there is too much of the product on hand, the people who own it may be willing to sell cheap to get rid of it. Thus, you buy at a sizable saving and sell somewhere near the going market rate. Before the embargo, this was the typical oil market condition. Refineries regularly churned out more gasoline than they were contracted to sell, and businesses who were willing to gamble a bit on availability of supply usually won out.

But with the oil crisis there was suddenly no surplus, and many of these businesses were unable to find any product at all. As a result, many of these independents suffered and some were forced to close down. But the suffering of the independents was brought on not by larger competitors, but by forces over which none of the companies, large or small, had any control, and by business gambles which did not pay off.

Later, however, after the crisis had been weathered and with supplies again abundant, the situations of those independents selling nonbrand products improved greatly. Suddenly, prices began to soar and customers increasingly shopped in those cut-rate, streamlined stations which offer few services beyond pumping gas—and that often on a do-it-yourself basis. High volume, quick turnover, minimal service gas sales put many independents in the black and the majors, unable to match their prices, began to think carefully about reorganizing their retailing methods. Most of us have noticed the new self-service sections at many of the brand-name stations. And some companies have begun to attempt to cut out paperwork by charging lower prices to those customers who pay cash rather than charge. This is the direct result of the challenge from the independents—competition, in other words.

The independents are having a definite effect on the majors. And they are also having an effect on dealer operators. Until the price hike, customers were at least as interested in service as they were in bargains and probably more so. Typically, a station gassed the same cars it serviced and a customer tended to buy his gasoline there because of the care taken of his car. But gasoline is increasingly coming to seem expensive to the average driver and there is, therefore, an increasing tendency to shop. Also, the automobile, thanks in part to the ceaseless stream of federal regulations, grows increasingly complicated, thus making it ever more difficult to work on at the corner station level. And there is also the problem of diminishing competence—how long has it been since a first-rate mechanic did a first-rate job on your car?

The reasons for this latter problem are complex, and no one has yet come up with satisfactory explanation. But it seems a commonplace thing to observe that something is very wrong with much of the work that is being done in America today. Conservatives, no doubt, would argue that it's the fault of the minimum wage and unionization. Liberals would say that too many sorts of work are dehumanizing, and it is thus absurd to expect people to perform it with enthusiasm. And still others would say that it is the result of affluence, that it is too easy these days in this fat society for people to get by. In times of hardship, they'd maintain—as, for instance, during the Depression—any man who had a paying job felt extraordinarily blessed. Thus, for several generations, the American work force, at perhaps its most productive period in our history, was made up of first-rate men who felt themselves to be working at what today we would call dehumanizing jobs—and those same men today, no doubt, would all be graduates of state universities and working at white-collar jobs.

But whatever the reasons, the decreasing quality of work, in addition to price increases and an ailing economy that forces more and more Americans to count their pennies, is leading to the success of the low-overhead, large quantity gasoline supermarkets. This has had its effect on the owner dealer, of course, and in many cases it has left him bitter, especially when he has, say, operated under the name of Exxon and suddenly finds that one of Exxon' company-owned Alert stations in the same general area has begun to drain off his business. It is understandable that he would feel he is being squeezed out of business, caught between the major company whose name he carries and the independents who are underselling that major. And if he hears on TV news that Congress is holding hearings on the matter, it would be understandable if he were to write letters to his senator, who woulu then read such letters into the record.

None of us want to see that full service station go

the way of the blacksmith shop, at least so long as it actually offers services. But in no way is monopoly involved here; instead, it is competition at its purest, which is what the divestiture proponents profess to want to promote. It is the misfortune of the owner-dealer to find himself caught between the two competing parties, and it is ironic that his plight should be brought on primarily by practices pioneered by independent dealers.

Still, the situation remains murky, and Congress has difficulty discussing it because of the confusion over that word *independent,* a confusion that extends to others involved in the marketing process, especially the jobbers. There are independent jobbers and company-paid jobbers and jobbers who are often peculiar combinations. Most jobbers sell gasoline to retail dealers who in turn sell the gas at the pump. The jobbers may also sell gasoline and deisel fuel directly to farmers, heating oil directly to homes, and lubrication oils and greases. They can be small companies with a half-dozen employees operating in rural areas, or huge firms operating in cities. They may be company owned—in which case the distributor is called not a jobber but a "commission agent" and draws a commission on the amount of the product he sells—or, as is more commonly the case, the company will be owned by the jobber, who buys products outright and sells them for his own account. Such a jobber, even though he is independent, might handle only the products of one major oil company and sell them under a brand name. Or he might buy on the spot market and sell under his own private brand name. Or he might do a combination of both.

On the retail level, then, the terms "major" and "independent" are confusing. An independently owned company, either a service station or a distributing firm, may be independent yet sell under a major company's name. Or it may be owned by one of the majors and sell under an independent brand name. Or it may be owned by an independent and sell under its own name. Thus, when the government decided to attempt to find out whether or not the majors were squeezing out the independents on the retail level, there was a great deal of confusion about who to count as what and where.

Under the Emergency Petroleum Act of 1973, the government was charged with preserving the independent marketers' share of gasoline sales. In 1974, under the provisions of this act, the Federal Energy Office (now the Federal Energy Administration) commissioned a consulting firm to study market shares. The conclusion of the study: the independents' share had fallen dramatically. It was subsequent discovered, however, that the data used by the company were faulty and that its definition of the term "independent" was different from the government's. Since these were the days when shredders were still routinely used in the executive branch, the copies of the study were destroyed. And since these also were the days when the worst was suspected as a matter of course—and kept coming true—the suspicion was that the government in collusion with big business was suppressing evidence that proved the majors were squeezing out independents.

However, according to four George Washington University scientists who were able to obtain and analyze copies of the flawed study, even when using that study's definition of independents, arrived at by determining the shares of gasoline sold under the brand names of nonmajor companies, it would have shown, had the comparative figures been correct, a slight increase in the independents' share of the market—from 45.4 to 48.2 percent.

Then, in the same year, the Independent Gasoline Marketers Council made public a study which purported to show that the independents' share of the market had fallen some 17.1 percent between 1972 and the first quarter of 1974. But again, the basis for the analysis was flawed. The IGMC studied only fifteen of the larger nonbranded independents—about 16 percent of the total market and these were the companies most likely to buy on the spot market in times of surplus gasoline. Many other marketers, among them most nonbranded independents, buy gasoline from refineries under contract. The study, however, was weighted heavily in favor of those independents who were spot buyers caught short during the crisis—businessmen who had lost a business gamble and therefore a share of the market.

Just to add to the confusion, a "quick survey" by Lewin & Associates, Inc., based on much the same sort of data as that used by the Independent Gasoline Manufacturers Council, indicated that the independents had lost 14.8 percent of the market. The FEA responded by commissioning yet another study by a reputable energy economist which showed that during the same period the independents' share of the market rose by nearly 4 percent.

Finally, swimming in a sea of contradictory figures, the FEA decided to undertake its own study. The FEA study, which defined "independent" sales as sales through outlets not owned and operated by the companies producing the gasoline, showed very little change at all in the market between 1972 and 1974. And subsequent FEA studies indicate that since the oil crisis, independents have not only regrouped but are actually gaining in market strength at a constant rate.

The FEA has increasingly narrowed the definition of independent so that it now includes only those dealers who both own their stations and sell unbranded gasoline. In 1974, these independents totalled 7.4 percent of the market. By April of 1975, according to FEA figures, the independents had 10.2 percent of the market.

Even according to the narrowest definition, then, the independents are hardly being squeezed out. And it is evident that as the independent's share of the market grows, it does so at the expense of the dealer-owned, full-service station. The majors, like everyone else, have responded to the proliferation of nonbranded, cut-rate, self-service gasoline stations with their own cut-rate nonbranded stations, and it becomes increasingly apparent that gasoline supermarkets will frequently corner the market in a given area.

But although many small businessmen would inevitably be forced from the market because of the new retailing practices, there would still be ample room for the franchise dealer who could in fact deliver the services he advertises. And there wouldn't just be room, for he'd be guaranteed all the work he could handle.

One of the effects of competition is always to winnow the least efficient and the least needed out of the market. And the fact is that today there are simply too many franchise dealers. There are, for instance, within about three miles from where this book was written, at least six Amoco stations, and as many Exxon and Texaco franchises, some of them barely a few hundred yards from one another. On one of the streets that approach our city, a small one, there is an interesting arrangement. It's one of those strip streets on which everyone is always making unexpected left turns, a couple of miles long, narrow and lined on both sides by McDonald's, Burger King, Fish 'n' Chips, little businesses that open one week and close the next, and gas stations —Texaco, Amoco, Gulf, Exxon, often two stations pumping the same brand. Near the beginning of the strip, where you turn off the highway, there's a dealer-operated franchise station which pumps only the gas of one major company and sells only that company's products.

Within a hundred yards, there are two other stations, located at important intersections, both of which pump name brands and carry a full line of products. And in the same general area as the name-brand franchise stations, are two of the best known cut-rate, no-service, fast-pumping independents, both of which sell their gas at significantly lower rates than the two major outlets.

Each of the stations is well located, each is clean and well kept, and all serve a mix of customers, both residents of the community and drivers from the major highway nearby, and because of this both the quick-service stations pump gas steadily, as do all the stations during the peak of the tourist season. For much of the year, however, you could fire a cannon through the service areas of two of the major franchises and seldom hit an automobile. But the two quick-fill stations are always full, and there are always customers at the one major franchise—the one at the beginning of the strip. At times these are drivers off the highway, but more often they are people from the community.

Why? The quick-fill stations are full, quite obviously, because they sell gasoline for less. But the major franchise at the beginning of the strip does a good, steady business because of the quality of the service it offers. In any community, the word spreads. Each of the major franchises carries a respected name, and consumers have seen each of the names time and time again on television. Each carries a superior line of products. But only one offers superior service. The man who operates the station, assisted by his family, is a first-rate mechanic, as is one of the men who works for him. Their reputations for excellent, careful work and for exceptionally reasonable bills has spread for miles, and just as in the days before the crisis, people are willing to pay more for gasoline in order to get the service their cars need. The other two franchise stations, on the other hand, although they bear names that most consumers generally respect, have community-wide reputations for sloppy and indifferent work and inexplicably high charges. Their business, as a result, has steadily fallen off. One group of customers, wanting only bargain-priced gas, goes down the street to one of the quick-fill places. Those wanting work done on their cars, either now or in the future, go to the major franchise at the beginning of the strip.

173

Thus, out of five stations in roughly the same area, there are three going, money-making concerns, and two which manage to squeeze by. Primarily their customers are unwary tourists who wander off the highway in search of a brand name they are accustomed to or the local who happens by with an empty tank, an empty wallet, and a company credit card. Eventually, one suspects, these two stations will be gone, and should another quick-fill station locate upwind of them before the next tourist season, their demise will be hastened.

The brand-name dealer at the beginning of the strip will be secure for as long as he wants to be, however. He will be secure, that is, unless Congress decides to legislate divestiture. His two brand-name competitors, competitively squeezed out by cheap gas on the one side and superior services on the other, will eventually be driven out by market forces. And this, of course, if we accept the validity of the free-enterprise system as the best means of ordering our economic affairs, is as it should be.

It is precisely these natural forces that divestiture would thwart, however, and the result would inevitably be that thousands of small businessmen who take pride in running their own operation and running it well, would be driven out of business indiscriminately. The man at the beginning of the strip, for instance, who under highly competitive but normal market conditions would continue to thrive, might very well go out of business in precisely the same way his two inefficient, franchised neighbors will go out of business. The market system is selective; divestiture is indiscriminate.

Under divestiture, it is highly likely that the

174

trend toward closing small outlets, eliminating franchised dealers in favor of salaried managers, and reducing repair services in favor of a gasoline supermarket would accelerate. And, as is likely, should the companies sell their marketing properties, the efficient as well as the inefficient small businessmen-operators would be driven out of the market. Most franchise operators simply can't afford the $350,000 or so it would cost them to purchase outright the service station and the land it sits on.

It would be likely then that a few big operations would sweep through the area buying up service stations and undercutting those independents left in business by setting up bigger and better multipump operations with super cut-rate prices. Thus, both the franchised small businessman and the independent would be most likely to go—again, an example of government victimizing precisely those people it sets out to help.

Also, of course, from the consumer's point of view, the whole thing would be chaotic. There is the problem of brand names, for instance. Perhaps dependence on brand names is bad for us, and no doubt when the new Consumer Protection Agency is established, a staff of experts paid for with our tax money will tell us how absurd it is to buy by brand. Some of us, however, set in our ways and no doubt suffering from some peculiar psychological aberration, still perfer to buy those brands with which we are familiar, even when experts tell us not to.

Divestiture will be welcomed by these experts, however, for it should effectively break us of branddependence. Once the companies are effectively broken up, we psychological cripples might very well be unable to find those brands. No one knows who would assume the name of the divested company. But even if it were the marketing segment, Amoco brand gasoline, for instance, is not Amoco brand gasoline unless it is refined by an Amoco refinery which guarantees Amoco's quality and composition. Under divestiture, however, although there might be an Amoco station, there would be no Amoco refinery. If, on the other hand, the refinery assumed the parent's name, then there would be an Amoco refinery, but since there would be no Amoco service station, the customer would have no way of finding Amoco's refined products, even if they existed.

And just as the government would break us of the brand-dependence habit, so too under divestiture it would break us of the habit of depending on a variety of credit cards. If the parent company's name weren't assumed by the service stations, then it's unlikely they'd take your Mobil card at some newly formed gas supermarket called Gasseroo.

All in all, slight exaggerations aside, the effects of divestiture would at the very least add up to years of total confusion in the retailing segment of the industry. If stations were forced to change their names, they'd be starting out cold, and one result would necessarily be years of costly promotional activity as they sought to reestablish rapport with customers. Retained retail names would be meaningless and contracts with their former refiners would be looked upon with suspicion—as attempts to wriggle back to monopoly status and would probably be challenged in court. And there would be no way for the retailer to assure the quality of his product, since the refiners, without brand-name

176

identification, would have little motivation to produce a product that did anything other than meet the minimum requirements of the government and the automobile manufacturers. It seems highly likely then, that the overall quality of gasoline would deteriorate dramatically, should refiners lose brand-name identification.

One sure result of divestiture, then, would be chaos for the consumer. And it would positively be tragic for the small businessman. The marketing of gasoline is perhaps a wasteful procedure. But it has been set up in such a way as to give individual and personal attention to the consumer, and to allow for adjustments to the business and service needs of individual communities. But perhaps most important of all, it has afforded small businessmen all over the country—station managers and jobbers as well—the opportunity to run their own businesses. And it is that opportunity, aided by the growth of the franchise system during the past few decades, which divestiture threatens.

This is not something that divestiture proponents like to admit, and indeed many of them no doubt sincerely misunderstand the stake the small businessman has in retaining a well-structured and coherent industry. Within it, as presently structured, he has a secure and meaningful place, and his customers receive service that they would almost certainly not receive were divestiture to become a reality. But without that structured industry, he is not then free to prosper, as some of the more naive of the divestiture proponents seem sincerely to believe. Instead, he is suddenly a small minnow swimming in a sea of wheeling-dealing sharks, and his life span would be very short indeed.

A small jobber from Georgia, testifying before the Senate antitrust subcommittee in 1976 put it this way: "It seems obvious to me that divestiture would cause marketing to consolidate into fewer and bigger marketing companies which would displace thousands of dealers and wholesalers with their own new high-volume, salaried chains because of their immense leverage to negotiate long-range contracts for refinery production.

"This revolution may work to the advantage of a few very large super-jobbers and private brand chains which have the money and the resources to create their own brand images, but it can only work to the detriment of small jobbers who have relied on their suppliers for major brand identification, image standards, credit terms, promotional product advertising, station design, engineering services, marketing experience, credit card programs, personnel training, and other forms of business support.

"It would seem obvious that the economics of size would force these new big oil companies, these 'Sears and Roebucks' of gasoline marketing, into existence, and there would probably be no room for the small jobber under their umbrella."

Another jobber from a rural area of the South describes how he believes divestiture and the growth of these "Sears Roebucks" of marketing would affect the people in his area.

"The impact of divestiture on the consumer will be one of less competition in the marketplace, fewer places to buy gasoline, increased prices for gasoline; and all of this to contend with when one is totally

178

dependent on the automobile for his livelihood.

"Regarding the farmers and home heating customers we serve directly ... Who is going to deliver to the small farmer who has a 280 gallon tank and wants to pay his bill once a year?

"Who is going to deliver to the heating oil customer who refuses to buy more than a 100 gallon storage tank and probably can't afford to? We have many such examples.

"Would the new marketing companies, with stockholders demanding marketing profits, be sensitive to the needs of these customers? I think not."

And a jobber from Virginia takes the time to remind Congress, which never seems to think about it and has yet to take one tentative tottering step toward devising a national energy policy, that the real problem is to find new energy sources. Time spent on divestiture legislation, says the jobber, compares with "the Berlin Symphony Orchestra continuing to give concerts while the Russians were at the city gates."

A New Jersey jobber then goes on to testify, with quiet eloquence, as to what it means to be a successful small businessman.

"I chose the oil business for several reasons—the most important of which is that it afforded people like myself, with limited financial resources, an entry into a good, clean business which was needed by society and which offered me the chance to be independent.

"I like to think that I have prospered and those around me have prospered because I was willing to get up a little earlier, work a little harder, and give a little better service than my competitors. ...

"My main point is this. If you are seeking to preserve and aid people like myself by legislation such as S.2387 [the divestiture bill], please don't do me any favors. I believe that this legislation is one of the biggest threats that has come along to my economic survival."

Thus, the consequences of divestiture to the marketing segment of the industry. Facilities would go up for sale, the prices for which could be swung only by organizations with vast amounts of capital. This means that independents would be forced out of business, and with less independents competing for customers, and with majors and franchises a thing of the past, the end result would be a few large "Sears Roebuck" marketing chains in control of the retail market. How precisely this could be described as a means toward "the creation and maintenance of competition," as the Bayh bill puts it, defies rational discussion.

We have here, it is true, been discussing the marigold Bayh bill, which would break up everything at once by demolishing the industry. But there are less explosive measures promising less spectacular fallout, that could have the same effect. There is, for instance, as mentioned earlier, a recommendation in a report of the House Small Business Committee that legislation be developed to prevent major oil companies from owning service stations, the first such recommendation to come from a committee of the House. This is also the sort of approach to divestiture that Jimmy Carter reportedly favors, for it would at least partially appease some of the more rabid prodivestiture members of his party, while at the same time not alarming some of these Democrats with no real knowledge of the issue but with conservative instincts.

The result of such limited divestiture legislation, however, while perhaps not quite as dramatic, would nevertheless have precisely the same effect on the retailing segment, and particularly on the small businessman making his living in that segment.

There is, especially among the senators who favor divestiture, a great deal of lip service paid to the idea that this small businessman is the rock upon which our nation was built and that therefore he must be protected legislatively from the depradations of the corporate giants who would squeeze every penny from the economy, and squeeze the small businessman out of business in the process. But this, of course, is nonsense. It is the major companies who in large part make it possible for the small gas retailer and jobber to continue to exist, and one suspects that those divestiture advocates who insist otherwise either haven't done their homework or really don't, deep down inside, care at all about that small businessman they like to champion rhetorically. In fact, from the evidence at hand, it often appears as if many of these self-proclaimed champions of small business are actually talking out of both sides of their faces.

Many of the newer regulatory agencies, for instance, whose activities are encouraged by prodivestiture legislators, while posing a threat to the large corporation, come down hardest on the small businessmen. Perhaps the most dreaded among them is the Labor Department's Occupational Safety and Health Administration (OSHA), the *bête noire* of small businessmen everywhere. Most conservative and centrist legislators in Washington will spend hours repeating OSHA horror stories reported to them by their small-business constituents, whose premises are subject to OSHA inspection without advance warning. One of the best of the true OSHA stories concerns a high-wire artist who, because he worked without a safety net, billed his act as "death-defying." The OSHA inspectors, however, decided the act wasn't occupationally safe, and so up went the safety net, and down came the "death-defying" billing. And that, of course, ruined the act.

In California, one of the most interesting examples of small-entrepreneurship concerns skateboards. In several of the state's cities, enterprising young people are successfully competing with the established regular delivery services by delivering small packages via skateboard. The word is, however, that OSHA is looking into the practice. Skateboards are certainly not safe.

Amusing examples, both of them. But to the small businessman, there is nothing amusing in what appear to be proliferating arbitrary and senseless regulations by agencies which seem at best remote and indifferent and at worst overtly hostile. And they all seem aimed most directly at him.

The small businessman forms the core of this country's middle class and to a significant number of middle-class Americans, it seems that Washington has lined up solidly against them. They pay the bulk of the nation's personal income taxes, yet have little to show for what they pay out. They make just enough money to disqualify themselves from receiving the benefits of the programs they pay for. Their dollars pay for the education of children of other less successful Americans, yet they no longer make enough to send their own children to college without going into hock.

Yet despite the fact that their government seems to have forsaken them, middle-class small businessmen keep trying, convinced, like that jobber from New Jersey, that if they just keep getting up earlier and trying a little harder than their competitors, they'll finally realize the rewards promised by the American dream. But the problem is that for the trendier of our national opinion makers, and among them are a good portion of the prodivestiture advocates, the American dream has become a nightmare. And this may help to explain the ambivalent and often openly hostile attitude that seems to characterize the new liberal intellectual attitude toward the middle class, of which the small businessman is the primary symbol.

We have all grown a bit more sophisticated than we were in the sixties, and the elitists no longer express themselves quite as bluntly as did, for instance, Professor Charles Reich, who saw middle-class Americans as a sad lumpy lot, stewing "in their sullen boredom, their unchanging routines, their minds closed to new ideas and feelings, their bodies slumped in front of the television to watch the ballgame Sundays."

Perhaps in part because the intellectuals have discovered pro-football and are writing about it, they don't talk that way any more. But one suspects the sentiment lingers on. "Scratch an intellectual," says Eric Hoffer, "and you find a would-be aristocrat who loathes the sight, the sound, and the smell of the common folk."

Now this may be somewhat extreme, and no one would claim that all—or even a majority—of the divestiture proponents in Washington are intellectuals. But the no-growth movement, which in many ways provides divestiture with an intellectual rationale, is an intellectual movement, and it is the American middle class, more than any other group, that represents everything antithetical to the goals and the vision of that movement.

The no-growth philosophy requires, by definition, that things must as much as possible remain exactly as they are. Thus, the upward mobility that has for long stood as the symbol of the best in the American system, is no longer desirable. If people insist on moving up, as that New Jersey jobber insists on doing, then their very motion is offensive enough. But even worse, as they ascend, they will also insist on acquiring all those superfluous, polluting trappings which the plants and factories persist in turning out, the symbols to the no-growthers and their environmentalist allies of the bad life.

But to the New Jersey jobber, those things are desirable in themselves and are rewards which prove the system is a good one. A better home in the suburbs where there are better schools, the best appliances, air conditioning, perhaps a boat or a swimming pool or both—the tangible symbols of success and progress.

And perhaps even the no-growthers would agree that they are. But the problem is, from the no-growth point of view, they should no longer be. And that, of course, sets up an unavoidable tension between those who aspire to better themselves and the no-growthers, for the no-growthers, for the most part, educated members of the upper middle classes, have long possessed all those things to which the upwardly mobile lower and middle-middle classes aspire.

The result, inevitably, is something that very much resembles a caste system, and perhaps, given the no-growth premises, this is as it should be. If things must stay as they are, which is simply another way of saying that things must no longer grow, then people's conditions must remain static. And perhaps this is why those who espouse the no-growth philosophy also tend to support massive social welfare programs, for no better means has ever been devised for insuring that the poor remain poor, a permanent subcaste born into dependency and encouraged to accept it as a way of life.

It is obvious, at any rate, that the middle-class belief in upward mobility and in progress, that belief which motivates every successful small businessman, is antithetical to the no-growthers. It may represent progress, they might admit. But progress is the result of movement, growth, expansion, and is therefore no longer desirable. And if progress is no longer desirable, then neither is the small businessman, for perhaps more than any other single figure in our society, he is the personification of that progress.

And that, perhaps, is why some of us find it just a bit difficult to take no-growthers seriously when they tell us that it is for the sake of the small businessman that they are attempting to dismantle the oil industry. Somehow, it just doesn't ring true.

# Chapter
# Nine

"We should not forbid the oil companies from engaging in research in other forms of energy or in acquiring other energy resources. They have the capital and the experience to develop them. More importantly, they know that if they do not find other sources of energy they will die when they run out of petroleum—and most of them see that day approaching. I don't think we have any interest in killing them, and if they are allowed to diversify they will have powerful incentives to develop new energy sources."

The speaker: James E. Akins, former White House energy adviser and ambassador to Saudi Arabia. The forum: a hearing of a congressional energy subcommittee. The subject: horizontal divestiture.

Up until very recently, it was thought in Washington that the best way to kill off the major oil companies was to dismember them vertically. And attempts at vertical dismemberment will continue, and may yet succeed, if the divestiture proponents are intelligently modest and content with a piece at a time.

But many enemies of the oil industry these days are taking the long view. It may not now be possible to do in big oil through comprehensive vertical divestiture legislation. But horizontal divestiture—that is, prohibiting the major oil companies by law from developing new energy sources—might just do the trick.

But horizontal divestiture, claim many experts, could be a colossal exercise in cutting off the nose to spite the face, especially since there may be only a bit more than a quarter-century of oil left. And what is more, given our 50 percent dependence on foreign oil, we live at the whim of the foreign policies of various Arabian states, not exactly fabled for the rationality of their dealings with others. Add to this the fact that the government which regularly promises us energy self-sufficiency has yet to deliver even a smidgin of performance of that promise.

We were given a huge bulge in the bureaucracy, to be sure, in the form of a new agency, but it is difficult to determine just what the FEA has accomplished. President Ford managed to sign one muddled major energy bill which confused everyone, including, according to White House aides, the president himself and his energy advisers on the Domestic Council. And Congress, galloping to the aid of the public with a televised flourish during the crisis, so far has done nothing to prevent such a crisis from recurring except to talk about breaking up the oil companies.

The congressional record has, in fact, been dismal. There is nothing more essential, for instance, if we are even to begin to make a start toward lessening our dependence on foreign oil, than the development of coal, with large-scale conversion of coal to gas and oil. Also, the development of technology to extract oil from shale should obviously be going full

187

speed ahead. But in 1975 and 1976, while spouting homilies about self-sufficiency, the House voted down bills which would facilitated shale and coal conversion. And in the area of nuclear energy, both the legislative and the executive branches, bowing to political pressure from a vocal group of critics, have begun to have second thoughts. Senator Percy, for instance, once an enthusiastic backer of the breeder reactor project, now has backed off and recommends transferring the project's funds to conservation and the development of solar energy. And Gerald Ford, outmaneuvered during the presidential debates and stung by the charge that his administration did not know what it was doing in the nuclear area, joined Jimmy Carter in expressing strong reservations about plutonium and breeders.

The fact is that in Washington, at this writing, little has been done. The environmentalists continue to oppose most new developments, opting for such things as windmills and discussions on how to develop a "conservation ethic" among those middle-class Americans they neither know nor understand. And the only solution they can come up with is to dismember the oil companies. Why? There is no one rational answer, for it is not a rational response. Like them or not, the fact is that the oil companies are actively engaged in developing alternate energy sources. And despite the rhetoric, no agency of government or environmental group can make the same statement. To be sure, there is occasionally an environmentalist group such as the one in the New York slum which made a media splash recently by erecting a windmill on the roof of a New York tenement. "We've become the first urban wind power system in the nation," said the group's leader proudly, and added, "It's a beautiful combination of what the environmentalists have been pushing for, and the needs of the poor." Unfortunately, however, the windmill, even on a day of high winds, barely generates enough power to light the halls of the tenement on which it sits. At a cost of $4,000 per windmill, it is hardly, one suspects, the answer to the needs of a city of six million people and hundreds of thousands of businesses.

Nevertheless, many find the windmill approach preferable to allowing the oil companies to develop alternate sources. Robert Sherrill, Washington editor of the *Nation,* for instance, puts it this way in a *New York Times Magazine* piece. "As a paying spectator, I'm entitled to say that I find it very easy to side with the divestiture crowd, although, in part, for the wrong reasons. It gives me considerable pleasure to see Big Oil quaking at the thought that the worm— the public—has turned. Smug, arrogant Big Oil has always had its way with us."

Now there are some obvious problems here, perhaps chief among them the suggestion that the Washington editor of the *Nation* knows what it is that the American public—or the worms, as Sherrill chooses to call us—is thinking about the subject of divestiture, or anything else, for that matter. But perhaps more important is that emotional tone and the name calling—"smug" and "arrogant," for instance—interspersed with the more intemperate and inaccurate statements about Big Oil by critics such as Senator Adlai Stevenson ("It [Big Oil] got to rip up the ecology of Alaska the way it wanted," said Stevenson in a patently untrue and ludicrous misstatement). Sherrill finally concludes his article with the ultimate emotional and uninformed argument against oil company development of alternate sources—the only one, in the end, that he is able to come up with.

"In terms of legislative strategy," writes Sherrill, "getting support for horizontal divestiture would be much easier than vertical. It can be reduced to one question: Do you want the same wonderful people who gave you the oil crisis of 1973 to get their hands on coal and nuclear power?"

Now it is demonstrably the case that those "wonderful people" who gave us the oil crisis were Arab producers and politicians and regulators in Washington, and few familiar with the facts would continue to argue today that the oil companies played the primary role in the crisis. Nevertheless, to those with certain ideological mind sets, the oil company conspiracy theory remains a comfortable one, for if we embrace it, as does Sherrill, we are able to avoid certain hard questions which might disturb our ideological or political preconceptions.

If we accept the oil company conspiracy theory, it is not necessary to come to grips with the whole concept of big government and what its encroachment into the private sector can lead to—an oil crisis, for instance. Nor is it necessary, if we accept the oil companies as prime cause, as does Sherrill, to examine certain aspects of our foreign policy which might make us uncomfortable. If we accept the notion that it is all the fault of the oil companies, then we have, in short, accepted a comfortable explanation. But comfortable explanations tend also to be simplistic and therefore dangerous.

In his testimony to the congressional energy sub-committee last year, James Akins put it this way: "Unfortunately, even today we find it difficult to accept the fact that our present difficulty in energy matters has been made worse by our gullibility to swallow the tasty but nutritionless pap fed to us by fools and charlatans; that nothing was wrong and nothing need be done. Perhaps the only adequate explanation lies in psychology, for now we seem to be searching for new myths to give comfort and new soothsayers to give the excuse to avoid unpleasant conclusions and difficult proposals. Many Americans still believe that the oil shortages and the price increases of 1973-74 were caused by the oil companies. Many of the 'solutions' which are proposed to avoid future shortages are restrictive or even punitive measures to be taken against the oil companies."

And this is precisely the problem with Sherrill's fatuous "same wonderful people" comment. It is a simpleminded observation, and one that is patently untrue. Whatever else the oil companies may have done, they did not bring on what Sherrill identifies as the crisis. That crisis was the result of the Arab embargo, and the embargo was the direct result of our support of Israel during the October war. Some critics charge that the oil companies were not unhappy to see the subsequent price rise, others say they may have let the Arabs know they were for it.

Perhaps. Our oil prices have for too long been kept artificially low, the industry believes, and from the market point of view, you're not going to have all-out development of alternate sources until prices find their real international level and people realize how much it will cost us to replace cheap oil. From this point of view, it is good not only for profits but also for national energy development.

The oil companies, therefore, may not have been at all unhappy to see those prices go up, and if they worked hard to discourage the price rise, then something was wrong with their business instincts. But to accuse them of bringing on the crisis is patently absurd. Because Sherrill here refers only to that immediate manifestation of the import problem, we need not discuss the long range situation—the period he identifies as the period of crisis, in other words, refers only to the period of the Arab embargo. Now how could the oil companies have "given" us that crisis?

Could they have persuaded the Arabs to attack the Israelis, or could they, perhaps, have persuaded the Nixon administration to go massively to the aid of the Israelis? If the oil companies truly "gave us the oil crisis of 1973," the only way they could have done so was to in some way or another cause the war and involve us in it on Israel's side, since it was the war and our position vis a vis Israel which led to the embargo and the embargo which led to the crisis. But Mr. Sherrill doesn't make this claim, of course. He just smugly makes his simplistic assertion, then lets it hang there. And that, one supposes, is one of the luxuries and privileges allowed those writers whose politics and ideology are sufficiently fashionable. They can be just as superstitious, just as emotional as they please, spinning their myths to fit their ideological preconceptions and by so doing avoiding all those "unpleasant conclusions and difficult proposals."

Among those unpleasant conclusions is the fact that we cannot continue as we are, although the government for the last several administrations seemed to want to do precisely that. One president or another periodically rose to read a speech on "energy independence," after which Washington fell back into a complacent doze again. And in the meantime, the dependence on foreign oil continues to rise and the world's supply of oil continues to sink. Thus, there are two threats, one immediate, the other long range, but both requiring that we do something to develop alternate sources of energy.

The first threat is the possibility of another outbreak in the Mideast, something that could happen at any given moment. And when and if it does happen, there is little doubt that if we once again threw everything we have behind the Israelis, just as we did in 1973, we would inevitably bring on another embargo. The Arabs now understand just how potent that that embargo was, the performance of their troops has improved in each confrontation, and the outlook therefore for the next time round is a longer war, more extensive damage to the Israeli forces, and a more stringent and protracted embargo, this one remaining in effect until we either managed to end the fighting on terms satisfactory to the Arabs or renounced our support for Israel. Would we do so? It seems unlikely on the surface because of the depth of our moral commitment to Israel. But we had a similar commitment to South Vietnam.

But our moral fervor could be short lived indeed, if we were sufficiently choked off from our oil supplies so that the cars one day stopped running and the heat or air conditioning went off. One

193

suspects that many Americans would begin to look at Israel in a new light. Why not, they might wonder, let the Egyptians move east to the pre-1967 borders? It's all desert, after all. And why not let the Syrians move south? And there's the West Bank for the Palestinians. And Jerusalem, of course, should not be controlled by any one nation. Thus the slippage would begin which could eventually lead to the destruction of Israel, a slippage that would probably be inevitable, given a total boycott and an increasing dependence on OPEC oil.

Even if there is not another war in the Mideast, there is still the long-range threat to be faced. Sooner or later that day will arrive when the last drop of oil on earth runs out. Whatever the precise date, it could easily fall within our lifetimes and the lifetimes of our children. And when it does, we have to be ready with alternate energy sources and new systems in place. Otherwise, the lights will go out, the machinery will stop running, and a dark quiet will settle over America.

This is not melodrama. The oil will one day be gone, first the domestic oil, then the rest of it. And to prepare for that day, we're going to have to make some hard choices. The objective has to be both to become as self-sufficient in existing sources as possible in the short run, and to develop alternate sources which in the long run will provide us with the energy necessary to maintain an industrial way of life and to insure eventual self-sufficiency.

Would preventing the oil companies from engaging in either of these activities help us to solve our energy problems? Perhaps, for some reason known only to thinkers like Sherrill, it would. But it seems more likely that such exclusion would instead effectively insure that the people most suited to solving those problems would be prohibited from doing so. The oil industry has the single best reason for working to develop these alternate sources of energy and that reason is self-interest. For unless the industry can expand into other fields of operation, it will within our lifetime go the way of the dodo. But no industry willingly paves the way for its own extinction, and oil companies now have two choices—they can expand into related energy fields or expand into nonenergy fields. In 1975, for instance, Mobil bought into Montgomery Ward, a move which, naturally, was criticized by the industry's enemies who, one suspects, join Robert Sherrill in hoping that all large profit making firms would just quietly lie down and die. But they won't do so willingly, of course, and their sudden interest in other investments is the direct result of the threat of horizontal divestiture.

Since the oil industry must diversify to survive, its natural choice for areas of expansion would be alternate energy sources. And while there is little in the experience of the companies which would equip them to run men's wear departments, their years of accumulated know-how and expertise would be extremely useful in alternative energy production. The lessons learned in exploring for oil, for instance, would be invaluable in exploring for uranium or their knowledge of hydrocarbons invaluable in the liquifying of coal.

Moreover, the oil industry is uniquely situated financially to expand into alternate fields. Oil still attracts capital and there is no doubt that such expansion will require massive capital infusions. If we

195

are to undergo even a modest amount of growth during the next few decades—and in the opinion of many, if we are even to stay even—then the sums required to develop new energy sources will be astronomical. Last year, for instance, the Senate antitrust subcommittee heard expert testimony that put necessary energy investments at approximately $1 trillion through the 1900s. And during the same period, between $95 and $200 billion will be needed for capital investments in nonoil related energy projects.

The amounts needed to begin a new energy production project grow increasingly exorbitant. A new coal mine in the East, for instance, which can be expected to yield about two million tons per year, would require, according to industry figures, an investment of some $79 million. A Western surface mine with a five-million-ton capacity would require a $60 million investment.

Other nonoil energy sources are even more expensive to develop. A new uranium mining and milling operation with a two-million-pound capacity now costs about $100 million to build. Standard coal liquefaction and gasification plants cost an estimated $1 billion. And the price tag for a tar sands facility of any size at all would be about $2 billion.

Not only are the costs for alternative source development enormous, but so are the risks. And the time between the investment of money in a project and when that investment may pay off is considerable. Extremely large amounts of money have been invested in synthetic fuel and shale oil development over the past several decades, for instance, yet today the chances that those massive investments will soon pay off grow increasingly doubtful. Or in the case of uranium mines, about nine years are required for development, and it is several years into the process before a company can begin to determine whether the operation will be profitable.

But it is precisely these sorts of risks that the oil industry is uniquely equipped to undertake. Oil companies have historically operated in such a way as to allow for long lead times, and they have proved their skills in managing these large-scale, capital-intensive, long lead-time projects. In addition, their size alone equips them to participate in the mammoth sorts of projects which will be increasingly necessary as the world's supply of oil runs out.

Nevertheless, the move in Washington to legislate the oil companies out of the alternate energy field is a serious one and, in the months ahead, given what are said to be Jimmy Carter's predilections, horizontal divestiture rather than vertical divestiture may become the fashionable cause. (In this area, as in others, most statements about Carter's position are more often than not educated guesses. During the campaign, one popular joke went this way. Question: Does Jimmy Carter favor horizontal or vertical divestiture? Answer: Neither. He's for diagonal.)

There are those like Robert Sherrill whose support for horizontal, or, for that matter, vertical divestiture seems to spring primarily from an emotional, perhaps unconscious, ideological hostility to profit-making business in general. But there are obviously more clearly thought-out reasons, although they tend to falter in the face of facts and statistics. Perhaps the best of them would run something like this. In the first place, the industry can be expected to put its own interests ahead of the interests of the nation. (It is no more fashionable these days to assert that self-interest and national interest can in fact frequently coincide than it would be to walk into the faculty club at Harvard and shout, with Calvin Coolidge, "The business of America is business." It may, in fact, very well be. But we are no longer allowed to say so.)

This selfish, totally self-interested industry, so the scenario goes, throwing its money around, muscles into the alternate energy field and corners research and development. And in some way, the mechanics of which are never explained, the industry freezes out anyone else who might be engaged in energy research. And then, suddenly, one of the industry's scientists discovers a Revolutionary and Ecologically Acceptable Source of Cheap and Unlimited Energy (RESCUE). At this point, the scenario can vary somewhat. Usually, among the environmentalists, RESCUE is solar. Occasionally it takes the form of wind energy. And in its more exotic forms, RESCUE can become something like a new chemical formula which, through a process resembling alchemy, turns ocean water into gasoline.

But whether the form it takes is exotic or mundane, RESCUE falls solely under the control of the powerful and monolithic oil industry which hides the fact of its existence from a waiting energy-starved world. For with RESCUE on the market, reason the unscrupulous captains of industry, their oil would be rendered worthless. And once the ultimate RESCUE is finally conceived, there would be no reason to attempt to continue to develop a variety of new sources. Ergo, with RESCUE, an end to

198

profits. Therefore, buy off the scientist and destroy the formula that could save the world.

Those who subscribe to something like a RESCUE scenario say that the oil companies should be kept out of alternate energy fields because, in order to insure that their oil remain profitable, they would not be interested in pushing full speed ahead in new energy source development and might also consciously tend to stifle innovative technologies. But, say the companies, such criticism is totally naive. Short of a government takeover, there is not now, nor will there ever be, the companies argue, a way to inhibit competition from smaller companies or competition between the major companies themselves. Each in fact will be working intently against a time clock as the nation's oil resources steadily run out, as inexorably as sand in an hourglass.

The company that manages to come up with something most resembling RESCUE to replace domestic oil will reap substantial rewards, and the competition to do so will therefore be fierce. Further, admit industry spokesmen, it might very well be that either government-sponsored or small-company research will produce the final RESCUE formula. But even so, they maintain, the nation, if it does not become totally socialized, will still need the size and the know-how of big industry to insure that the RESCUE formula is translated into reality.

Further, argue industry spokesmen, the idea that big oil might be motivated to sit on new technology flies in the face of everyday energy facts. Tomorrow, for instance, if a scientist were to shout "Eureka" over a RESCUE plan for storing solar energy, we'd still require petroleum products well into the foreseeable future. Even with a stunning RESCUE solar formula, it's highly unlikely that solar energy could run automobiles. Nor would the world overnight close down its current power plants and home heating systems. For years after that stunning RESCUE discovery, oil will still be needed to run those existing energy systems, and there would be no worry whatsoever about domestic oil reserves lying untouched.

If, instead of RESCUE with solar energy, the industry came up with a quick and easy method of turning coal into petroleum or natural gas, the national switchover would be less difficult, but the tasks would still stretch as far into the future as the remaining supplies of gas would take us. It would be necessary to construct new gasification and liquefaction plants across the country, and new mines with new top-speed coal mining and coal transporting technology would have to be developed and put into operation. And the same is true of each of the conceivable alternate energy sources. There are no magic wands, and the country will need well into the next century every remaining drop of the nation's oil that the companies can produce.

And because there are no magic wands, the chances are minimal that even with dramatic breakthroughs in technology we will become self-sufficient, Messrs. Nixon and Ford to the contrary. One unpublished study, commissioned by the American Petroleum Institute, predicts that our national energy demands will require at least a doubling of our energy resources over the next decade. Even with higher costs and conservation, says the study, American energy demands will rise by 1990 to nearly 60 million barrels in oil equivalents per day, up from the 1975 demand of 36.4 million in oil equivalents.

And when that 60-million-barrel in oil equivalents *per day* figure is coupled with the industry's estimate that there remain only some 40 billion barrels of proved domestic crude and liquid gas reserves, it becomes obvious that if there is to be even the vaguest hope of energy self-sufficiency in this century, then we must embark on very serious programs for developing alternate sources of energy, and do so immediately.

The most obvious of these alternatives to oil to be developed is coal. According to the Federal Energy Administration, coal represents about 90 percent of our nation's proved energy reserves. We have, in other words, enough coal left to carry us well into the next century. Unfortunately, however, as with each aspect of the energy picture, things aren't quite that simple.

There are, for instance, the enormous complications caused by the ubiquitous environmentalists and the legislation for which they lobby so effectively in Washington. All coal is not alike, and because of the Clean Air Act Amendment of 1970, passed in a year when Richard Nixon was trying to steal a march on his liberal opponents by supporting even more liberal legislation than they, less than half the minable reserves of coal in the United States can legally be burned. The sulfur content is too high. And of the remaining half, a significant portion can be used only after the installation of expensive stack scrubbers to remove the sulfur after the coal has been burned. The air around the factories is cleaner now, of course, but there is, as with all environmental measures, a cost as well and among those harmed are the industries and the miners of the East, where the high sulfur coal primarily occurs. The miners will continue to lose work and the industries of the energy hungry East must surmount vast transportation problems in order to bring coal from the West, where most of the low-sulfur fields lie.

And if these problems are solved, there are always mining problems. Coal deposits that are too thin or lie too deep cannot be mined economically, at least not at current market rates. Therefore, if western low-sulfur coal is to be brought to market at a competitive price with oil, it must be strip-mined. But the future of strip mining remains uncertain, and the whole western coal mining operation has been and may continue to be bogged down in law suits brought by environmentalists. (Quite recently, boring tests that began in February 1976 have found millions of tons of usable, low-sulfur, clean-burning coal deep under the soil of New England. New England, which now mines no coal and which relies heavily on foreign oil for its electrical generation plants, currently has by far the highest utility costs in the nation and is the region that would be most seriously affected by another OPEC embargo. The coal is there and is needed, but enormous problems would have to be surmounted before it could be mined. Also, some of the coal lies beneath densely populated areas, and one suspects that it would be difficult indeed to sell the denizens of Cambridge on the need for digging big holes beneath Harvard Yard.)

Adding to the problem still further is the instability of the coal market. In response to the oil shortage during the embargo, the Energy Supply and Environmental Coordination Act of 1974 prohibited the burning of natural gas or petroleum in power plants, whenever coal could be burned in compliance with Clean Air Act standards, thereby increasing the market for coal. But other governmental policies have precisely the opposite effect. As the Council on Wage and Price Stability recently put it, "A major obstacle blocking expansion of long-term coal demand has been uncertainty regarding federal policy for sulfur oxides control. Coal customers have been reluctant to make long-term commitments until questions on possible revisions to the Clean Air Act of 1970—currently being debated in Congress—and about EPA implementation and enforcement are resolved."

Coal, which would seem the most obvious answer to our most pressing energy needs, is now caught in a push-pull battle between environmentalists and industry, and precisely at that moment when we should be moving rapidly to develop it. The government and the courts, which are refereeing the battle in a rather desultory fashion, rule occasionally for one side, occasionally for the other. But without hard and fast decisions about whether the environment or which of our energy needs should take precedence, the whole question of whether coal can serve as an adequate replacement for oil may become moot.

Also in doubt, and for many of the same reasons, is the future of uranium in our national energy picture. At present, the principal use of uranium is as a fuel for operating nuclear electric generating plants, the construction of which communities are increasingly opposing, in part because they fear being blown out of their beds. (The Energy Research Development Administration prefers to call it a "disassembly process," induced by "autocatalytic recrecriticality.") But perhaps even a larger worry is that the wastes from these facilities cannot be disposed of in any safe and reasonable way. Nevertheless, despite the growing negative popular reaction, which is resulting in an increasing number of ballot initiatives in the western states, the ERDA continues to predict that by the end of this century, nuclear energy, which now generates approximately 9 percent of our electric power, will be the major factor in meeting our energy needs. And the Federal Energy Administration predicts that by 1985 nuclear power will generate more than one quarter of the nation's electricity, a figure which will increase to 50 percent by the year 2000.

If so, says the Nuclear Task Group of the National Petroleum Council, then in order to meet the demand for uranium, we should be drilling forty to sixty million surface feet per year. However, surface drilling peaked in 1969 at thirty million feet and by 1976 had fallen off to fifteen million feet. This means, in other words, that even were the current questions of safety to be cleared up, at the present rate of drilling we will not have enough uranium to run the power plants of 1985, to say nothing of 2000. Present drilling, in fact, would meet only a third of our projected end-of-the-century needs and it is doubtful that it will increase quickly enough. The siting and licensing of new nuclear power facilities grows increasingly controversial, and the purity of an elected official's intentions toward his constituency is frequently measured by environmentalist groups in terms of how strongly he opposes the construction of those facilities. The depth of the growing antinuclear sentiment was demonstrated in the 1976 primary election in California—where national trends are often set—when an antinuclear initiative appeared on the primary ballot. Proposition 15, which would have effectively functioned as a shut-down measure, was soundly defeated. But the fact that it made it onto the ballot at all was highly significant. Not too many years ago, Californians, who constructed their first plant in 1957 under President Eisenhower's Atoms for Peace program, routinely spoke of nuclear power as the energy wave of the future. Today, however, that attitude is undergoing a profound change, and nuclear opponents intend to continue to introduce ballot initiatives in most of the western states. Whether these initiatives will eventually attract majority support is doubtful. But the questions that have been raised—especially those questions concerning disposal of wastes and accidents—are valid ones and should concern thoughtful people.

And there is still another problem here that very much concerns the government, although it is extremely reluctant to discuss it. That problem is sabotage. In 1976, as primary election day approached, the Nuclear Regulatory Commission quietly called alerts at each of California's nuclear plants. No one at the NRC would say why officially, but one NRC spokesman told these writers off the record that a well-known underground group—probably the Weather Underground—intended to attempt to blow up a plant to dramatize the issue. At least in part because of beefed-up security, the NRC believes, the attempt never came off. But the threat is far from an idle one. As a result of the civil war of the sixties, a terrorist underground has become what appears to be a permanent feature of the seventies. This underground may disappear in a decade or so as the survivors of the old New Left such as Bernadine Dohrn and Mark Rudd sidle into middle age. But for the time being, its existence is a fact of contemporary American life.

But even without the problem of sabotage, no doubt a minor one, nuclear energy development is in trouble, and the resulting slowdown means that when and if the government finally convinces opponents that the problems that alarm them can be dealt with, a crash program of exploration for uranium will be necessary to make up for lost time. The process of turning uranium into power is a lengthy and complicated one. Unlike coal, uranium can't be shoveled out of the ground and into the furnace.

First the uranium ore has to be milled and refined to produce various concentrates. These concentrates are then converted to uranium hexafluoride. Next comes a process called isotopic enrichment which turns the hexafluoride into reactor-grade uranium fuel, which in turn is converted to uraniumn dioxide. That dioxide is then assembled into fuel elements which are loaded into reactors and the resulting heat is used to generate electricity. After the electricity is generated, the spent fuel is reprocessed to recover remaining fissionable uranium and plutonium from radioactive wastes. And finally comes the increasingly difficult and costly process of disposing of the radioactive waste material, which may stay hot for millions of years—not exactly what most Americans would like to have buried in their backyards.

The whole process requires a lengthy lead time. It takes up to nine years to move from exploration to production, and the average life of a uranium mine is only ten years. And then there is the problem with the enrichment stage of the process, which requires a separate facility. There are only three such facilities in the United States, each owned by the Energy Research and Development Administration and operated by private industry under contract. According to FEA estimates, this enrichment capacity must be expanded dramatically by the early or mid 1980s if we intend to carry out even a minimal program of nuclear development. But it takes $3 billion and at least eight years to design, construct, test, license, and put a new plant into operation. Thus, if such plants are to be there when we need them, construction would have to begin immediately. The government hopes to see a three-fold increase in the use of nuclear energy by 1985, and a five-fold increase by 2000. If this is to be realized, industry estimates that a capital outlay of some $30 billion will be required.

In the face of these massive technical, political, and financial problems, then, the business of generating energy through nuclear reactors seems extremely difficult and perhaps not quite capable of realization, and it is little wonder that many laymen are increasingly inclined to look for other ways to do the whole thing. And as doubts spread, the critics of the government's approach to nuclear development are ever more telling arguments against that approach. The federal government, they maintain, having blindly invested in nuclear power as the mid-term solution to our energy needs, now refuses to reexamine its policy, despite rising costs, technical difficulties, and real threats to the population.

And as anyone who has studied government in action realizes, such a charge must invariably hit the mark, if the program under discussion is indeed flawed. Whenever the federal government embarks on any large-scale course of action, be it energy development, bussing, or the assuring of occupational safety standards it is seldom able simply to stop and back off. Government is inflexible. It is managed by men who feel they cannot afford to make mistakes and its response to any problem tends to be more of the same of whatever caused the problem in the first place. And, of course, there is always a certain momentum involved in the inception of any new technology such as that involved in nuclear development which is difficult to slow down, even if the value of the results becomes questionable.

The potential problems inherent in nuclear generators are hair-raising, most recently dramatized in a gripping but less than reliable book called *The Day We Almost Lost Detroit*. But although the hazards are great and are increasingly well publicized, there are nevertheless distinct advantages to nuclear development, and many experts feel that barring a miracle, such as the immediate development of a cheap, efficient solar cell or the adoption of a stringent new life style by millions of Americans, then nuclear energy is absolutely necessary.

According to nuclear advocate Rep. Mike McCormack (D-Wash), the energy equivalent of forty-eight million barrels of oil a day is the minimal amount that will be required by 1985 to keep the country running. For each million-barrel equivalent less than that, he estimates, some nine hundred thousand people will lose their jobs. And even with an aggressive conservation program, insists McCormack, the nuclear portion of the 1985 energy consumption figure will translate into six million jobs.

"There is," says McCormack, "no substitute for nuclear energy." And federal energy officials apparently agree. But they have as yet mounted no effective informational campaign to convince the rest of us and have also left too many questions unanswered. One of the most important of these, and a subject of intense current controversy, is the question of the breeder reactor. A nuclear breeder, which can eliminate the expensive and energy wasting "enrichment" process, "breeds" fuel from what would otherwise be waste products in uranium processing. In fact, it creates more fuel than it consumes. Without the reactor, it is estimated that our 3.6 million tons of proved uranium reserves, provided we can get them out of the earth in time, can probably get us through the next decade. But if we can develop a workable breeder reactor, then, according to the Energy Research and Development Administration, those 3.6 million tons of uranium on hand would take on an energy potential equivalent to 126 million tons—an amount sufficient to supply nuclear power plants well into the forseeable future.

The government is reluctant to proceed with the development of breeder reactors, however, and although several European nations have launched a joint project to develop a breeder for the commercial market, Congress refuses to allow private companies to get into the business of building breeders, stating that the technology which produces a peacetime breeder also can be used to produce nuclear weapons.

But while that is true enough, congressional logic here seems a bit less than convincing. France, England, and other European nations are moving full-speed ahead on commercial breeder development, which means that if they succeed, any nation with the funds can have its own breeder. And our own government showed no hesitation at all in supplying India with a breeder. Why Washington trusts India, which is using the technology for warlike purposes, and mistrusts General Electric, which has yet to threaten to go to war with anyone, remains a mystery. But apparently here, as in so many of those public policy decisions of this decade, emotional considerations seem more important than reason.

This is not to say that the critics of nuclear development fail to marshall convincing arguments to buttress their positions. They do argue well and convincingly, especially in the areas of safety and waste disposal. But the breeder controversy is another matter altogether, a 1970s extension of the old ban-the-bomb brouhaha of the fifties. The sentiment behind the idea was no doubt admirable, but because we were required to disarm unilaterally in order to put it into effect, few found it worth the risk. And the attitude toward breeder reactors seems similarly impractical and unrealistic. Preventing private industry from developing them will do nothing to prevent nations with warlike intentions from acquiring them, any more than nationalizing our armaments industry would prevent anyone who wanted them from acquiring tanks or guns. If there is a chance that breeder development, carried out under proper conditions, could solve our energy problems and perhaps make us self-sufficient, then many believe we should be launching the same sort of combined federal and private developmental program that sent our astronauts to the moon.

The problem is, however, that many of the most articulate critics of nuclear development are really critics of development *per se.* If they genuinely fear the potential problems growing out of an all-out nuclear program, there is no reason, for instance, why they should not urge the government to concentrate on coal. But in fact, they find coal mines offensive for aesthetic and environmental reasons, and fight against them just as fiercely as they fight the breeders.

Their objective, they frequently maintain, is to keep energy consumption at current levels, something which will simply be impossible to do if we expect our children to enjoy such conveniences as central heating and modern transportation. The current decline in the birth rate will not begin to affect energy consumption for another fifteen or twenty years and until then, there remains a large crop of teenagers and children waiting to inherit their share of our energy resources. But if fifteen or twenty years from now energy is still being consumed at current levels, then those grown up children and teenagers, as well as the rest of us, will have to cut back drastically on our share, which means not just cutting back on personal consumption of electricity and gasoline, but cutting back on jobs and material goods as well, since jobs and the creation of material goods require the expenditure of energy. And that is why economists insist that standing still is actually going backwards.

Not all critics of nuclear and coal development are backwards looking, however. Some recognize the problem but look far into the future for the solution, which usually takes the form of one of the more exotic forms of energy, frequently either solar or geothermal. But the problem, say energy experts, is that while these are desirable alternatives and should be developed, they won't alleviate the mid-range problem. And if we don't make it through the next few decades with sufficient energy resources, then what happens in the long range will be academic.

Of the most frequently mentioned "exotic" fuels, geothermal energy is closest to being practical. Geothermal energy is the earth's natural heat, generally considered to be the result of radioactive decay under pressure, deep beneath the earth's crust. In some regions, this heat, instead of seeping up to the surface, is trapped and concentrated; the result is a geothermal reservoir from which heat can be extracted to produce electricity.

There are four types of these reservoirs, classified by the sort of substance in which the heat is trapped. In some cases the heat is trapped in steam, in others in superheated fluids called "brines." Some consist of water and dissolved methane gas, and in some the heat is trapped in rocks. All have one thing in common, however: in each case harnessing the energy from them is extremely difficult, and the technologies for doing so have yet to be fully developed.

212

The dry-stream type of reservoir is the easiest to tap, but it is also the rarest formation. Only three have thus far been discovered in the United States and two are in parks and consequently unexploitable. The third, the Geysers site in California, has been developed and is currently generating 500 megawatts (MG) of power. But Geysers is the only geothermal project currently in operation.

Of the other three formations, industry is currently focusing attention on hot-water systems, primarily those which flash to the surface as steam. The problems here are formidable, however. The brines in the hot-water systems are often highly corrosive, for instance, and tend to clog up machinery. If they are disposed of on the surface, they cause contamination problems and if they are pumped back beneath the surface they can possibly cause seismic disturbances.

And finally, there's the whole question of what would be considered in this country—although not in Europe, where this type of reservoir is now in use —unacceptable pollution problems. The process of harnessing this hot-water energy releases toxic and foul-smelling hydrogen sulfide, for instance, something which no one has yet devised a method to control. Given our current sensitivity to anything which affects air quality, it's doubtful that our various environmental regulatory agencies would tolerate the development of anything that results in great clouds of foul gasses being belched into the atmosphere.

Perhaps the most promising of the forms are the hot dry rock reservoirs. The technology for developing these reservoirs is still highly experimental; the

213

major problem is to find an efficient and effective way to shatter the rocks which hold the heat. Nevertheless, energy experts believe the technological development will be worth the effort. One dry rock field in Montana, for instance, contains temperatures so high that its potential energy value is estimated to be equivalent to all the oil under Alaska's North Slope.

Eventually, as in Iceland, heat from geothermal fields might be pumped directly into homes. But at present, the primary market is the utilities, which, because of the expenses involved in building new power plants, have been extremely conservative in geothermal development. Another holdup in such development is caused by what the energy industry views as cumbersome and overlapping regulations. In order to drill, for instance, it's necessary to obtain local, state, and federal permits, the requirements for which are often conflicting. There is also the delay which is the result of the inevitable and increasingly frequent environmental law suits, a problem compounded by the haziness of the laws as they touch on the geothermal area. Are these resources mineral, for instance, and therefore subject to mining laws? Or are they water, governed by water allocation regulations? Or will it finally be decided that they fall into an entirely new category?

These are just a few of the unknowns which will have to be cleared up before investors leap enthusiastically into the geothermal market, which requires large sums for lease acquisitions and plant costs. Based on its experience in the relatively inexpensive Geysers field, for instance, Union Oil has projected an estimated initial investment for a 100 MW plant of $32.8 million, and that figure may be low, since many facilities will require at least a 200 MW field to justify the investment. And then there is the lead time, which is estimated by energy experts to run between five and fifteen years. All in all, the risks in the development of geothermal energy still significantly outweigh the benefits, and investment has not been heavy.

Nevertheless, geothermal energy will be very much a part of our nation's future. How much a part and when is difficult to say and predictions have varied widely. Former Interior Secretary Walter Hickel asserted in 1972 that by 1985, geothermal sources would supply some 132,000 MW of energy. At about the same time, however, the Bureau of Mines was estimating only 4,000 MW. But even if Hickel's sanguine estimate were to come true, it would still be dismally inadequate for our needs. The Federal Energy Administration, for instance, says that the nonfossil fuel needs of California alone by 1985 will exceed the Hickel figure.

Geothermal energy holds great promise, and there are great long-range schemes for using it being developed, among them a science-fiction-like plan for supplying most of the eastern United States, as well as portions of Europe and Africa, with energy from Iceland's geothermal sources, transmitted by a satellite system which even the scientifically oriented have problems comprehending. But well into the future, one suspects that most of the effective use of geothermal energy in the United States will be primarily on the local level and limited to the fourteen western states, where all the nation's geothermal sources have thus far been discovered. In Portland,

Oregon, for instance, the Northwest Natural Gas Company hopes to tap reservoirs of hot water under the west slope of Mount Hood and transport it into the city through insulated pipes, eventually heating both industries and homes. If successful, Northwest Natural Gas estimates that geothermal sources will provide one-fifth of Portland's total energy needs.

That would be a highly significant step forward for Portland. But precisely because most geothermal sources lie beneath often remote lands in the Far West, it will be technologically difficult and extremely expensive to get the energy to the midwestern and eastern industrial centers where it is most needed. It is one thing to run an insulated pipe from Mt. Hood to Portland, but quite another to extend a number of such pipes to New York. Eventually, of course, as both geothermal and then solar energy are developed, American industry, if it is to survive, may find it necessary to relocate massively in the Far West. Should solar energy ever become technologically feasible, the Sun Belt could become the economic center of the nation. But in terms of the needs of our near future, none of the most discussed alternate forms, be they geothermal or nuclear, will be enough, even given the increasingly unlikely prospect of a crash program. Geothermal and nuclear power will run electric generators, but we are also going to need synthetics to replace the petroleum products we use in our homes, our cars, and our industries. And even should the wildest dreams about successful alternate energy development and the growth of a national conservation ethic come true, the Energy Research and Development Administration estimates that the demand for natural gas and crude oil will outstrip our natural domestic supplies by an increasingly widening margin. We must, therefore, either continue to import from potentially hostile sources, and by so doing ransom our means of national defense, or we must develop synthetic fuels.

According to ERDA figures, in order to keep oil imports at 1975 levels during the next decade, we would require approximately five million barrels per day in synthetic fuels. And if we are to begin to phase out our foreign dependency in the decade ahead, says the ERDA—and again, this presupposes that all of us will be doing our best to conserve energy—we would need to be producing eleven million barrels in synthetic fuel. Obviously, then, programs for developing this synthetic fuel should be well underway. But the fact is, apart from a few experimental programs, we are not producing a drop.

That is not because the potential does not exist. It does, and in abundance. There is, for instance, our virtually unlimited shale oil potential. There is more shale out there than most realize. But again, there are tremendous problems involved in developing it. Oil shale, which has been formed underground by pressure in the same way crude oil was formed, is primarily, like geothermal formations, a western phenomenon. The only significant deposits thus far discovered, in fact, are found in a twenty-five thousand-square-mile area covering parts of Colorado, Utah, and Wyoming. But within this limited area, according to informed estimates, there are some 1,800 *billion* barrels of crude oil.

Unfortunately, however, the process of extracting that oil from the shale, which has developed in arid regions, requires vast amounts of water. It has been estimated, for instance, that an above-ground shale oil restoring facility producing three and a half million barrels of oil per day would use *all* of the water in the Colorado River Basin.

Another problem arises with techniques for removing the organic substance called kerogen from the marlstone rock which imprisons it. When the kerogen is removed it can be refined exactly like crude oil, but removing it requires a heating process which has yet to be perfected and, although more than two hundred patents have been granted for such a process, none has yet been judged to be economically feasible or environmentally acceptable. Many experts are pinning their long-range hopes for shale oil on *in situ,* or, in the case of shale, underground recovery techniques, which could save handling, waste disposal, water, and manpower requirements. But an *in situ* recovery process is still at the drawing board stage, and it might be years before such a process could be applied to commercial production.

As in the case with all synthetic fuels, recovery of shale oil is technically possible, but the prohibitive price of that recovery makes full-scale production infeasible. In early 1976, for instance, it was estimated that an above-ground shale oil recovery plant producing fifty thousand barrels a day would cost anywhere from $800 million to $1 billion and would therefore have to charge a price per barrel well above both the going domestic and foreign crude oil rates. Thus the development of shale oil, like other synthetics, is not at present considered economically feasible and will not be until there is a sharp increase in world oil prices or a technological breakthrough which could significantly lower the cost of production.

Also increasingly discussed as means of filling the energy gap are synthetic petroleum products made from coal through two processes, coal gasification and coal liquefaction. In the gasification process, the carbon and hydrogen in coal are separated from the bulk and form a gas, the trick being to create a gas with a high methane content. Natural gas contains enough methane to produce a heating value of about 1000 BTU per cubic foot, but it is not technologically possible at the moment to produce coal-derived gas with similar heating properties. At present coal gas with a low BTU heating value is being produced to provide raw materials for chemical plants and is used to a limited extent in foreign countries but remains too in efficient and too costly to pipe for domestic production. Experts predict, however, that there may be breakthroughs soon in the production of high BTU coal gas. And if natural gas prices were to be deregulated so that the price of synthetic gas could become competitive, then coal gasification would become an important energy industry.

There is less optimism about the future of liquefaction, however, a process which turns out an oil product that, like oil shale, resembles crude and can be similarly refined. The only known process for producing coal oil is considered too inefficient to approach commercial feasibility and energy experts rate it behind both coal gasification and shale oil recovery processes. In one industry survey, for instance, not a single company believed that coal liquefaction, even if the processes were to be dramatically improved, could provide for one-twentieth of U.S. oil needs through the next decade. And several companies predicted that liquefaction would not be commercially feasible for two decades.

Another potential source of synthetic fuel is tar sand, a mixture of crude oil, coke, sand, and sulfur which can be broken down into its separate substances. When placed in hot water, the sand settles to the bottom, the coke and sulfur are removed by another process, and for every 300 tons of sulfur and 2,300 tons of coke separated out, there remain 50,000 barrels of tar to be refined into petroleum products.

There are three major tar sands deposits in the world—the Orinoco deposit in South America; a deposit at the juncture of Missouri, Kansas, and Oklahoma; and a huge deposit in the Athabascan field of north central Alberta. The Athabascan fields alone are believed to contain 700 billion barrels of oil, representing more energy than the world's total known oil reserves. The tar sand field of the United States is more modest, with an estimated 160 billion barrels, but that in itself is an impressive deposit, and one of potentially great significance.

As is the case with each of the synthetic fuel sources mentioned above, however, extracting tar sand presents considerable difficulties. In the winter, when they are solid, surface deposits can be scooped out, but in the summer the sand will not support the weight of the machinery, and working with it is thus extremely difficult. No one has yet come up with a method for mining deposits under the surface, and in the Athabascan fields, at any rate, only about 12 percent of the available oil can be extracted through strip mining. And finally, there is the prob-

220

lem of waste disposal. Whoever processes the tar sands must be equipped to handle two tons of sand and one ton of overburden for every ton of oil yielded, a waste ratio greater than that for shale oil. Tar sand development is further along than shale oil but is still not economically feasible at the present market price.

There is, however, one source of potential energy which presents no problems of waste disposal. Unlike several of the sources discussed above, it is clean, universally available, and inexhaustible, and one of the few potential sources acceptable to politicians and environmentalists of every stripe. This source is solar energy, the potential of which has only begun to be imagined. As one writer points out, the amount of sunlight which falls on Lake Erie on an average day is greater than the total of all the energy consumed in the United States during that same day.

As yet, however, our methods and plans for harnessing and using this energy source are at best primitive and imperfect. While solar energy could well be the primary energy source well into the next century, it can do little or nothing to meet our midterm energy needs. There is no way, for instance, that it could propel the motor vehicles we now depend upon or act as a substitute for many other of our petroleum products. This is not to say therefore it is not to be taken seriously. No doubt we will one day find better methods of transportation and will also develop an industrial capability which has nothing to do with oil or synthetic products. If we don't, in fact, we will not survive. But that is the long view, and while the day will probably come when solar energy is the most common and efficient

221

source, it cannot be so for as long as our society and its day-to-day operations remain as currently constituted. We cannot, in other words, adapt solar energy to our most pressing needs as they exist today. Eventually, we might very well restructure our society and our industry and technology to adapt to solar energy. However, although such change might very well prove both desirable and inevitable, it will take the better part of a century to bring it about.

In the meantime, there are some relatively practical uses for solar energy, although they are still somewhat inefficient and uneconomic. There is, for instance, the use of solar energy to heat homes and buildings, a simple operation that is still very uncommon but in which interest is growing. Usually the process involves collector panels placed on rooftops which heat waters in pipes. The hot water is then circulated through the building. It's a simple system, and if the sun shone day and night, and if many of us didn't dwell in dank and murky places, no doubt we'd all be heating our homes with solar energy. But since there is seldom twenty-four hours of sunshine below the Arctic Circle in summer, and since many of us live in dreary climes buried beneath close-growing trees, we have to find ways to store the hot water and preserve the heat during those periods when the sun fails to work for us. One of these ways, unfortunately, requires the installation of a total system that can cost two to four times as much as installing a conventional system in most parts of the country. And then it is usually considered prudent to go ahead and install a conventional system anyhow as a backup.

The difference in cost here can run into the thousands of dollars for a modest house. An aesthetically satisfying system, no doubt, and one suspects that there will be a national solar boom among the back-to-nature, vacation-home owners. But it is much less likely to catch on among those Americans of more modest means. It takes money to get back to nature.

Whatever the costs, however, major problems such as storage to assure regular supplies of energy have to be worked out. Solar cells may well emerge as the most common means for gathering solar energy. If so, they must be made much more efficient than they are now. If mirrors or reflectors become the chief conductors, then there will be problems of adjusting them to catch the sunlight as the day progresses. And there are all sorts of nearly unimaginable environmental problems which could arise from all this intense concentrated reflections of the sun's rays, problems which might, in fact, dwarf the problems caused today by more conventional fuels.

In the distant future, then, as our way of life gradually evolves and our technology begins to realize its potential, there will be sufficient new sources of energy to sustain us for as long as our will to survive prevails. In addition to solar energy, there will be wind energy, energy from the ocean, and, if our space programs don't completely atrophy, there will no doubt be undreamed of sources of energy from outer space, harnessed and transmitted in ways for which we have at present neither words nor concepts to describe.

The years of great trouble, however, will fall between the last several years of this decade and the beginning of the next century, a period when, if we are to survive intact, we must make the wrenching transition from petroleum products and the society they have in many ways structured, to the new sources and technologies waiting to be born. This is a profoundly important transition period, for it will determine whether we enter the new era still strong as a nation or whether, unable to bridge the gap from one era to another, we collapse, our economy no longer able to sustain national life and reasonable growth, and therefore unable to provide the base we need to effect those necessary changes, societal and industrial, essential to survival.

George Ball, former undersecretary of state and adviser to presidents, put it this way in 1973: "I agree that there is light at the end of the tunnel. I agree also that there is no long-term energy shortage in the United States, because we are sitting on vast amounts of potential energy. The question is not whether there is light at the end of the tunnel, but what happens in the middle of the tunnel. . . . I think the problem is from now until, say, the middle or latter 1980s. This is the period when these political pressures and developments could take place in a way that could be extremely disturbing and disruptive."

Mr. Ball's metaphor is an apt one. There is always, by definition, light at the end of tunnels, and it is not the end that one worries about. The most dangerous part of a tunnel is always the middle. And since Mr. Ball testified four years ago, the roof of that tunnel has begun to sag. The world situation has changed little, but the optimistic estimates of when alternate energy sources will be widely available, bruited about so carelessly by opportunistic politicians, have been pushed back significantly.

Today, almost no one predicts that we will make meaningful progress toward lessening our dependence on petroleum products before 2000.

Congress has at nearly every turn bowed to the will of the environmentalists, small in number and nonrepresentative in view, but well organized and highly vocal, their utterances on any subject under the moon sure to attract major media attention. Thus, the needless and wasteful provisions of the Clean Air Act which make the mining of vast amounts of middle-sulfur coal economically unfeasible remain in effect, as do numerous other economically wasteful environmental provisions.

And perhaps most important of all, Congress is now debating and politicians are seriously considering a bill which would prohibit the major oil companies from investing their know-how and their capital in the development of alternate energy resources. Should such a bill actually become law, it will be very difficult indeed to continue to shore up the roof of Mr. Ball's collapsing tunnel.

# Chapter Ten

In the past, we have relied totally on our national knowhow and technology to carry us from era to era and we have never been disappointed. For perhaps the first time in our history, however, faced with the real energy crisis of massive proportions which will soon be upon us, there are signs that the will of our energy industry is being sapped. The technological progress that is essential for developing whole new energy sources is lacking and reluctance to meet the capital requirements necessary to fund production to form those sources is growing.

In the end, however, the blame must rest not as much with industry as with Washington. The government and the politicians who run it have persisted in looking only to short-term, expedient goals, rather than to the future.

Congress has refused to vote for increased federal financing for the development of synthetic fuels, fearful that the Naderites and other consumerists would accuse them of subsidizing big business. Yet it is on this sort of project that industry and government have always worked best together, the government supporting research and industry providing the know-how, the equipment, the personnel, and the capital to turn the results of that research into reality. That is what happened, for instance, in the space program.

Similarly, Congress has refused to vote for a natural gas price deregulation, a move that nearly every expert with a knowledge of energy problems favors, and a move that would vastly increase our supply of natural gas, the cleanest and most efficient of our current fuels. As a result, during the past winter, we suffered from shortages that would never have occurred had natural gas been sold at a fair market value.

What those shortages conclusively demonstrated is that prices held at an artificially low level render uneconomical the recovery of more costly replacements, which means that supplies inevitably dwindle. As was the case after the oil embargo of 1973-74, politicians are busy attempting to pin the blame for the shortages on profit-hungry private companies. In 1974 there were rumors sweeping through Washington of tankers lying just off the coast, waiting for price hikes before unloading. And during the past winter, there was a similar spate of rumors about companies withholding gas for the same reasons. No doubt there are companies that did precisely this, hoping to bring on deregulation. But such instances were mere symptoms of the larger economic malaise brought on by governmental policies which hamstring the energy industry.

This is especially true of natural gas. In many ways, gas is the most valuable of our energy products. It burns efficiently. It is cleaner and less polluting than other fuels, and when geography allows, it is easier and less expensive to recover. There is one major drawback, however. Without a pipeline to deliver it, it is no longer inexpensive. It can be shipped by truck or tanker, but this requires that the gas be liquified, a process that increases the price of gas many times over.

Thus, if gas is to remain an economical fuel, it must come from domestic sources. Unlike oil, it cannot be imported, and thus shortages cannot be disguised by importing foreign replacements. We are now importing nearly half of the oil we use, but the American consumer, although he does increasingly resent higher heating bills and gasoline prices, really doesn't feel any immediate pinch of intolerable proportions. Gas, however, is another matter, and a natural gas shortage is felt immediately and directly, as we all dramatically discovered last winter. Factories and schools closed down and hundreds of thousands of Americans, who had come to take such things as central heating as part of the natural order of things, suddenly found themselves shivering in their homes. It all happened just a few months ago. And unless the weather is extremely mild, it will happen again next winter.

It is too late to avert such shortages through next year. But future shortages can be averted if the government finally agrees to deregulate and allows gas prices to find their natural levels. At this writing, the Carter administration has not yet unveiled its comprehensive energy program, but the word is that a partial short-term program of deregulation will be proposed. If so, it will not solve our natural gas problems. As matters now stand, companies can be sure of a profit only if they do not go out to search for new supplies. Exploration and production are costly and risky long-range operations, and companies will engage in them only if they can be sure that their products will be sold at prices that make up for the costs involved in finding and developing them, something which is not possible under current regulations. Industry can hardly be blamed for refusing to embark on ventures certain to be unprofitable, although during the past winter, many politicians seemed to be demanding that they do precisely that.

The problem has been building for decades. In 1935, the Federal Trade Commission (FTC), at the request of Congress, submitted a study recommending that interstate gas pipelines be regulated. The case for pipeline regulation, as was earlier explained, is a solid one, primarily because an unregulated pipeline owned by a private company could discourage competition by refusing to move a competitor's product.

The FTC, however, had no intention of setting up the sort of system of regulation that exists today. In 1938, when Congress responded to the FTC's recommendation by passing the Natural Gas Act which empowered the Federal Power Commission to regulate the interstate flow of natural gas, the act stipulated that it "shall not apply . . . to the production or gathering of natural gas." And the FTC itself gave no indication of lusting after the controls over natural gas it exercises today. In case after case over the following sixteen years it asserted that it had no jurisdiction over natural gas producers but merely over their pipelines.

In 1954, however, the Supreme Court handed down a decision which many believe sowed the seeds that recently grew into our full-fledged natural gas crisis. By a 5 to 3 vote, the Supreme Court ruled that the FPC must take jurisdiction over natural gas rates. Thus, all producers and gatherers of natural gas became subject to federal price controls. In his minority opinion, Justice William O. Douglas expressed a concern which today sounds prophetic. The decision, he noted, would result in mass confusion as the FPC attempted to regulate thousands of producers, all with different cost bases and methods. "The effect is certain to be profound." he wrote. "Regulation of the business of producing and gathering natural gas involves considerations of which we know little, and with which we are not competent to deal."

As an immediate result of the decision, a flood of rate applications poured into the FPC from producers seeking approval of their going rates and permission to sell their gas. The FPC, awash in paper, attempted frantically to back out of the whole business. Testifying at a congressional hearing, its chairman said, "We are firmly convinced, from every aspect of public interest and national defense, that Congress should not single out natural gas as the only one among those fuels over which an artificial ceiling should be placed." He then went on to plead with Congress to enact legislation which would exempt from controls those producers who sell gas wholesale to pipeline companies, but who do not themselves engage in interstate transportation.

Congress agreed that gas regulations were unfair, unworkable, and unnecessary, and in 1956 attempted to undo the damage done by the Supreme Court by passing the Harris-Fulbright bill, freeing producers from regulations. At first, President Eisenhower seemed favorably disposed toward the legislation. "I must make quite clear that legislation conforming to the basic objectives of this bill is needed." he said. "It is needed because the type of regulation of producers of natural gas which is required under the present law will discourage individual initiative and incentive to explore for and develop new reserves of gas."

But then, having put the presidential finger on the heart of the problem, Eisenhower, having gotten wind of questionable monetary dealings between a senator and gas industry representatives, vetoed the bill as a matter of principle, and subsequent attempts to enact the legislation never regained momentum.

What followed was twenty years of chaos in the natural gas industry. The FPC kept trying, but was totally incapable of fixing a fair market price for the nation's 2,300 gas producers. Regulatory delays dragged on for years, and resulted in hundreds of law suits. Five years after the Supreme Court decision, the FPC estimated that even if its staff were tripled, it could only hope to catch up with its producer rate cases sometime after the year 2043.

The FPC, unable to make a case by case method of regulation work, finally attempted a geographic approach by mapping out twenty-three areas and then devising a pricing formula for each. At the end of five years, it managed to come up with a pricing recipe for the first of its areas, the Permian Basin of West Texas and Southeastern New Mexico. The same tedious process was then repeated for each of the twenty-two areas, a process which spawned a spate

231

of lawsuits and great uncertainty in the industry. And as a result investment, exploration, and production fell off dramatically. Supreme Court Justice Tom Clark, along with Justice Douglas, a dissenter in the original rating decision, predicted that there would be "serious legal questions lurking in the application of 'area' policy . . . causing additional delay, delay, and delay, until the inevitable day when there is no more natural gas to regulate."

As Justice Clark predicted, the confusion was massive, and one inevitable result was that investors grew increasingly cool toward the idea of throwing their money into holes from which they could not count on salvaging profits. Consequently, the search for new gas supplies fell off sharply, and in the following five years, 1965 to 1970, exploratory drilling dropped by more than 50 percent, with proved reserves in the lower forty-eight states dipping from twenty-three times the annual production of gas to only ten times annual production.

Then, in 1967, for the first time we began to consume more gas than we produced, and since then our reserves have fallen dramatically. According to industry figures, between 1965 and 1974 we consumed 202 trillion cubic feet of natural gas, while adding new supplies of only 127 trillion cubic feet. At this rate, as *Barron's* puts it, we now sit on "considerably less than a fifteen-year supply."

Compounding the problem is the increase in natural gas use which has paralleled the decrease in exploration. Had our energy situation remained stable during the past few years, natural gas use would still have increased, but at nowhere near the going rate of consumption. But the energy situation has

232

not remained stable. One factor has been the rise of the environmental movement and the federal clean air standards it has given birth to. Factories and utilities, rather than investing in the expensive equipment required for the legal burning of coal, switched instead to gas. And of course the price of gas, held at an artificially low level by federal controls, has added significantly to the demand. Because gas costs only about half as much as oil, and because it is a more desirable fuel, approximately 40 percent of our industries and 50 percent of our homeowners now depend on it.

Thus, the crisis had been brewing, and the natural gas industry had been warning Congress and the country about it for years. For the past two winters it had been predicting serious shortages. But those winters were unusually mild, and the cutbacks they predicted were confined primarily to industries with the capacity to switch to other fuels. Thus, with no immediate and direct effects visible to most of us, we tended to join those congressmen who accused the industry of attempting to frighten them into deregulation. The industry, they maintained, was crying wolf, an attitude that continues to prevail among many Americans. A Gallup poll, for instance, taken in February during the height of the gas crisis, showed that nearly half the people surveyed east of the Rockies believed there was no real crisis at all.

Finally, however, experts within the government have come to disagree. James Schlesinger, for instance, Carter's energy adviser, was asked by a reporter last winter whether the natural gas crisis was real or manufactured.

"With this winter weather," he answered, "we

were bound to be in trouble. . . . The shortage is real and the United States will run out of oil and gas in the next thirty or forty years. The single most important fact is that we will run out of oil and gas early in the twenty-first century and we will have severe supply problems in the 1980s on a worldwide basis and we must begin now to plan for that."

At this writing, no one outside the administration knows the particulars of Carter's energy package. But energy experts across the country almost universally agree that it should at the very least call for a step-by-step program of decontrol of the natural gas industry. As early as 1974, for instance, Stephen Breyer, a Harvard law professor, and Paul Macavoy, an MIT economist, told Congress that "the arguments against the present system of gas field market regulation are compelling. Price control is not needed to check monopoly power, and efforts to control rents require impossible calculations of production costs and lead to arbitrary allocation of cheap gas supplies. In practice regulation has led to a virtually inevitable gas shortage. It has brought about a variety of economically wasteful results, and it has ended up hurting those whom it was designed to benefit. Thus, less, not more regulation is required."

Dr. William Johnson, a George Washington University economist, asserted in 1973 that "in no segment of the industry have our policies been so wrong or created such damage as in gas. . . . The conscious decision of past Federal Power Commissions to keep gas prices as low as possible, regardless of the consequences on future exploration, and, worse, to change retroactive prices already approved by the FPC, has discouraged investment in drilling.

234

. . . We must deregulate natural gas, not only to assure the higher prices necessary to produce more gas, but to enable the industry to operate free of uncertainties about changes in future FPC policies."

And Stanford professor of finance Ezra Solomon summed it up for the Senate in this way: "One of the arguments sometimes used in favor of low ceiling prices on gas is that this would tend to keep the price of competing fuels down. This would be true only if the low price of gas were due to large supplies of gas. But artificially mandated low gas prices produce exactly the opposite effect. It lowers gas supply and creates shortages. Unmet demands for gas are then transferred to other fuels, and the result of higher demand for those fuels is rising prices.

"This is what occurred beginning in 1970. Given the depleted level of reserves, domestic gas output virtually reached its limit and deliveries to some users had to be curtailed. . . . The root cause lies in a decade-long attempt to hold natural gas prices at artificially low levels. . . . Rationing existing supplies of natural gas does nothing to reduce the overall shortfall of supply—it simply shifts the problem and the burden to another sector, creating new problems there.

"Regulation hurt, and will continue to hurt new residential and commercial consumers—usually those in new and growing population centers—who were and are willing to pay more for gas but cannot obtain supplies; it hurt the producing industry directly and indirectly hurt those who participate in the overall exploration, development and producing process; it hurt the public at large through a fall in tax receipts below levels that otherwise have prevailed; finally, it hurt users of competing fuels by upward pressure which the gas shortage has exerted on the price of such alternatives.

"The case for more controls is a weak one. It also ignores some clear and important lessons. . . . A continuation of FPC price ceilings means that the shortage will get worse. . . . Rationing a commodity which is in short supply can do nothing to increase its total availability or to hold down the potential growth in demand. . . . The basic issue is what happens to those numerous users who will be forced to do without gas under a long-term system of price control and rationing: either they will suffer deprivation or they will be forced to turn to alternative forms of energy which cost more than they would have to pay for gas in a free market."

As Professor Solomon cogently points out, the economic argument for controls is a specious one. Yet it persists, its primary appeal no doubt lying in the mistaken notion that consumers would be stuck with intolerable gas bills. But this concern for the consumer's wallet, although no doubt a sincere one, proved last winter to be dramatically misplaced. Consumers—industrial consumers, state officials, and homeowners—would have been glad to pay significantly higher prices to keep factories running, schools open, and homes heated. But because price ceilings had steadily been slowing down production, there was no gas to be found and many Americans came to realize the governmental overprotection of the consumer had led inevitably to more privation than a free market could have caused.

Nor is there any solid evidence to substantiate the charges, widely bruited about by consumerists and

236

their friends in Congress, that decontrol would lead to extreme and unaffordable price increases. Such charges, in fact, have been heavily based on thoroughly discredited cost studies. One such study, entitled "Economic Impact of S. 2310 Pricing Provisions," estimates that decontrol of natural gas would cost consumers more than $20 billion. The study, widely quoted in Washington, has had a powerful impact on congressional attitudes toward deregulation. But it is a deeply flawed study, showing profound ignorance of the operation of the natural gas market and little understanding of even the simplest economic theory. Perhaps its most unforgivable error was to figure in as a consumer cost the cost of gas which, under deregulation and consequent increases in supply, would replace imported oil. According to the study, this additional use of gas would result in a cost to consumers of $7.5 billion. But what the authors of the study seem unable to understand is that the consumer who switches to gas would of course *not* be required to pay for the oil he was no longer using.

It is this kind of elementary mistake that no schoolboy should make that has persuaded many energy experts that the authors of the report are either slanting the case against deregulation or are so intent on pushing their thesis that they've misplaced their wits. At any rate, whatever the condition of the authors, the Council of Economic Advisers looked the study over after its release and concluded that even if most of the study's imprecise forecasts were taken into consideration, the increase would nevertheless be closer to $5 billion, rather than $20 billion.

And analysts for the natural gas industry itself insist that even that figure may be too high. In fact, they maintain, deregulation will have very little long-range effect on the cost of energy. For one thing, they say, even if all ceilings on gas were removed tomorrow, most of the gas available is "old gas"—that is, gas already contracted for which would remain at its original selling price. And the Federal Energy Administration has estimated that five years after a policy of deregulation went into effect, about 60 percent of the interstate gas supplies would still consist of gas previously contracted for.

Furthermore, say the industry analysts, because 80 percent of the homeowners' monthly bill presently goes to transportation and distribution, only about 20 percent of that bill would be affected by deregulation, even if the homeowner burns only new gas. And the rest of the bill, they maintain, that 80 percent that goes for transportation and distribution, would actually go down under decontrol. It costs a pipeline just as much to run at half capacity as at full. Therefore, as gas became more plentiful, transportation costs would be spread out and averaged in with the cost of the new gas, thus decreasing the total price the consumer must pay. Under continued controls, however, that portion of the bill could well continue to rise. From May 1974 to May 1975, for instance, the average wellhead price of natural gas paid to producers by interstate pipelines increased only 6 cents per thousand cubic feet. But because pipeline companies and distributors had less gas to work with, they were forced to charge their customers an additional 30 cents. And some pipeline companies now predict that if federal price controls continue, their portion of the homeowner's gas bill will double.

Finally, there are the indirect costs to the consumer. An industry manager endangered by potential cut-offs of gas supplies will face several difficult decisions. If he retains his gas burning facilities, he will have to be prepared in the event of a cut-off to turn to synthetic gas made from imported naptha, at a cost currently equal to about $30 for a barrel of oil, or he can use liquified natural gas at up to five times the current price. If, on the other hand, he converts to oil, the change will be costly, as will the product, and there remains the threat of cut-off. And if he switches to coal, he must contend with environmental laws, which require costly equipment and which invariably result in interminable delays as the red tape untangles. And all these costs, of course, are passed on to the consumer.

And then there is the cost to consumers of unemployment. At various times during the past winter, directly as a result of the gas crisis, some two million American workers were laid off. One suspects that the cost to the families of these workers was infinitely greater than a slightly higher gas bill would have been. Had there been adequate supplies of gas, those lay-offs would not have occurred. And had there been no controls, those supplies would have been more than adequate.

Many energy experts and economists believe that decontrol would not only prevent job loss but would also create new jobs. A study by the International Institute for Economic Research, for instance, entitled *Energy and Jobs: A Long Run Analysis*, concludes that immediate decontrol of gas and oil prices could increase the Gross National Product by nearly $1 billion by 1980 and create significant numbers of new jobs throughout the energy industry as fuel producers expanded production.

As the study points out, artificially low prices in effect put a cap on the development of alternate nonpetroleum energy sources. "The production of these alternative sources is artificially constrained because their major competing energy input (oil and gas) is given an advantage on the market through the control system." If oil and gas prices are allowed to seek their natural market level, in other words, other energy sources will be developed and perfected and thus will become less expensive and increasingly competitive with gas and oil. (A case in point: the use of solar panels to heat homes. As petroleum prices rise and as a growing number of people come to realize that our supply of petroleum products is finite, more and more homeowners are becoming interested in solar heat, and thus companies that produce solar heating equipment are motivated to develop increasingly economical and efficient products. But if a petroleum product such as gas is kept artificially inexpensive, consumers will shy away from more expensive alternate sources and those sources lack the opportunity to develop into cheap sources.)

"And finally," concludes the report, "as the price of energy rises, firms will tend to substitute toward more labor-intensive means of production. In addition, as energy-intensive commodities experience larger price increases relative to labor-intensive commodities, consumers are induced to substitute away from the former to the latter. Both GNP changes and substitution effects tend to drive up the demand for labor and hence increase total employment." If the cost of running machines becomes excessive, in other words, an employer will hire men to do the job instead. Thus, under decontrol, employment would increase and everyone—consumers, workers, and businessmen—would benefit.

But although the societal benefits of decontrol become increasingly clear, and although those who argue against it can marshall few convincing economic arguments, it has come to be treated in Washington as a political issue, and arguments over political issues tend to be emotional rather than logical. Just now, the consumerists and the environmentalists are riding high in Washington, and although there is compelling evidence that these movements have crested, a majority of Congressmen would still rather confront a crying woman than risk the wrath of the various "public interest" lobbies. Thus, up until last winter, many of our most articulate Congressmen continued to insist, in the face of overwhelming evidence to the contrary, that there was no natural gas shortage. The argument was the same one trotted out to use against the oil companies during the Arab embargo—all the warnings and the evidence amassed over decades were simply a ruse. What the producers wanted to do was frighten the government into enacting decontrol, and thus reap windfall profits. And the opponents of decontrol went well beyond rhetoric in attempting to make their point. In one case, for instance, they even went to court to suppress warnings which contradicted their own unproved assertions. In the autumn of 1975, the Federal Energy Administration predicted that the natural gas shortage would be felt by Americans during the coming winter. The *Wall Street Journal* describes what ensued.

"The FEA staff was hauled before Congress to be browbeaten by Representatives Dingell and Moss for crying wolf in support of administration efforts to decontrol prices of natural gas. The American Public Gas Association, which represents various local gas utilities, even took the agency to court, accusing it of violating federal statutes that prohibit lobbying by government employees. Judge Sirica, the famous Watergate Judge, split the difference by barring the agency from 'mass' distribution of its warning brochure, 'The Natural Gas Story.' In fact the FEA's warning was a year premature for the winter of 1975–76 was an unexpectedly mild one."

The next winter, however, was not, and those largely responsible for keeping the lid on prices and thus bringing on the gas crisis attempted with some quick political footwork to shift the blame from themselves to the industry. Gas producers, they maintained, were holding back supplies in the hope that prices would soar. It was, essentially, the same thoroughly discredited charge leveled against the oil companies during the embargo, the implication being that industry would allow Americans to freeze in their beds if there were windfall profits in sight.

Now there is, of course, a great deal wrong here. One wonders why the procontrol forces hold American business in such total contempt, almost as if capitalism is by definition an evil which must be subordinated to the dictates of government. And one wonders why so many Americans seem to accept the presumption, unsubstantiated by any solid evidence, that the politicians and bureaucrats who manage our government are more deserving of trust than the people who manage our free enterprise system. Is the profit motive inherently more distasteful or venal than the power motive which drives the men who run our government?

The problem here is a complex one, compounded in this case by the complexities of the energy industry and the forums available for explanations of that complexity. Politicians as a matter of course simplify, their public utterances pitched at what is frequently the simplest common denominator among their constituents. The successful politicians, like the acupuncturist, know precisely where the nerves are and how to hit them. Thus, Congressmen intent on escaping their share of blame for something like the natural gas shortage can simply point again and again to those proven reserves untapped by the gas industry as sufficient proof that gas is being withheld from the market. But the industry has neither the highly visible public forums enjoyed by its antagonists nor the simplistic examples which strike emotional chords. The producers invariably find themselves on the defensive, forced to respond to demagogic, shifting attacks, and as they attempt to explain themselves, their voices are seldom heard above the shouting.

The problem, essentially, is that the business of extracting natural gas from the ground and selling it is extremely complicated, its intricacies not easily explained to the American public. There is, for instance, the difference between inter- and intrastate sales. Gas produced and sold within a given state is not subject to federal price controls. Last winter in

Houston, for instance, gas was selling for up to $2.50 per thousand cubic feet, as compared with the FPC ceiling on interstate sales of $1.42, with an average interstate price of about 60 cents. And further complicating the picture is the federal decree that natural gas cannot be withheld at the well, but must be shipped, even in slack seasons. Those states, therefore, that had planned ahead and had built sufficient storage facilities for gas so that it would be available in peak winter months were far better off than those who had not, among them most of the eastern states, in which gas was sold during the summer for marginal use, with little concern for what winter might bring.

The result, predictably, was federal bailout, something that eastern metropolitan areas have come increasingly to expect as a matter of course. The Carter administration, responding in what was probably the only way open to it, given the need for immediate action, moved supplies around, shifting, as the *Wall Street Journal* put it, shortages from one part of the country to another.

As a stopgap measure it was relatively successful, but the practice of taking gas from those states who had it and giving it to those who did not understandably stirred a good deal of resentment. Louisiana Governor Edwin Edwards, for instance, is threatening to curtail the flow of gas from his state to the northeast. Edwards, angry that supplies of gas off the Atlantic seaboard have not been tapped, says that the South will soon be drained by the New England states and the federal government. Said an Edwards adviser: "The attitudes today are just like the Civil War. The North wants everything its own way. This time they won't get it."

The *Chicago Tribune,* speaking for much of the Midwest, took a similar but perhaps more convincingly argued position.

"There is nothing wrong," editorialized the *Tribune,* 'with gas from one area of the country going to another area if the latter is willing to pay for it and the former is willing to sell. But that decision should be based on the realities of the market, not some new bureaucratic scheme which likely would penalize sellers and reward buyers. . . .

"Our reluctance to see natural gas diverted away from the Midwest is not a matter of regional chauvinism. What we object to is this new version of the bailout theory, one that penalizes the planners and the frugal and benefits the short-sighted. If the easterners had not exerted so much political pressure to keep gas prices down, they would have more of it today.

"In short, we have no particular desire to see our eastern friends shiver, but neither do we see any reason to reduce ourselves to shirtsleeves simply because they didn't buy a sweater during the summer sales."

And even the editorial writers at the *Washington Post,* traditionally a very liberal group sympathetic to the objectives of those who favor ever-expanding controls, began to feel the chill last winter. Reviewing the recent history of attempts to deregulate gas, the *Post* editorialized: "The country is going to have to pay more for the stuff, unless it wants to institutionalize the winter gas shortage as an annual event."

Indeed. But as the *Post* goes on to point out, the process of pushing legislation through Congress to deregulate "the stuff" is very difficult indeed.

"Just a year ago," said the *Post*, "a Senate bill to deregulate gas prices came to the floor of the House where it encountered vast indignation at the unseemly haste with which it was being pushed forward. The bill was set aside for more mature consideration. Then the weather got warm and everybody forgot about gas—everyone, we ought to note, except the Federal Power Commission, which in July published a forecast of the winter's shortages. But it was hot in July and who takes fuel shortages seriously in midsummer? Then, in a strange and utterly unexpected turn of events, in November it started to get cold again. What could be more surprising than to see the FPC's forecasts actually becoming the reality?"

The appropriate analogy, suggests the *Post,* is the fable of the grasshopper and the ant. "When you think what Aesop extracted from those two mere insects in the way of moral instruction, you can only wonder what he might have done with the 535 members of Congress and the natural gas industry."

Had it wanted to belabor the analogy, the *Post* could have gone on to quote one of the most famous lines from that fable: "It is thrifty to prepare today for the wants of tomorrow." Or to push it to the outer limits, were Aesop here to instruct Congress in its dealings with the industry, he might repeat another well known line from *The Dog and the Shadow:* "Beware lest you lose the substance by grasping at the shadow." For the fact is that Congress has been baying at the shadow while ignoring the substance, and by so doing it has both misled the American people and intensified our energy problems. Last winter, for instance, instead of doing anything substantive to assure supplies of gas, Congress instead chose to bay at the companies for leaving gas in the ground. And any politician who wants to capitalize on this sort of accusation can quote numbers of cubic feet ad finitum and cite examples of untapped reserves to buttress his case. But this again is a case of barking at shadows. The substance is much more complex and requires a serious attempt to understand the way gas is produced and the effect of both geography and regulations on that production.

Natural gas is found in reservoirs in areas surrounded by harder rock which confines the gas geographically and prevents its escape, and any given well may sit on top of several others. One deposit, for instance, may lie at the 8,500 foot level, another below it at 10,000 feet, and a third beneath the first two at 15,000 feet. And each of these reservoirs, unless they are very large, requires separate pumping facilities.

Traditionally, when producers discover a number of reservoirs at various depths, they begin with the deepest and then move up to the shallowest, the most economical method of recovery. Should a producer decide to produce gas from more than one of these vertically stacked reservoirs at the same time, then he must install duplicate platforms and drill additional wells, and must also build a larger pipeline. The gas can be recovered more quickly this way, but at far greater expense than would be the case if the producer simply waited until one well was exhausted and then moved up to the next one with his original equipment.

To go through all this makes little economic sense when the size of most of these "behind-the-pipe" wells are taken into consideration. Over 70 percent of them in the Gulf of Mexico, for instance, contain less than five billion cubic feet (Bcf) of natural gas. An offshore platform costs between $10 and $20 million to install. After that platform is installed, it remains in place as a production base. And if the producer decides not to install a new platform but to comingle the new reserves in one stream of production, then the conversion of the platform is approximately as expensive as the installation of a new one. When additional wells are drilled from a platform that is already being used for production, then for safety reasons production must be halted and production equipment removed while the additional drilling is in progess. Then once the drilling is finished, the drilling equipment must be removed and the production equipment reinstalled. It is an expensive process and a time-consuming one, often taking three to four months, during which time no gas is being produced at all.

Thus, if that producer wants to avoid the charge that he is in fact withholding gas, he more often than not faces two unattractive options. He can install a new $10 million platform to recover the five Bcf that will result in gross revenues of $2.5 million. Or he can remove existing production equipment for a few months on a well that is producing perhaps 100 million cubic feet per day, thus insuring the loss of production of nine Bcf during the conversion period in order to tap a well which contains a total of less than five Bcf of reserves.

In its October 1975 report, the House Subcommittee on Oversight and Investigation examined such a situation in a Louisiana natural gas field.

"A number of the untapped reservoirs are 'behind the pipe'; that is, they are penetrated by wells that are currently producing from deeper reservoirs. . . . Certainly, the producer cannot be criticized for waiting several months to recomplete an existing well rather than to drill into a small reservoir. For example, [one such] reservoir, containing approximately 1.7 Bcf, penetrated by the Williams No. 1 well which is expected to deplete in a deeper reservoir in 1977. A $200,000 recompletion of Williams No. 1 in 1977 appears economically feasible; a $1.4 million investment in a new well does not. Nor does it seem in the public interest that $1.4 million be spent in tapping such a small gas deposit when that money can be used for exploration or development elsewhere."

Thus, there is indeed natural gas lying in the ground; it lies there because it cannot be economically extracted. But this does not, of course, deter those who confuse shadow with substance, and any governor in a gas-poor state or any congressman or consumer advocate can broadcast figures to the nation which prove that production of gas is being withheld in the hope of future profits. And they will be perfectly correct. Producers are indeed holding back on production, especially on expensive federally leased off-shore drilling operations, the contracts for which dictate that producers sell on the interstate market at low ceiling prices. And those producers are holding back in order to realize a profit. But what the critics don't mention, and what the producer seems rarely able to get across to the general public, is that if he did not do so he would lose vast amounts of money and perhaps eventually go bankrupt. And then, of course, there would be no gas production at all. To accuse a gas producer of being interested only in profits is a bit like accusing a drowning man of being interested only in his life.

Another accusation being increasingly leveled at producers is that when they are not shutting off production, they are slowing it down. The producers, say their critics, are not pumping gas fast enough from existing wells, and some members of Congress are demanding that the government require acceleration of production from those wells. But here again, these demands ignore the realities of the gas production business. And in fact, in some cases, compliance with congressional demands would require that gas producers actually break the law. In the contract between a producer and the pipeline that will move the producer's gas, the producer promises to produce a certain amount of gas within a certain amount of time. It is necessary to so regulate this production rate, for if gas is produced too rapidly, the reservoir can be seriously damaged, with large quantities of gas lost as water or sand rushes in to fill the vacuum created by the too-hasty removal of gas. Thus, the kind of fast production currently being called for is in fact illegal and could frequently result in a loss of fuel.

And then, just to complicate the matter even more, and in the process to provide more ammunition for the critics, there's the whole hazy business of the maximum production rate (MPR). Producers are required by law periodically to submit to state and federal authorities the MPR for each of their wells, and once those rates are fixed, producers are not allowed to exceed them. But at the time he submits his MPR, the producer often has no sure way of knowing how much his well will produce. He will, therefore, tend to submit the very highest rate that he feels his field can produce without damage. When he actually begins to get the gas out, however, he may discover that his reservoir will simply not produce as much as the ceiling set by his MPR. Or, as is often the case, he finds that when he first starts pumping he reaches his ceiling, but as pressure decreases, so does the amount of gas he can produce.

For the critics, however, it's all a paper problem. Their approach is to look at the MPR's submitted by gas companies, to compare these estimates with actual rates of production which are very often considerably lower, and to conclude that the companies are not producing gas as rapidly as they could. These purely paper comparisons by critics who lack the most rudimentary knowledge of production operations are of course sophistic and do nothing to encourage the production of natural gas. But they do make for good speeches and press releases read avidly and usually believed by those consumers who are forced to curtail or cut down on their gas consumption. We all nurse grievances, and it can be comforting to have our anger directed at what seems to be their cause.

Yet another complication arises because of production tie-ups due to bureaucratic red tape and, more recently, bureaucratic intrusion into producer-pipeline contracts. One recent case involves Mobil Oil and an offshore field, Grand Isle 95, off the coast of Louisiana in the Gulf of Mexico. Typically, the contract between the pipeline and the producer is first written up, a formidable chore in itself. Then, if the government owns the land on which the drilling is to be done, which is usually the case with off-shore oil, the Federal Power Commission must approve the contract, even at the best of times a time-consuming process. But in the case of Grand Isle 95, production was delayed for ten months because of a contract dispute. As a result, Mobil could not begin production until autumn and was unable to achieve maximum production through last winter.

The dispute centered around the length of the contract. Years ago, when gas was easily accessible and prices were reasonable, the normal contract time between a gas company and a pipeline was twenty years. Now, however, with uncertainty over prices and a buyers' market, companies usually insist on a shorter contract of five, ten, or fifteen years. The pipeline no longer needs twenty years' surety to finance construction of the proposed line, and the producer, as a businessman, is unwilling to commit himself to sell gas at the current artificially low base for the next twenty years.

In the case of Grand Isle 95, however, although Mobil and Trunkline Gas, an interstate pipeline, had already agreed to a ten-year contract, and although the FPC had accepted those terms in previous contracts, this time around it decided, for reasons unknown, to assert itself by insisting at the last

252

moment that it would not give production approval unless the contract was lengthened to twenty years. Mobil, quite naturally, protested the ruling. Not only would a twenty-year contract locking in the price of gas produced by Grand Isle 95 be a bad business venture, but worse, according o Mobil, the FPC's intrusion into contract terms of this sort was illegal. Were it allowed to do so without a fight, Mobil believed, it would set a dangerous precedent for contracts throughout the industry.

Eventually, Mobil reluctantly agreed to a compromise fifteen-year contract. But interestingly, in the meantime, the price of new gas had risen, and had the FPC not decided to initiate the dispute, Mobil would have been selling the gas that is now being sold for 93 cents per thousand cubic feet for 53 cents. Critics, of course, predictably charged that Mobil purposely fought it out in order to hold up production until prices rose. Mobil, however, calls the charge asinine. If it had intended to hold up production, its spokesmen assert, it certainly would not have gambled on the FPC issuing an unprecedented and previously unheard of contract ruling. In fact, says Mobil, it proceeded so rapidly in the development of the field that it was ready for production ahead of all the other tracts but one that it had acquired in the lease which gave it Grand Isle 95. Rather than slowing down production, according to Mobil, -it was, at the time of the FPC interference, working full speed to get it ready.

The fault, according to even semiobjective observers, lay with the FPC. One congressional critic of Mobil, for instance, while lecturing the company that "profit incentives should not be blinders to the public welfare," nevertheless concluded that "bureaucratic ineptitude [and] the inability of the FPC to make a timely determination that would result in increased natural gas production and delivery demonstrates a total insensitivity for the public health and welfare."

The Grand Isle 95 dispute is just one example of the way in which bureaucracy inevitably complicates and intensifies the problems it sets out to solve. The intention was to push the industry into speeding up production. The result was that production was held up. And that is how bureaucracy seems so often to work.

As we have attempted to point out, the charges against the gas industry are not baseless, as far as they go. But the problem is that the critics are careful not to proceed beyond a certain point. Producers do in fact delay the development of certain wells. But they do so for solid geographical, technological, and economic reasons. They do not attempt to shorten contract lengths. And they do attempt to divert their products to intrastate markets rather than feeding them all into the interstate or industrial market, where they make minimal profits, or no profits at all. Last December, for instance, Damson Oil sold a two thousand-acre gas field to the Libbey-Owens-Ford company. Its three most prolific wells had been capped since 1975. The reason: the gas in those wells could only be sold interstate, and at interstate rates Damson could not make a profit. Only by selling to a private industry could Damson resume natural gas production at a profit. And this is a route that other gas producers, victimized by the price system, have begun to follow.

Under present interstate pricing policies, the problem will intensify, and in the end, only Congress, in conjunction with a cooperative administration, can solve that problem through a coherent program of phased deregulation.

# Chapter Eleven

Deregulation of natural gas prices will undoubtedly stimulate production which was otherwise economically unfeasible but it will not erase the hard fact that natural gas is a finite resource. Oil, our other main source of energy, is even more limited, especially as a domestic product. If Congress were smart, then, it would pass a bill forbidding the oil industry to invest in anything *other* than alternate energy sources.

The myth that the oil giants will come sweeping into the alternate energy field, wiping out small companies as they pass, is just that—a myth. In some cases—coal for instance—there would continue to be small firms operating alongside large ones, for the same reason that there are now small oil drilling firms operating alongside large ones.

In other fields, however, such as the mining of uranium or the extraction of shale and tar oil, the whole thing will have to be done by a large company or a large group of companies or it won't be done at all. The cost, the risk, the lead time involved, all dictate that only very large firms with vast capital resources behind them will be able to come up with the billions of dollars required to proceed with such projects.

This doesn't necessarily mean that big oil would have to invade the field. But if it didn't, then something equally big would have to. That something could be the federal government, of course. But if the federal government were to come into the energy field on the scale that would be necessary, then we would have to find a new word or phrase to characterize the economic system under which we live—perhaps state socialism, or something like it, would do. And if that's what most of us want, then fine. But one suspects that no matter how enervated the national will, we're not yet quite ready for that.

More likely, were big oil banned from the field, then big everything else would come slowly and hesitantly in—General Electric, for instance, or Anaconda, or Union Carbide, or Westinghouse. And since the energy business is a vast one, then any company which moved in to fill the vacuum would soon expand to fill the space available to it. And there is no guarantee that the new energy companies would not be dominated by three or four rapidly expanding giants, rather than the eighteen or twenty currently involved in oil. Eventually those critics who are attempting to prevent big oil from expanding would find themselves faced with companies wielding the same sort of power—although after horizontal divestiture, that power would be concentrated in fewer hands, thus bringing on the very monopolistic situation which the original divestiture proponents feared.

One would like to meet the best arguments of those who advocate horizontal divestiture head on.

But the problem is that critics of oil company expansion are invariably vague when the talk turns to what harm oil involvement can do if it enters the alternate energy field. They tell us that if oil moves horizontally it will become "too powerful," although they never attempt to explain how powerful is "too" powerful and more to the point, what nefarious activities oil can be expected to engage in if it becomes "too powerful." Will it drop bombs? Throw people into camps? Outlaw free speech? Mandate the separation of the nuclear family?

Hardly. Marxists, revisionist historians, and alienated American intellectuals cloistered safely within the middle-class confines of the middle-class universities in which they teach that ours is a repressive society try desperately to convince us that the root of all social evil is the capitalist system. But when one looks out over the rubble and human devastation that makes up so much of the history of this century, it requires a great imaginative leap to arrive at the conclusion that it is the fault of capitalism and the profit motive. One thinks, for instance, of National Socialism, of Leninism and Stalinism, of Maoism, the curtailment of freedoms and the millions upon millions of corpses that these ism's have created. In contrast, it is unarguably the capitalist system that has distributed the greatest amount of the best things available in life to the greatest number of people on earth. If it is intent on oppression, and if it is intent on keeping poor people poor, it has done a bad job in contrast, say, to the Soviet Union or in any other state in which the capitalist system has been dismantled and profits prohibited.

No doubt the profit motive is at the heart of the problem. Perhaps because of the peculiar eclectic intellectual flummery upon which several generations of unfortunate liberal arts majors have been undernourished, it is common these days for those with sufficient stamina to make it through a university to speak of profits in a tone once reserved for sloth or avarice. In fact, one suspects that if a college graduating class, chosen at random, were asked to choose the seven deadly sins from a list including the profit motive, many of them—probably primarily the liberal arts majors—might well choose profits at least as frequently as lust.

Someday, no doubt, perhaps after the system finally collapses, someone will undertake a study explaining why those who benefited most from that system and were spectacularly unequipped to live under any other, worked so hard to tear it down. But for the time being, suffice it to say that the capitalist system and the men who make it run have never been held in such low repute.

Consider, for instance, our popular culture and the medium which is primarily responsible for codifying the manners, morals, and mores of that culture. It is not surprising, for obvious reasons, that businessmen are villains among the denizens of the campuses. If they weren't, something would be very wrong. It is surprising, though, that they have become villains to regular American TV watchers. But they are. At this writing, two of the boffo new series shows on TV are NBC's "The Moneychangers" and CBS's "Executive Suite," both of which shows, especially the CBS offering, depict the class of businessmen as, among other predictable things, venal,

259

lustful, shallow, soulless, callow, banal, driven by ambition to make a buck, never taking time out to enjoy those finer things, which by definition are denied to businessmen if they are successful.

Both shows may well have folded by the time you read this. Nevertheless, the fact that they were aired at all gives rise to several intriguing questions. Why should CBS and NBC, themselves profit-making big businesses operated by hard-driving executives, be interested in stereotyping themselves? Why should business be interested in buying advertising on such shows? Why doesn't business put its foot down?

Nearly every other group in the country has done so. One show that portrayed doctors in an unflattering light was driven from TV by organized medicine. For a time Archie Bunker nearly succumbed to attacks from various unions. Police organizations, trial lawyers, ethnic groups, airline stewardesses— nearly all have at one time or another protested successfully about the way TV treated them.

Not long ago, we watched the host of a national TV talk show spend several minutes apologizing abjectly for having made a derogatory crack about bed-wetters, who were, apparently, sufficiently organized to elicit not only an apology, but also a promise to devote the top of a major talk show to a discussion of their problem. And homosexuals are treated by TV not only as healthy, but also downright admirable in their sexual predilection. And for that we can in large part thank the National Gay Task Force for bringing pressure on TV.

But, one wonders, if the National Gay Task Force can actually persuade television moguls that people will respond positively to homosexuals, why in the

world can't the National Association of Manufacturers or the Chamber of Commerce of the U.S.
convince some of those networks its members support that just occasionally it wouldn't hurt to show
the businessman as at least as heroic and as
sympathetic a figure as the homosexual?

Myth is a powerful force, and we live for the first
time in history in a period when through the mass
media it is possible to mass produce myth. Thus, the
myth of the soulless businessman has gained a certain power and as that myth has grown, so too has
the corollary myth that making profits is somehow
evil. Now there are scores of absurdities here, perhaps chief among them being that the men who
build the myth make a great deal of money by doing
so. But the myth has nevertheless been successfully
created, it has given rise to what may well be permanent stereotypes, and these stereotypes have become
real for many of those who tend to shape their view
of the world according to what they see on television,
even as girls used to draw their pictures of life from
the gothic novels they read.

No doubt this comes as no surprise to those who
study the effects of mass media on the mass mind.
But it is surprising to discover that those who pre-
sume to lead us seem frequently just as vulnerable
to succumbing to the influence of stereotypes as any
of us more humble citizens.

Mr. Otis Ellis, an attorney and petroleum marketing consultant, touches on this in his comments on
the nature of the oil industry before the Senate antitrust subcommittee. "Just who or what are the
major oil companies? There are some within and
without the Congress who would have us conjure up

a vision that a major oil company is owned and exclusively functions for a group of officers and directors who gather in a mahogany paneled room in some distant city, sitting around a long mahogany table with their computerized brains thinking up new ways to gouge the American public as their thin lips volley back and forth the best means of doing it, all the while greedy spittle drips off their respective chins."

Mr. Ellis, whose stereotype is really not too far from that created by television and accepted unthinkingly by large numbers of Americans, then goes on to discuss the ways in which this stereotype is inaccurate. Such directors and officers, he points out, even if they did exist, would not own as much as 1 percent of the stock in any major company. Who profits? George Keller, vice-chairman of the board of Standard of California, explains it this way: "A recent study by the New York Stock Exchange indicates that the shares of the six largest oil companies in this country are owned—either directly or indirectly through pension funds, state employee retirement plans, or mutual funds—by some 14 million American citizens.

"Almost half of this number are retired people, who depend on dividends from these companies to supplement their Social Security income. Their average annual income is only slightly above $14,000 a year."

It is a fact of American corporate life that the chief beneficiaries of profits are those millions of average Americans who are also shareholders. And the corporate structure itself, together with an effective body of laws, would make it impossible today for any one small group of greedy men to succeed in ripping off the public. Yet the stereotype persists, often, one suspects, because many people, chief among them politicians, have a vested interest in seeing to it that it does persist.

One such politician was Senator Abourezk, chief sponsor of the horizontal divestiture bill. Consider, for instance, his opening statement as hearings on his bill began. His subject was the recent rise in coal prices, which he implied came about as the direct result of big oil's constitutional inability to resist ripping off a vulnerable public.

"I believe," said Abourezk, "that it may be useful to ask whether oil ownership of coal companies and coal reserves has already limited competition between the two fuels. The fact is, that coal could right now be a substantial competitor with oil. We have a commitment to switch our electric generating capacity from oil and gas to coal.

"This policy decision would be supported by good business practices if coal had remained anywhere near the price it was three years ago. Now we are seeing coal sold at a BTU equivalent price, regardless of cost, and regardless of the fact that the price of two-thirds of our oil is set by an international cartel. The advances in profits by coal companies come from higher prices rather than from the increased volume of sales."

Now the best that can be said for all this is that it is extremely simplistic. The recent increases in coal prices, if they are to be analyzed sensibly, must be looked at within a context much larger than that of oil's involvement in the coal industry. Until very recently, for instance, coal was a depressed industry with an extremely low profit margin. In 1969, coal was selling for $4.99 per ton—precisely the same price it had sold for in 1948. When Senator Abourezk spoke of "advances in profits by coal companies," therefore, he was talking about advances from a very low base.

The first increase to which Abourezk refers, occurring between 1969 and 1971, had nothing whatsoever to do with oil's involvement. T.D. Duchesneau, an independent economic analyst, explains it this way: "Critics have been quick to assert that oil entry into coal represents an attempt to monopolize and that rising coal prices during 1969-1971 are the result of an oil company conspiracy to restrict output. A review of price and output patterns of coal firms fails to support such an assertion. No substantive evidence exists to indicate that oil-coal companies have restricted output in order to elevate price.

"The sharp price increase during the period 1969-1971 appears to be not due to oil company entry, but rather the result of a marked increase in wage costs and a sharp decline in productivity levels. The tight coal situation in 1969-1971, often taken to be evidence of a conspiracy, appears due to a sudden rise in utility demand, an unfavorable climate for investment in new coal capacity in earlier years, and a sudden growth of coal exports. Thus, difference in conduct between the period 1969-1971 and earlier periods are real but were caused by differences in economic forces between the two periods rather than due to any conspiracy to restrict coal production."

The price rise, most experts now agree, was the result of natural market forces, and in terms of our overall energy picture, probably a good thing.

The industry was depressed, and expansion of coal mining had consequently ground to a halt, with a growing shortage of coal and a consequent increase on oil dependence. But as a result of the modest gain in coal prices between 1969 and 1971, there was a corresponding modest increase in coal mine expansion.

And then, in 1973-74, a much more dramatic coal price rise took place, and the charges of conspiracy by such critics as Abourezk intensified. But the problem with those charges is that it is extremely difficult to get a handle on what precisely the conspirators were supposed to be up to. The oil companies, said some of the critics, having bought into coal, were holding back supply in order to raise prices and thus make money on their investment. Other critics charged that the companies were holding back supply in order to raise prices so that coal would not be economically competitive with oil. Still others claimed they were holding down supply so that there would not be as much coal available and people would thus turn to oil. Well perhaps, but there are some four thousand independent coal companies producing in the United States and it seems a bit difficult to believe that a significant number of these companies were persuaded to hold back production, thereby working against their own best interests and in the interests of big oil.

In fact, as the President's Council on Wage and Price Stability discovered, there was a much more sensible explanation for the price leap. First there was OPEC: "The rapid rise in coal prices which began in November of 1973 . . . was in large part the result of dramatically higher prices for imported oil.

The unanticipated strength of the oil embargo and subsequent OPEC cartel pricing which drove up the price of oil to electrical utilities by 180 percent in the year ending June 1974 created an abnormal increase in the demand for coal. Substitution of coal for oil by a small number of users combined with inflexible demands from coal-dependent utilities placed upward pressures on prices. During this period, delivered spot prices rose by 148 percent and average contract prices by 38 percent."

And the second force was labor unrest:

"Anticipation of the United Mine Workers' strike was a major factor putting upward pressure on spot coal prices during the second half of 1974. This pressure intensified as the expiration date (November 12, 1974) of the contract approached and it became clear that contract negotiations were proving unsuccessful. Strenuous efforts in the second half of 1974 by the steel industry, electric utilities, and foreign purchasers to build stock piles reached near-panic proportions."

A sluggish industry, then, with a greatly reduced output, suddenly found that because of abnormal external circumstances its product was very much in demand, and that it was unable to meet that demand. The price of noncontract coal, therefore, skyrocketed, a very obvious result, and a theory infinitely more plausible than convoluted and contradictory conspiracy theories.

And finally, despite the picture painted by critics such as Senator Abourezk, the intervention of oil into coal production has not, in fact, been massive. None of the big eight, for instance, ranks among the nation's top twenty coal poducers and three of the big eight are not involved in coal production at all. Altogether, sixteen of the twenty-two major oil companies are not now producing or delivering coal and Conoco, the leading oil company currently producing coal, ranks only thirteenth in the U.S. crude oil production.

There is little evidence of an oil company take-over. But should the prospect nevertheless make the government nervous, it could solve the whole problem without resorting to a complex and costly horizontal divestiture bill. The oil company most deeply engaged in coal owns only 3 percent of our coal reserves and the other firms only 12 percent. The remaining 85 percent is controlled primarily by federal and state governments. This means, then, that if the government is truly worried about oil expanding into a monopoly in the coal field, it can simply refuse to lease such lands to big oil. As matters now stand, the oil industry cannot move in on these reserves unless the government allows it to do so. A divestiture bill, therefore, to the extent it is intended to prevent an oil takeover of coal, is superfluous, since the government already possesses the means to exclude big oil and to do so very simply.

Why it should want to, however, is a different question. Oil has certain services to offer the coal industry and the coal industry has certain services to offer the nation. If we are to become energy independent, then coal will be vital. And if the environmentalists have their way and succeed in halting the development of nuclear power, coal will be indispensable.

Since the beginning of the fifties, however, the coal industry has not done well. Part of the problem has grown out of coal's intense and protracted struggle with the labor movement. And as the nation's standard of living and therefore its expectations continue to rise, it becomes increasingly difficult to find men willing to go underground for any wage at all. Low market prices, combined with escalating labor costs, have decreased production dramatically. And just as it grows increasingly difficult to find men to work the mines, so does it grow increasingly difficult to find men willing to sink badly needed capital into an industry whose future seems at best cloudy and risky. Financing coal development is a gamble. There are problems growing out of governmental policies and there is the problem of uncertainty over future OPEC actions. If the cartel were to crack completely, for instance, and the price of oil were consequently to plummet, then coal would become overnight an uncompetitive product.

Coal is not, in short, an industry that acts as a magnet for capital investment, yet the amounts of capital required for its development continue to increase. Continental Oil, for instance, estimated in 1975 that increasing output from 604 million tons per year to 1895 million tons by 1990 would require the opening of 482 new mines, thus necessitating additional investments of up to $27.5 billion.

"What we are talking about," said National Coal Association president Carl Bagge to the Southern Governors Conference last summer, "is a fourfold increase in the amount of capital required for building a new coal industry in less than a decade."

Oil is uniquely situated and uniquely motivated to make that investment, and thereby provide a shot in the arm for a depressed but vital industry. Coal, like most depressed industries, has been extremely slow in innovating and in attempting to increase efficiency. To the extent that oil is involved in the industry, however, it has contributed significantly to industry research and development. In addition to basic work on mine safety and increased production, oil interests are working on a hydraulic transportation system for continuous transportation from the mine face to the preparation plant; on methods for removing methane gas from coal mines; on a seismic mine monitoring system for detecting roof falls and locating trapped miners; and on more efficient ways to design mines themselves.

The capital alone that oil can bring to the coal industry can make a dramatic difference. Prior to its acquisition by Conoco, for instance, Consolidation Coal Company was spending $13.5 million per year for new mine expansion. After the acquisition, such average annual capital spending increased to $36.5 million. But in addition to providing capital, oil believes it can also, because of its expertise, devise ways to mechanize and automate, thereby reducing reliance upon an increasingly limited and discontented manpower pool. (Should national reliance on coal increase significantly, we will also become increasingly dependent on the United Mine Workers Union, an organization which in the eyes of many rivals the Arab states in terms of self-serving irrationality.)

At present, in spite of its critics, oil does not participate to any dramatic extent in the development of coal, although it could be argued that it should. And the same is true of the mining of uranium. Seventeen of the twenty-two major oil companies neither produce nor deliver uranium, and the leading oil company involved in uranium production ranks twenty-ninth in the production of crude oil. In general, wherever oil has involved itself in uranium production at all, it has stuck pretty much to the exploration end. Oil and uranium tend to occur in the same sorts of ground formations and exploration methodology therefore overlaps. According to the Energy Research and Development Administration, twenty of the eighty-three companies that drilled for uranium in 1974 were petroleum companies but only five of those companies were engaged in mining and milling as well as exploration.

Compared to other energy fields, the uranium industry is relatively concentrated with a few leading companies—Kerr-McGee, Union Carbide, Anaconda, and Utah International—controlling about 54 percent of the market in 1975. But Kerr-McGee, the premier producer of uranium with 15.8 percent of the market, ranks only twenty-ninth in U.S. crude oil production. Of the other companies, only Exxon, Getty, Pioneer, and Continental were as of 1975 involved in producing significant amounts of uranium. As for the rest of the industry, the feeling in the past has been generally that because uranium, like coal, produces very low profit margins, there is no compelling reason to rush into the field. Between 1976 and 1977, an investor in uranium earned an average 5.6 percent return on his investment, a figure considerably lower than the comparable figure for all manufacturing.

Kerr-McGee, the uranium industry leader, sank $105.6 million into its nuclear operations between 1971 and 1974. Its net return on that investment was only $8.7 million and that figure includes a $2 million loss in 1972. Because of the nuclear energy program slowdown, which may develop into a permanent stall, and because of the low rate of return, there remains, despite a recent rise in uranium prices, a reluctance among investors to enter the field. More than coal, uranium requires a long lead time from the day the money is invested until the day when that investment yields a return. And here again, the experience of the oil companies, accustomed as they are to sinking hundreds of millions of dollars into such large long-range deferred payoff ventures as offshore oil development and pipeline construction, makes them natural potential investors in the uranium industry.

If the nuclear development program is not permanently curtailed, and if Congress does not interfere, experts agree that increased uranium production is most likely to come from the oil industry. And again, as in the case of coal, oil company participation would be beneficial. For one thing, it would insure continued competition. As in other infant industries, concentration in the uranium industry is high, and without oil company participation, uranium is vulnerable to a one or two company takeover. And should nuclear energy become the dominant energy alternative for the rest of the century, then those few companies controlling the uranium market could be very powerful indeed. It makes sense, then, for those who fear monopolies actually to encourage oil companies to get involved in uranium production.

As with coal, oil has introduced innovation into the uranium field. Gulf, for instance, has developed and is manufacturing a high-temperature, gas-cooled

271

reactor to compete with the standard light water reactor. Gulf claims that its plant, cooled by helium rather than water, can increase thermal efficiency by about 7 percent. Exxon is sponsoring a research effort aimed at enriching uranium by laser. And the Energy and Research Development Administration reports that two of the three acceptable proposals it has received for building gas centrifuge enrichment capacity came from petroleum companies.

Research in uranium, like research in all exotic new fuels, is a risky business, leading down numerous blind alleys and often losing millions of dollars in the process. Both ARCO and Continental, for instance, have invested heavily in and then backed out of experiments in the fabrication of reloaded nuclear fuel, and many of the research projects in which oil is presently engaged will lead to nothing whatsoever. Yet it is precisely this that makes big oil's participation in the field so valuable. Not only does it bring a unique expertise to uranium development that no other industry can duplicate, but it also can afford to invest sizable sums of money in what may often be dead-end but nevertheless necessary research and experimentation.

Defenders of the oil industry maintain that its participation in uranium development is essential. Such participation, they say, will guarantee competition and will insure rapid development. And what is true of uranium, they claim, is equally true of the geothermal industry. Of the fourteen firms thus far awarded federal leases to develop geothermal energy, eight are oil companies. No one knows the extent of the unleased geothermal fields in the country (like offshore oil, geothermal sites are leased rather than bought). But most experts agree that it is vast and that most undiscovered sites, like those already leased, will be found primarily under government land—thus, again, insuring that should any one group of companies gain excessive control, competition could be restored through the rationing of leases.

Currently, knowledge of geothermal fields or the forms they are apt to take is still at the kindergarten stage. Oil does have a head start in the area, for its geologists have been trained in a similar field. And as is the case with oil, extraction depends on drilling. But there are, at present, other industries involved in the field, among them railroads, paper companies, utilities, and municipalities. And since geothermal development seems suitable for a variety of small plants rather than a few large ones, a variety of smaller companies are expected to enter the field once exploration risks are lessened.

But even these smaller companies can be expected to turn to oil for help. In the Geysers field, for instance, two smaller companies originally attempted to develop the project. For a decade they struggled to generate a mere 50 MW of power. Then, in 1967, because their limited resources would not permit the kind of development they felt their holding could yield, they asked Union Oil for help. Union took over as the operating company on existing wells and the drilling company on new ones, and as a result Geysers is a 500 MW and is expected to be generating 850 MW within the decade. And this can be expected to be the pattern as the field of geothermal energy expands—more joint ventures between small companies with leases and oil companies with capital and expertise. This pattern could not develop if Congress were to pass horizontal divestiture legislation, however. Such legislation would effectively prevent these joint ventures. And should such joint ventures be outlawed, it could well be that the development of geothermal energy would remain at the present kindergarten stage. Thus far, except for the Energy Research and Development Administration, only the oil companies have invested substantial amounts of research and development in geothermal energy. Without that investment, many experts believe that geothermal energy will not develop beyond its present stage throughout the next two decades.

The industry is even more heavily involved in synthetics, in large part because they provide direct substitutes for its major product, with refineries and pipelines and outlets already in place and functioning. There is as yet no current commercial oil shale production, but those existing research programs judged most likely to succeed are either financed by oil or by a consortium including oil companies.

Here again, however, as in the case of uranium, the danger of monopoly control is negligible simply because it can be prevented federally. The government owns about 80 percent of the country's oil shale lands and of those lands in private hands, according to the FTC, oil companies control as little as 8 percent. Furthermore, existing federal policies already prohibit the leasing of more than one plot to any one individual or corporation. And since the size of each plot is limited to 5,120 acres, that provision alone assures that as the oil shale industry develops, there will be ample land available for competing firms. Thus, as is the case with each of the other sources, it is difficult to understand just why horizontal divestiture legislation is necessary.

This is not to say that at present oil companies seeking new sources of crude do not dominate oil shale development. They do, for several reasons, among them the necessity for large infusions of capital. Unlike geothermal development, economies of scale will almost certainly prevent the extensive use of smaller plants in the shale oil field. And, of course, given the structure of the industry, it seems natural that it would figure heavily in the development of shale oil. The refineries are there, the pipelines are there, the equipment is in place, and the research is extensively underway. Bar the oil companies from entry into the field, say industry experts, and the result might well be that shale oil research will halt altogether. Although mining and chemical companies have been mentioned as participants in such research, they have shown little interest in involving themselves and, as matters now stand, without oil company involvement there would be little if any shale oil research being carried out.

Oil has shown less interest in gasification experiments, with such companies as Westinghouse, General Electric, and Central Power and Light of Texas carrying out the bulk of gasification projects. There has, however, been major oil company involvement in liquefaction research, especially on the part of CONOCO and Gulf. As is the case with shale oil development, coal liquefaction seems a natural area for oil company participation, one in which they possess impressive credentials. And in fact, between 1964 and 1974, oil companies took out some forty-nine different patents in the coal synthetic field.

Similarly, between 1965 and 1975, oil companies were granted ninety-one patents for tar sand development, another natural and logical area for their participation. Most actively engaged in tar sands is a subsidiary of Sun Oil, at present the only commercial extractor and processer of tar sands. The plant, located in Canada, lost $90 million during its first seven years, but has shown a profit since 1975, and a number of other companies have expressed interest in a similar venture.

As with oil shale, the oil companies are nearly alone in carrying out serious tar sands research. And without horizontal divestiture, that research would grind to a halt. The tar sands and oil shale segments of the industry would attract little attention on the market where they would be split off from the parent companies, without whose financial backing significant development would be extremely unlikely. And according to many experts, were horizontal legislation to be enacted, it might well take years simply to regain the levels of research already completed in these fields.

Interestingly enough, while the oil industry is bombarded with criticism for entering or entering too heavily the alternate energy fields mentioned above, it is also criticized for not entering the solar energy field with similar gusto. "When it comes to solar energy," says one industry spokesman, "oil companies are rarely criticized for seeking control of that source. Rather, we are often accused of not doing enough to develop it."

Oil's apparent lack of total enthusiasm, say critics, springs primarily from a fear that it might contribute to the development of a cheap method of harnessing solar energy, thus making the industry's oil holdings worthless. But because no one has yet seriously considered running this century's transportation system on solar energy, and because therefore even with cheap solar energy, oil would still be needed for that system, such criticisms seem at best specious. A much more sensible explanation is that solar energy development, unlike other alternate energies, requires a totally different sort of expertise and experience than is required by the extraction of oil from the earth and the processing of that oil. Nor would solar energy naturally substitute for oil, as could most alternates. The development of these alternates could be carried out within the established structure of the industry. To develop solar energy fully might require the structuring of a wholly different industry.

But even though solar energy, like wind and waves, is not a natural field and in spite of the criticism for their alleged indifference, oil companies have nevertheless been active in developing solar cells and thermal electric conversion processes. Exxon scientists are attempting to develop a silicon cell which would be cheaper than present cells and are also attempting to solve the solar storage problem by developing a cell composed of liquid dye which will store energy in a chemical form. And a subsidiary of Exxon is selling silicon cells and working at ways to reduce their cost.

Other companies are similarly involved. Shell owns a large interest in a firm which is doing research on cadmium sulfide cells. Mobil is engaged in a joint venture with Tyco Laboratories to develop silicon ribbons for use in solar cells. And Gulf and Shell jointly own and finance what energy experts consider to be one of the most innovative companies in the solar energy field.

Oil involvement in the solar energy field may not be as dramatic as its involvement in shale oil or tar sands. But its involvement is significant and it will become more involved if it is allowed to. Other large companies—chemicals, for instance, or electricals and steel—may, with an eye toward diversification or as a long-range gamble, dabble with some of the more exotic but promising forms of energy. They have their own product-development projects to work on, however, and their major developmental thrust will be aimed at improving the products in which they specialize. But oil finds such research integral to its major operation and as the oil runs out, the energy and expertise and especially the capital of the industry will be increasingly diverted into the search for new sources. For it is oil, and oil alone, that is threatened with extinction if those sources are not developed.

Simply in terms of its ability to raise capital, the oil industry's contributions to this search would be invaluable. Consider the figures. As the economy now stands, it would require an investment of $70 million to open a new eastern underground coal mine capable of producing two million tons per year. A western surface mine with a five-million-ton capacity would require $60 million. At least $1 billion would be required for a coal gasification plant, a coal liquefaction plant, or an oil shale plant with a significant producing capacity. And a tar sands facility capable of producing one hundred thousand barrels per day would cost about $2 billion.

Yet despite these figures and the massive capital requirements they represent, proponents of horizontal divestiture continue to talk about removing oil from the alternative energy field in order to make room for small innovative firms. They fail to explain, however, why those small firms could not work alongside the oil industry. Nor do they face up to the fact that developing alternate sources is not like developing a better mousetrap. No brilliant young inventor struggling alone in his basement is going to come up with a cheap method for removing oil from tar sand. Research in such fields cannot even begin without the development first of huge plants and laboratories, costing millions and millions of dollars.

Nevertheless, despite what it has to offer—unique experience and expertise, impressive research facilities, and massive capital investment—the oil industry will, if the advocates of horizontal divestiture have their way, be prohibited from bringing any of those resources to the development of alternate sources of energy. And ironically enough, they would be barred in a way which, were it attempted by private industry, would be promptly declared illegal. For the horizontal proponents would create by legislative fiat an artificial barrier to entry into certain fields of industry, thereby decreasing competition in those fields and increasing the likelihood of an energy monopoly, or of an industry dominated by governmental regulation.

Horizontal divestiture, in short, would place unnatural restraints upon a natural process, one which is part of the natural development of most of those companies which respond to changing markets and social needs by expanding into related areas of production. Textiles have naturally expanded into synthetics, rubber producers have shifted to plastics, and newspapers have moved into other media. The *Washington Post,* for instance, is owned by the same people who own *Newsweek* and major television and radio stations in the District of Columbia. But as the *Washington Post* and *Newsweek* would certainly maintain, there is nothing particularly sinister in the process, and there may well be something decidedly unhealthy about being prohibited from participating in it. The only other American industry so prohibited was the railroad industry, which was legislatively barred from entering other fields of transportation and has since been dying a slow and painful death. If oil is legislated into a similar situation, forced to watch itself being inched toward extinction and powerless to take those natural steps with which it could save itself, business experts feel that industry morale and initiative would inevitably suffer and production could fall off significantly, well before the oil runs out.

Thus, horizontal divestiture might just succeed in putting the whole energy industry on the same track previously traveled by our railroads. And what is perhaps most ironic of all, horizontal divestiture would legislatively mandate the very thing it is supposed to prevent. If coal and oil, for instance, were to get together and enter into a voluntary agreement to stay out of each other's markets, they would be guilty of engaging in a hard-core antitrust offense, and the executives involved could find themselves facing jail sentences. But this same sort of arrangement, presently illegal under antitrust laws, would under horizontal divestiture be legislatively approved in the *name* of antitrust.

At present, without horizontal divestiture legislation, the oil industry, as FTC statistics demonstrate, is one of the most highly competitive in the nation, and as its members move into the alternative energy fields they follow their own courses. Some have moved into coal, some into uranium, others are experimenting with exotic sources. This movement is in no way monopolistic or centrally choreographed by oil company conspirators. Nor, as some critics claim to fear, are the largest companies carving out the biggest slices of alternative development. Continental, for instance, which accounts for only about 2 percent of our crude oil production, accounts for more than 8.5 percent of our coal. Exxon, on the other hand, which produces 8.5 percent of our oil, accounts for only 0.4 percent of our coal production.

Senator Abourezk's charge, then, that companies conspire to withhold alternatives in order to raise the price of oil—a formidable feat in itself, given the fact that the major alternatives do not naturally compete with oil—simply makes no sense in the light of the facts and figures of industry involvement. And for as long as the industry is allowed to expand and diversify, this will remain the case. But exclude big oil, with its twenty-plus firms, from the alternate energy fields, and chances are that you will also be excluding a vital source of competition. The result might well be either a domestic energy cartel controlled by a handful of very large companies or a federal monopoly which would eventually do for the energy industry what massive governmental intervention did for the railroads.

# Chapter
# Twelve

In *Enterprise Denied: The Origins of the Decline of American Railroads,* Albro Martin discusses the motivations of the populists who led the assault on the railroad industry at the beginning of the century.

"The archaic Progressives, as I have chosen to call them, never were so numerous or so strong politically as to explain their overwhelming influence on the [demise of the railroads]. It was their intense concentration on this one issue which must account for their success. . . . Like the secessionists of 1860, they had little in their favor except the fantastic energy which came from the blind passionate feeling in their guts that they had been conspired against and robbed."

In many ways, Martin's description of the "archaic progressives" who helped destroy the railroads fits those archaically progressive proponents of divestiture who hope to deliver a similar blow to the oil companies. Most of them think of themselves as liberals, thus embracing an ideology which is not shared by the majority of Americans. And their political impact, while still strong, grows less potent each year. But they are articulate, their concentration on this single issue is almost fanatically intense, and there is a powerful emotional factor which fuels their fight against the oil companies. Many of them, such as Representative Udall, are men of great integrity who act from the best of motives. But others, as were the antirailroad forces, are also inspired by emotionalism, paranoia, and in some cases, hatred —not necessarily hatred of oil companies *per se*, but hatred of what such large companies symbolize.

It is this intense emotional factor which may explain the success of the divestiture proponents in focusing serious senatorial attention on what is essentially illogical and often sloppy legislation. Both the vertical and the horizontal divestiture bills receiving most attention during the last session of Congress were poorly written and showed little evidence of any real concern with the legal and the practical problems that would inevitably grow out of industry dismemberment.

Consider the Bayh vertical divestiture bill, for instance, which would involve oil companies with total assets of more than $146 billion and aggregate long-term debts of $21 billion. Obviously, it would be difficult for companies of this size to dispose of their divested segments through sales alone. There simply isn't sufficient money floating around to buy the assets, especially when members of the industry themselves would be prohibited from buying. The most likely result therefore would be a "spin-off" of the various dismembered parts, which would become separate companies, with shareholders, through a series of complicated procedures, eventually ending up holding stock in only one of the parts. One of the immediate and major problems with such a "spin-off" arrangement, however, is that oil companies

284

have debts and contractual obligations with outside interests, including not only banks and institutional lenders, but foreign governments as well.

The amounts of money involved here are so great that lenders have written provisions into the loan contracts to protect their interests. These provisions require, among other things, that the oil companies retain the same essential structure that prevailed at the time the money was lent. Thus, S. 2387, the Bayh bill, would require that the oil companies break the basic agreements written into their contracts with other institutions. And this, in turn, because of clauses written into the contracts to protect those agreements, would allow the lending institutions to call in their loans.

At this point, no doubt, because S. 2387 charges the FTC to come up with a "fair and equitable" plan for dealing with such problems, the government would step in and attempt to deny the lenders the right to follow through on these contractual provisions. Thus, the FTC might well find itself in the business of writing new debt contracts for institutional lenders, something it simply isn't equipped to do. Given the number of companies the bill covers, the complexity of the issues it raises, and the variety and magnitude of the interests involved, the FTC would be forced to expand into a huge bureaucracy, which might well, in the opinion of many legal experts, spend the rest of the century writing new contractual agreements and arguing its decisions in the courts.

Nor would it be reasonable to expect foreign interests and governments to submit docilely to the rulings of the FTC. Their most likely course of action would be to call in their loans and sue for damages in their own courts, under their own breach of contract laws. But there is also another course of action. Lenders could challenge the right of the FTC to involve itself in such contractual agreements between private parties. And if the courts were to decide that the FTC had no such right, it seems likely that given the shakiness of a newly dismembered industry, lenders would call in massive amounts of money, in many cases bringing on bankruptcy, and in all cases drying up funds and enthusiasm for the whole business of producing energy for the nation.

The potential consequences of this single aspect of the divestiture bill could be discussed here ad infinitum and without exaggeration. But what is equally disturbing is not this particularly fuzzy provision, but the thoughtlessness and apparent unconcern that permeates the bill. As it stands, for instance, a company which is defined as a major in any area at the time of the bill's passage, will forever remain a major. If Gulf, therefore, divested itself of all pipelines, it would nevertheless still, under a literal reading of the bill, remain a major pipeline company. Thus Gulf, as a major pipeline company until it dies, would be breaking the law by remaining in production or marketing or refining. And so, if we were to take the bill seriously, we would have to conclude that no oil company can remain in oil.

Exaggerated, perhaps, but it says something about the way in which the bill was written that it is possible to construct such examples. And there are numerous other thoughtless provisions which would cause real problems and unnecessary agony. In certain key areas, for instance, the bill uses such crucial phrases as "substantial," "long term," or "control" without defining such terms at all, or defining them so vaguely that one wonders how the companies could understand them or how the FTC, whose job it would be to enforce the provisions in which they appear, could decide precisely what it is supposed to be enforcing. The bill's use of the word "control," for instance, as it applies to how the majors could interact with their dismembered parts, would seem to preclude them from doing business with anybody. Any contract among independent producers, refiners, transporters, or marketers involving more than a small amount of crude oil could well be criminal, for the bill defines "control" as any transaction involving "long term" or "substantial" contracts. Since the latter two terms are in no way pinned down, the law could well be interpreted to preclude all sorts of contractual arrangements, without which independent companies would be unable to function in the marketplace.

There are other problems. A nonmajor company, for instance, which makes a major discovery of oil after the bill becomes law but before the time limit for divestiture expires, becomes a candidate for criminal prosecution unless it can perform instant divestiture within the time limit set up by the bill. Such problems are legion, each of them providing sufficient fodder for suits and prosecutions to keep the nation's lawyers deep in cases for the next quarter century. But perhaps nothing better illustrates the bill's basic impracticality than that time limit itself—three years, possibly amended to five—

287

within which companies are expected to dismember themselves. According to the most liberal estimates of legal experts, if everything moved with extreme rapidity and without any major hitches, divestiture might just be carried out within ten years. But most experts agree that it would probably take at least the rest of the century. Thus, even were the oil companies to act in total good faith and actually attempt to expedite their own suicide, they would simply not be able to get the job over with before the time limit ran out and they thus became liable for criminal prosecution. Therefore, in addition to everything else, the bill is open to attack on procedural due process grounds.

Peter Bator, a corporate lawyer whose firm does no substantial business with the majors, put the case against divestiture this way in his testimony before the Congress: "The drafting inadequacies of the bill itself raise questions as to whether this kind of simple-sounding legislation is a legally viable approach to disintegrating the largest and one of the most complex industries in the world. Moreover the inevitability of legal challenges to the bill and to its implementing the break-up of all the major oil companies in the United States, should also make it abundantly clear that a divestiture statute is not at all a simple, swift, unbureaucratic or inexpensive way of resolving what is perceived to be wrong with the oil industry. . . .

"In addition, Congress must ask itself the question: what happens to this country's energy industry during the ten to twenty years of litigation which will inevitably result from passage of S. 2387? As divestiture programs are proposed by the various interests affected, this enormously complex and vital sector of our industrial economy will be in what amounts to a state of chaos. Until plans are finally approved, litigation concluded, and plans put into effect, literally no one will know who owns what, what kind of companies will emerge, what their capital structure will look like, or how viable and competitive, both domestically and overseas, the fragmented components will be."

Ironically enough, proponents of divestiture who argue for legislation rather than a court ordered breakup insist they do so because our judicial system is too unwieldly and moves too slowly. But the legal ramifications of divestiture under the legislation they propose are profound, and it is difficult to conceive of how such legislation could, as its proponents rather feebly insist it could, save courtroom time. And most important, such proposed legislation does not carry with it the same sorts of checks and balances which have over the years been built into the legal system.

Proposed horizontal divestiture legislation also raises legal questions. As we have mentioned, such legislation, proposed in the name of antitrust, contradicts the basic thrust of antitrust policies by in effect legislating artificial divisions of markets and erecting artificial barriers to entry into the energy industry. The result could well be the growth of precisely the sort of cartelization and anticompetitive restraint of trade from which our antitrust laws were written to protect us. In fact, the whole legal rationale for horizontal divestiture legislation is suspect. The Clayton Act, for instance, which governs business acquisitions, makes a careful distinction between pro- and anticompetitive acquisitions and recognizes that business growth through acquisition may actually foster competition by introducing new blood into established markets. The courts have watched oil very closely as it has moved into alternate fields—and especially coal—and have concluded that oil company acquisitions are not anticompetitive and may in fact be fostering competition.

Nor do the antitrust enforcement agencies within the government agree upon the necessity for horizontal divestiture. Thomas E. Kauper, the assistant attorney general in charge of the antitrust division, has testified that "the factual justification for legislation to categorically prohibit cross-ownership of energy sources has yet to be demonstrated. Absent from such an analytical base, and considering the potential adverse effects of such legislation, we cannot recommend its passage."

Similar sentiments were voiced by Owen Johnson, director of the FTC's Bureau of Competition, who testified that "the broadness of S. 489 [the Abourezk horizontal divestiture bill] could actually retard growth and development in the alternate energy industries. Potential entrants, having sufficient sources of capital, technology, and other resources, would be precluded from entering these energy fields, even though their entry would not cause an adverse competitive effect. Nor does the bill make any distinction between entry by way of internal expansion of development—which in some cases could be pro-competitive—and acquisition of existing companies and technology."

In addition to the possibility that horizontal divestiture might prove to be a way of legislating anticompetitiveness, there are numerous other problems inherent in the Abourezk bill. There are, for instance, the constitutional questions which will inevitably be raised and which will take years to resolve, during which time research in the alternate energy field will almost certainly be seriously impeded. And as in the case of the vertical bill, S. 489 is sloppily written. The Supreme Court has ruled, for instance, that due process is based upon the ability of those subject to legal liabilities to ascertain their status and obligations. Yet although Chapter 6 of the bill imposes heavy legal liabilities on those who fail to divest properly, it is unable to state clearly just who must divest what and to whom. Another section of the bill prohibits anyone who holds oil stock from holding stock in any alternate sources. Thus, if the bill is interpreted literally, the mutual fund holder who owns stock in Mobil and Anaconda could become a criminal. And a similar provision might forbid any financial institution which lends to oil and gas companies from also lending to alternate energy firms.

And due to ambiguous wording, the very act of developing shale oil or of liquefying coal might well be illegal. S. 489 would prohibit companies engaged in the production and refining of petroleum or natural gas from engaging in the oil shale or the coal business, with the coal business defined to include the ownership or control of the liquefaction of coal. But the bill does not define "petroleum," and in our *Webster's Seventh Collegiate Dictionary,* we find that the second definition of the term is "a substance similar in composition to petroleum." This means, therefore, that according to common definition the

291

oil in shale is petroleum, as is the oil in coal, and any company engaged in the liquefaction of coal or the development of shale oil is therefore by definition engaged in the petroleum business. And since the bill makes it illegal to be engaged in both, a strict interpretation would require that no one be allowed to engage in either.

The list goes on. S. 489 uses the word "reserves" in a way which could, if the bill as written ever became law, cause massive problems. Companies engaged in the production and refining of oil or gas, says the bill, would be prohibited from having interests in "reserves of coal, oil shale, uranium, or geothermal steam." But since it is nowhere defined in the bill, the term "reserves" could mean several different things. It could, for instance, refer to resources which can now be profitably extracted, as defined by the U.S. Geological Survey. But resources which can be profitably extracted through existing technology and under this year's price structure might undergo a change of status next year. Thus the scope and applicability could change from year to year, making it impossible for this provision to be enforced.

If, on the other hand, the term "reserves" were defined in the broader sense to mean store or supply, and if the bill which defines it that way were to become law, then the results would be chaotic. Oil-rich land containing small supplies of coal or uranium, for instance, could not be exploited by the oil companies, if the common definition of the word "reserves" is applied. And because if we dig deeply enough we will always find hot rock, then under this interpretation no oil anywhere in the country could

292

be extracted, since every inch of the earth's crust covers a geothermal reserve.

There are numerous other problems resulting from similar instancs of sloppy thought and draftsmanship. Language can be changed, however, and no doubt will be when the bill is reexamined. But it is another thing altogether to change the sloppy thinking which conceived the bill in the first place. Many provisions are illogical because the basic idea of divestiture is illogical. Others are illogical because the bill's authors simply don't care about the details. They are out to get the oil companies, as their spiritual progenitors were out to get the railroads.

Things are changing and our place in the world grows less certain. The World Bank tells us that there has been a stagnation of growth among industrialized nations since 1973, the year of the boycott. And since then a whole new group of nations has begun to outstrip us economically. There are now five countries with higher per capita income than the U.S., among them Kuwait, the United Arab Emirates, and Qatar. And although it still rides relatively far down on the list, Saudi Arabia, the world's largest oil producer, had the largest real increase in per capita income of any nation on earth since 1974 and could conceivably overtake the U.S. within the decade.

The world is changing rapidly, and the energy problem, more than any other single problem, is the cause of that change. We no longer can afford the luxuries. The party is over, and the time has come to refocus on the necessities. If we are not to become one of a newly formed group of have-not nations, depending entirely on the new have nations of a new world order—like Qatar—to care for our national energy needs, then we are going to have to make real rather than rhetorical efforts to become self-sufficient in energy. The only way that can be done is to give our energy industry its head; the way it cannot be done is to smash that industry into fragments.

Both the horizontal and vertical divestiture bill carry the stamp of the sixties, and like so much of the emotionally inspired legislation that came out of that period, they would, if passed into law, accomplish precisely the opposite of what they were intended to accomplish. The desire for divestiture is emotional rather than logical, and in the seventies we can no longer afford the luxury of emotionalism as a prime determinant of national policy. It's pleasant, perhaps, to dream of a return to nature, or an end to all smoke and noise, or even of zero growth. But we will never recover Eden. Things are changing rapidly, and those luxurious concepts which shape the dreams of the New Romantics may have to be put away once more, as they always are when societies seem on the verge of hitting the shoals. The day of the archaic progressive may once more be about to pass, not to return until the free-enterprise system of which he tends to be so contemptuous has again made the nation prosperous, and therefore safe for archaic progressives to legislate in.

# Chapter Thirteen

In *The Control of Oil,* John M. Blair's major thesis, previously argued in Anthony Sampson's *The Seven Sisters,* is that the major oil companies who do business in the Mideast—Exxon, Standard of California, Mobil, Texaco, Gulf, British Petroleum, and Royal Dutch Shell—act in concert with OPEC to control the flow of oil from producing nations, thereby assuring constant prices. Without such an arrangement, says Blair, the market would soon be flooded and prices would drop drastically.

This is an old and basic argument, and there is evidence that such arrangements may in fact have existed in the past. But it is also a dated argument, its relevance increasingly questionable since about 1970, the year in which Blair retired. If you buy the argument, you must first buy the premise, advanced by Blair and others who make it, that those five major producers are indispensable to the Arab decision makers and that they keep those decision makers firmly under their thumbs.

But this is simply no longer the case. For one thing, with the exception of Saudi Arabia, OPEC nations nationalized industry oil holdings in the first half of the 1970s. According to the Petroleum

Industry Research Foundation, the percentage of OPEC oil owned by the companies has dropped from 95 percent in 1971 to 30 percent in mid-1976. Their vast reserves were appropriated without compensation, and they were forced to sell their capital equipment at much below its market value.

Now it seems fairly obvious that an industry which has the final say in the operations of a nation would not let that nation to nationalize its holdings. Hardly, one could argue, is it compelling evidence of oil company control over the governments of OPEC nations. And perhaps even more damaging to the Blair argument is the fact that the nations that have nationalized the companies' holdings are increasingly bypassing the major companies to set up their own distribution facilities and create their own companies. Direct sales to parties other than the seven sisters have risen from 4 percent of total OPEC production in 1971 to an estimated 24 percent in the first nine months of 1976, as Abu Dhabi, Iraq, Iran, Algeria, Kuwait, Qatar, and Venezuela grow increasingly confident of their own ability to move their crude in the world market.

There is, of course, still the matter of Saudi Arabia, whose proved reserves are equal to nearly 30 percent of the total reserves of the other OPEC nations. The Saudis have up to now, largely as a matter of convenience, allowed Aramco to dispose of their crude oil rather than set up their own bureaucracy. Most of the charges that the Arabs and the oil industry are in collusion stem from this special relationship between Saudi Arabia and Aramco. However, these charges fail to take into account the difference between production and distribution.

Saudi Arabia controls the rate of production. The Saudis control nearly 30 percent of the entire OPEC reserves and in addition, Saudi Arabia owns some 70 billion barrels of probable reserves. Since Saudi Arabia is sparsely populated, it can cut production without affecting its economy. On the other hand, since its reserves are vast, it can vastly expand production without seriously draining its reserves. And herein lies its real power—a power which has nothing to do with big oil interests whatsoever.

Thus, if Saudi Arabia so chooses, it can control the price of OPEC oil simply by turning off or beefing up the amount of oil in pumps. And that decision is entirely up to Saudi Arabia. The oil companies have no bargaining power with Saudi Arabia and therefore have no control over the price of OPEC oil. If Aramco attempted to pressure the Saudi Arabian shieks for lower prices, those shieks are in a perfect position to tell Aramco to take its business elsewhere. Saudi Arabia is fully capable of selling and distributing its own oil, it is now in total control of its own pricing policy, and it intends eventually to nationalize. The companies stay on only because the traditionalist Saudis know them and are accustomed to doing business with them. But if they should decide to protest OPEC pricing policies too vigorously to the Saudis, as Blair tells us they can do, then the Saudis would very likely tell them to pack up and leave.

The dramatic changes in OPEC's role in the world and the way in which it views that role, a change that has taken place within three short years, means that the major companies, or for that matter any organization or government from any

Western nation, no longer call the shots. As MIT economist Morris A. Adelman puts it: "The oil companies are now hired hands who supply their services. It's the OPEC nations who are running the show and taking the rest of the world to the cleaners."

Blair's book also fails to take into consideration the current and significant datum that the international industry is not profiting from the OPEC price rise. In fact, the profit margins of those companies dealing with OPEC have been drastically reduced. In 1973, due to a tight supply of crude oil and an increase in world demand, the profit margins did rise, but at the same time OPEC was in the process of fine-tuning its pricing mechanism so as to set limits on those margins. And when it saw that the industry had begun to make higher profits it quickly brought the market down again.

OPEC obviously understands that if the oil companies' profits are too high, they will be able to unload OPEC oil at beneath OPEC price levels, thereby threatening the existence of the cartel. In fact, there is evidence that this concern is precisely what caused the adjustments of September of 1974. There was an OPEC miscalculation which allowed the industry at that time to make $1.32 in profits per barrel, and the feeling grew that the industry was beginning to undercut OPEC. According to the Middle East Economic Survey, prices for Arabian light crude were ranging between $9.60 and $9.80—nearly a dollar below the published Saudi price for direct sales. As a result, a group of OPEC nations, sensing danger, met at Abu Dhabi to map strategy. Some of the results: the companies' income taxes were raised by 85 percent and royalty rates by 20 percent. Company profit margins on Saudi oil were reduced that month to 22 cents per barrel, after production costs, and remained fairly constant ever since.

The major oil companies do not now profit on the international level from OPEC pricing policies, nor do they any longer exercise any measure of control over those policies. Nevertheless, Blair insists on constructing theories which would explain why the companies surreptitiously pushed for an OPEC price hike. He implies, for instance, that the whole exercise—the nationalization of oil company holdings and the OPEC price rise—might have been part of "a carefully engineered, precisely executed plan" to freeze out service stations and independent refineries in the United States. But surely, the problem of the refineries does not lie here. The notion that the major companies would give up their foreign holdings and shake up the world economic order just to close a few domestic refineries is nothing less than ludicrous. And even if it were their intention, the conspirators have failed miserably, for their share of the market has fallen since 1974.

Many of Blair's charges are similarly fanciful or misleading, especially those growing out of events occurring after 1970.

But that, of course, is not Blair's fault. A half-decade ago, when he was compiling the arguments for his book, few Americans would have believed it, had they been told that in 1977 our single most important international ally would be King Khalid of Saudi Arabia. Nor would they have believed that we would be moving rapidly toward total dependence for the fuel that keeps our country running on nations like Qatar and the United Arab Emirates. But it's happening, and as it does it breeds dismay among those who still can't believe our lives are being increasingly controlled by a group of Arab shieks. The *Washington Post,* speculating on the outcome of the meeting of OPEC oil ministers in Qatar, last year said of what Blair had no way of forseeing:

"The truly dismaying thing about it is that the choices are entirely up to OPEC. Three years after the great oil revolution and the embargo, OPEC still holds the initiative and the United States still has no very clear ideas for recapturing it."

True. But the problem is that there may very well be no way to recapture that initiative if to do so means returning to a world in which industrialized societies once again float on a limitless sea of cheap oil. The hard fact is, as the *Post* points out and the Blair book does not admit, that "Things have changed in the world, truly and fundamentally." Not too long ago, if the average American thought about Arabs at all, he probably thought about them with a mixture of pity and contempt. But since 1973 there has been a fundamental shift in the structure of world power, rendering the arguments of Blair academic, and today the average citizen of an oil-producing Arab country is no doubt inclined to view us as we once viewed him.

The fact is that for as long as we remain dependent upon oil as our primary fuel we will also depend heavily upon the Arab members of OPEC. The oil producing nations of the Persian Gulf rest atop more than four hundred billion barrels of crude oil, or two-thirds of the free world's total supply. It is their oil, just as surely as the wheat that grows in Kansas is ours, and they can sell as much or as little as they choose, for whatever price they like, and there is, quite simply, nothing we can do about it. Nor perhaps should we.

The country is buzzing just now with ingenious schemes designed to loosen the grip of the OPEC cartel. Some suggest that we should make the government our central purchasing agent and let it play off one nation against the other. Others suggest certain foreign policy trade-offs in return for guarantees of supply and price stability. And still others suggest that we break up the oil companies.

The first suggestion is totally unacceptable. The government is already too heavily involved in the private sector and its involvement invariably drives prices up and efficiency down. And as we have mentioned above, in the case of another Mideast flareup, government would not have the same room to maneuver enjoyed by private companies. Our current energy problems have to a great extent been made in Washington over the past few decades by an encroaching federal government. It makes little sense to attempt to solve problems created by that encroachment by inviting government to encroach even further.

The second suggestion, that we make certain modifications in our foreign policy, has from the beginning had supporters at the highest levels of government, an articulate minority which argues that our support of Israel is too inflexible and that we owe it to our other friends in the Mideast, especially the Saudis, to become more "even handed." There is no doubt that the Saudis would like to see this happen, and there is no doubt that if it did happen we would have all the oil we needed for as long as it lasts at any reasonable price we named. But most of us would want to think long and hard before opting for a policy of "even handedness" which would probably in reality mean the end of Israel.

The third suggestion, advanced by Blair, that we break up the oil companies and therefore break up the cartel, is apparently based on the assumption that if we break up the major American comanies active in the Persian Gulf, we open the gates for independents to swarm in and replace them. The consequent increased competition, the assumption seems to be, would lead to a dramatic drop in prices as the producers battled to undersell one another.

In some ways this argument once sounded plausible, resting as it does on some very basic market assumptions. But the problem is that in this case the assumptions don't apply. There is, for instance, the matter of competition. International oil is already notably competitive. "During the period 1953 to 1972," writes Professor Neil Jacoby in *Multinational Oil*, "more than 300 private and 50 state-controlled companies either entered the foreign oil industry for the first time or significantly expanded their participation in it." And today, new and independent companies own a third of the world's crude oil reserves, half its refinery capacity, and 80 percent of tanker capacity. And their share of the marketing of petroleum products overseas amounts to about half the total volume.

The competition is there, but the prices don't drop, for competition has no meaning in a one-way sellers' market controlled by a cartel. Robert Krueger, project director of a Federal Energy Administration study that probed the relationships between the industry and OPEC, puts it this way: "History strongly indicates that where there is a real or potential cartel among producers, competition among consumer-national companies will not result in a more stable supply or lower prices in international petroleum markets. If anything, the contrary is more likely to be true."

Competition is not a factor in setting the price of Mideastern oil. And even if it were, divestiture would do nothing to increase it. The independents are no match for the cartel, nor would our newly fragmented companies be any match for the large foreign multinationals and government owned firms that would move in quickly to fill the vacuum left by our previously integrated major companies. As a result, we would very probably end up buying much of our oil from foreign firms and their governments, something which makes no economic sense, and certainly makes no sense from the point of view of foreign policy or national defense.

There is an even more basic illogic running through nearly all the plans for dealing with OPEC, however, and that is the almost compulsive concentration on questions of price, frequently to the near exclusion of considerations of the much more important problem of supply. There recently appeared in the *New York Times Magazine,* for instance, a long and complex article entitled "How to take on OPEC," in which two writers constructed an elaborate scheme for making the federal government the sole importer of oil, which it would auction

303

off through a system of sealed bids. This import-auction system is not a new one, having been kicked around for several years now, primarily by academics. And like all systems structured in universities, it has a certain symmetry which lends it plausibility, although to make it work in practice would require that our own government and the governments of other nations operate in ways consistent with the objectives of the scheme—something that seems very unlikely to happen.

But it is not the scheme itself that deserves attention, as much as the basic attitude of the authors and the way they order their priorities. Near the beginning of their article, they say, "The problem is not that the earth is about to run out of oil—though, undeniably, we do need to work at conserving energy. There are proven reserves today of 660 billion barrels, enough oil, at present levels of consumption, to last the world beyond the year 2000 even if we never discover another drop. But more will be found."

This is a thesis also pushed by Blair. But it is a flawed thesis, for the problem is *precisely* that the world is soon going to run out of its unreplaceable supply of oil, and therefore we must do a great deal more than simply worry about conservation. Nor is it realistic to discuss the life of that supply in terms of today's levels of consumption. In order to demonstrate that consumption is not rising, the authors compare today's figures with those of 1973. But what they do not mention is that consumption dropped sharply during the period following the embargo, when people were still sufficiently frightened to cut back. The figures are rising sharply, again, however, and threaten to soar through the roof in the near future. The economy has improved, people are consuming unthinkingly again, and utilities and industries use increasingly large quantities of oil because of dwindling natural gas supplies. (Interestingly enough, the authors nowhere discuss the effects of governmental policies upon our energy problems. The shortage of natural gas, for instance, is the direct result of federal regulations which hold its price at an artificially low level and thus discourage exploration and production. The authors acknowledge that "U.S. reserves of low-cost oil and gas continue to dwindle." But this they can accept with equanimity, their only real fear being that if OPEC prices rise there is a danger that American producers will also raise prices, "especially if all price controls are removed." Than which, apparently, there is no greater potential evil. Intriguing, that people with a certain mindset find it easier to undertake to restructure our government and rebuild the existing world order than to let industry make a modest profit.)

It is this preoccupation with prices that acts as a smokescreen, distracting us from our real energy problems. But prices may be the least of our problems. The Saudis will continue to hold them at reasonable levels, not because King Khalid loves us, but because he loathes communism and fears that outrageous oil prices might bring on recession in already unstable Western European nations, thus opening the door for Communist takeover. (Ironic, that our energy prices remain relatively reasonable because of fierce anticommunism growing out of profound religious beliefs.)

And although the recent price hike hurt, just as all price rises hurt, oil is still one of the world's best bargains. The Saudis believe this very deeply, and they make a convincing case. Consider, for instance, the arguments advanced by Saudi Ambassador Ali A. Alireza before the National Foreign Trade Council in late 1976:

"Surely an audience of economists and businessmen like this recognizes that the ultimate economic cost of anything is what alternative supplies or services would cost. By that long-established standard, oil is still one of the very best buys available.

"Or if I might use another, not-at-all facetious test, how many Americans know that the cost of a barrel of oil is still cheaper than what we are charging for a barrel of Pepsi-Cola or other cola syrup? More specifically, a barrel of cola syrup costs well over a thousand per cent more than a barrel of oil.

"Yet which is really the more precious and should be conserved? And where are the values and priorities of those in the West who are complaining about oil prices?

"Instead of the self-posturing and niggling criticism of OPEC sometimes heard, it should be recognized that organization has made an important historical contribution in finally bringing about a sense of reality on the spendthrift depletion of a resource which had taken many millions of years to come into being.

"At a moderate and rational pace, OPEC is acting as a major force for conservation, for correcting long-prevailing wrongs which had been done to key parts of the world by the exploitation of their principal resource—oil—primarily for the already developed countries, for now providing a significant additional segment of the human race with the opportunity for development, for opening up major new markets for everyone, and for offering a case history of hope for all of the developing world."

Surely, given the fact that we charge more for a barrel of Pepsi syrup than the Saudis charge for a barrel of oil, we really can't argue with any great conviction that OPEC has a moral duty to charge even less for its oil than it does at present. As the ambassador points out, it is in no one's best interests to drop prices to the point where the world market would be flooded with cheap oil. Should this happen, then we would very likely not even make it to year 2000 before running out.

Reasonable but not exorbitant prices are, as the ambassador asserts, "a major force for conservation." And one wonders, given the absence of compelling arguments, how critics of OPEC's pricing policies justify their criticism. Should the Saudis, for instance, simply open their spigots and let it all drain off within the next decade or so? Is that in their own best interests? They do, after all, own that oil, and after it is gone, how will they maintain their place in the world? There is a certain arrogance here which seems almost inexplicable, involving as it does the views of some of the most liberal members of our society. These are the critics who find traces of imperialism in nearly every activity of America abroad. Yet here they call for what amounts to nothing less than the exploitation of the Arab nations for selfish reasons. Surely there could be no more quintessentially imperialistic attitude. Or perhaps they just don't consider the citizens of Arab nations quite as valuable as citizens of Western nations—in which case, the attitude is racist as well as imperialist.

But whatever the reasons, we seem adamantly opposed to giving any credence at all to the stated positions of the oil producers. At a 1974 conference on world oil problems in Washington, for instance, sponsored by the American Enterprise Institute, a panel discussion and question and answer session featured Senator Jackson, former FEA administrator John Sawhill, George Ball, Donald MacDonald, and Sheikh Ahmed Zaki Yamani, Saudi Arabia's oil minister. Again and again, in response to questions on prices, and discussion of a "financial crisis," Yamani attempted to outline the position of the producers.

"I look at it for the long term, and I know for sure that what you are discussing today will be history maybe in two or three years. I think when we are discussing oil, we do have two problems to face— number one, the price of oil, and number two, the availability of oil. Unfortunately, we are focusing nowadays only on the price of oil and forgetting for a while the main problem the whole world will face very soon: the availability of oil."

Three years later, Yamani's comments on the problem preoccupying his American co-panelists, the abrupt price rises of 1974, have become history. We have learned to live with the increase and have found it much less difficult than expected. But now we worry about future price rises, and in our preoccupation still seem not quite willing to face the more important question of availability and what will happen when the oil runs out.

Yamani puts it this way:

"You will be irresponsible in this country if you don't work very hard to find some additional sources of energy, whether it is oil, coal, atomic—whatever it is. I think you will be responsible, and everybody is responsible in this country for it. We also feel responsible, though we are far away from the problem. But since we have the huge reserve, we think that you should share the burden with us.

"I want you to adjust yourself to the new economic reality that there is a transfer of wealth from the industrial world to a group of developing nations, the oil-producing nations. You cannot do anything about that by saying, 'We don't want it. We have to stop it. We have to reduce the oil price; we have to do this and that. You have to recycle the money the way we want it.'

"I think such an approach is very unhealthy, and you won't solve the problem this way."

No one at the conference seemed to be listening. But there is, as Yamani points out, a new economic reality structuring international affairs and there is little we can do about it as it stands. True, the OPEC cartel might yet crack and if it does, prices will drop. But in the end that may not serve our best interests. There is only one sensible course of action, as Yamani states. We must develop alternative forms of energy. It is in our own best interests. And it is also in the best interests of the oil producers. They naturally don't want to deplete their greatest resource for what they no doubt view as the frivolous uses to which oil is put in Western society. That oil will be gone one day, and it makes no sense at all to hasten that day along. Thus, from their point of view, there must be something very suspect about our intentions. We insist that they increase production and lower prices for our comfort and convenience, yet we seem to be doing nothing whatsoever to help ourselves. Mobil president William P. Tavoulareas sketches the picture we present to them: "Domestic crude production is falling. Increased coal production is hampered by the combination of economic uncertainties and environmental restrictions. Similarly, growth of nuclear power has dramatically slowed down. Those who oppose increasing our energy supplies offer only conservation as an alternative."

It is not a picture to inspire confidence, and it might be well for us to remember that we are not dealing with dunces. The way to make an impression on OPEC is to begin immediately to develop our domestic energy potential and to put aside all complex, crack-brained academic schemes involving the radical restructuring of our economic system. Such schemes impress no one, least of all the oil producers. Howard Page, a former president of Exxon who spent much of his career negotiating with the Arabs, puts his finger on one of the central weaknesses of all such proposals: "I have the feeling that many of the proposals and theories start with the premise that the OPEC people are stupid and naive and can be easily fooled or frightened. My personal experience is that those OPEC representatives I have dealt with are far smarter than any of the people who make these kinds of suggestions."

We are caught in a situation over which we have no immediate control. We are dependent on the OPEC countries as we never have been dependent

310

on foreign powers since our independence. And were divestiture legislation to be enacted, we would be totally dependent on them until the day the oil ran out, upon which day the lights would go out and the machinery would stop running and this nation as we know it would quietly pass into history.

We must have a long-term policy for the next century and a short-term policy to carry us to the beginning of that century. And for the short-term, in matters pertaining to OPEC, the best possible policy, until someone develops a more sensible one, is to stay with the system under which we currently operate.

The day of cheap oil is past, and even if a crash program began tomorrow, we would still not achieve energy independence by 2000. And in the meantime, like it or not, we will remain tied to the oil producing countries. Over that period, the devising of complex schemes to refashion our relationship would simply be a waste of time. If, for instance, we were to go ahead with the idea of turning it all over to the government under some sort of import-auction system, it would take years, given the way the government proceeds, before it actually began to work and the bugs would just be getting worked out on that day when the oil supply dried up.

By far the smartest thing to do would be to encourage the oil companies—and anyone else with the skills and resources—to launch a crash program to develop alternative sources for our long-term needs and over the short run to allow them to carry on business as usual. It may be distasteful in the extreme to many liberal critics that the companies should be allowed to make profits. And dark theories about conspiracies will continue to whisper through Washington. But the fact is that they have done and are doing nothing illegal in the Mideast and are, in fact, by serving their own best interests, also serving the best interests of their nation.

Robert Krueger, the consultant to the FEA, after extensive study concluded that the oil companies may indeed have been too close to the producers. Nevertheless, he says, the companies "remain an important component of the U.S. presence abroad. Even today, despite the continued threat of disruption and higher prices, the petroleum industry serves the logistical demands of the modern world well and—it is worth noting—did so during the energy crisis, itself."

And James Akins puts it more bluntly: "The oil companies foiled the oil embargo in large part by shifting to the United States oil which would normally have gone to Europe and Japan, thereby equalizing the burden among all consumers. The oil companies were not, however, acclaimed in the United States for this patriotic act which jeopardized their holdings in both OPEC and the developed world."

And this, of course, is one of the most telling arguments of all against vertical divestiture. "It should not be assumed," says Robert Krueger, "that the firms which would surely desire to displace the U.S. majors in foreign markets would do so on better terms or would serve the U.S. or world markets as well."

Indeed it shouldn't. The producing countries value the technical expertise and assistance that the American firms provide, and as a result the firms are able to protect American interests. If the companies were dismembered, however, and therefore unable any longer to provide that advice and assistance, other firms and nations, as William Tavoulareas puts it, "could be expected to step into our shoes before they were scarcely cooled to provide the services we had offered."

Divestiture is a bad idea indeed, in terms not only of process but also in the larger terms of foreign policy and national defense. And it is an idea, one suspects, whose time has passed. Not too many years ago, we could afford such luxuries. But today we are no longer in control and over the short run it is incumbent upon us to make the best arrangements possible with those nations that control the bulk of the world's remaining oil supplies. And no one has yet come up with a plan superior to the one the oil companies already have in operation.

And after all, it isn't really for very long. Surely, even the most vitriolic critic could swallow hard and live with the distasteful thought of the oil industry making modest profits for a bit longer. And unless oil is allowed to put those profits into the development of alternate sources, there may only be about twenty-five years that we'll have to live with it all.

In the meantime, there should on the domestic front be a serious attempt to work loose from our growing dependence by formulating a coherent national energy policy and a program which will develop oil, gas, coal, shale oil, tar sands, geothermal, and solar energy. That program should begin immediately and the oil industry, with its capital and its expertise, should play the primary role in getting it off the drawing board and into operation.

It would be tragic indeed if through divestiture legislation our government prevented the oil industry from playing that role, for it is difficult to imagine who else could do it. Perhaps over a half century or so others would gain the same sort of know-how and experience. But we may not be able to afford the wait. Time, like the earth's supply of oil, is running out.

"It is not fanciful to believe that the public decisions to be made on oil and energy over the next four years will affect American national security more deeply than those made at the Pentagon," the *Washington Post* editorialized recently.

Indeed, they may. And none of those public decisions will be more profound than the decisions on whether or not to break up the oil companies. The decisions we make on divestiture will very probably determine not only our energy future but the future of the civilization fueled by that energy. Let's hope the right decisions are made. None of us wants to live through that day when the machinery stops running and the lights go out.